The Great Satan

Shadow Squadron #1

By David Black

Reprinted 2012

ISBN-13: 978-1480216532

ISBN-10: 1480216534

Published by David Black Books

Acknowledgements:

To my agent, Humfrey Hunter -

Sincerest thanks for your sage advice, patience and

friendship....

Also a great debt of thanks to Cass and Paul at Pennant
Books,

to the unsinkable Clare Conville at Conville & Walsh,

and not forgetting Rob Dinsdale for his able direction.

Finally, to the men of 21 SAS (v)

*'True unsung heroes with whom I am proud to have shared so
many incredible adventures, in a world full of dark shadows. '*

D.B.- 2010

Dedication:

To Pam and Ryan - 'Love never dies …. '

Other great books by David Black:

Dark Empire

Shadow Squadron #2

Playing for England

Siege of Faith

Eagles of the Damned

http://www.david-black.co.uk

ABOUT THE AUTHOR

David Black and his main character Special Forces team
leader Pat Farrell - are so close as to be synonymous. 'I
served as a part-time SAS Special Forces soldier leading
exactly this kind of bizarre double life,' says Black. Like his
main character Pat Farrell, Black worked as a London taxi
driver during a long tenure as a Territorial SAS member,
ready to be called into action in times of national
emergency. The principal difference is that the author is
now retired from the army, while his fictional counterpart
is left to contend with 'the real world' … with direct
relevance to the grisly global horrors being perpetrated
today.' 'David Black' is a pseudonym, used to protect the
author's identity and the integrity of his former Regiment.

Join David on Twitter - @davidblack21

http://www.david-black.co.uk

Chapter One

Afghanistan/Iranian border - 2004

As the early morning sun threw its first brilliant shafts across the jagged Namakzar Mountains, SAS Troop Sergeant Pat Farrell heaved the last sandbag onto the firing parapet of his newly dug slit trench. Settling the sandbag into position, he hammered it firmly into its final resting place with his fist. Nodding with satisfaction that the job was finally finished, he turned and said.

'Last one Dusty, we're just about set. Be a good lad and get the Primus going, while I go and check on the rest of the Troop.'

Dusty Miller, Pat's radio operator, and other occupant of the small two-man fire trench grunted.

'Yeah, great idea Pat. I'm gagging for a hot brew after digging all night.'

Resting his hand on top of the row of sandbags, Dusty lent down to pick up his small cooker, to begin boiling a mess tin of water for tea. Suddenly, with the deafening sound of a cracking bullwhip, the sniper's high-velocity bullet slammed into the sandbag above him, raising a small cloud of dust, and neatly removing the tip of Dusty's index finger. With a yell, Dusty Miller dropped to the floor of the trench, cradling his wounded hand.

'Jesus, that hurts!' He hissed through clenched teeth, using his other hand to try and staunch the bleeding.

Pat Farrell had involuntarily ducked when the sniper's bullet hit Dusty. Now he knelt beside the radio operator, busy pulling out a field dressing.

'For Christ's sake, hold still! Stop waving it around while I get a dressing on your hand.'

As he worked on the wounded trooper, Sgt Farrell yelled to the rest of his men, who had also ducked into their fox holes when the bullet hit.

'Anyone see where that shot came from?'

A chorus of men answered, but not one of them had seen the enemy's muzzle flash. Pat finished tying off the bandage, and grinned at his companion.

'You'll live, son,'

9

Dusty groaned, eyes flashing at the khaki dressing covering his wounded hand.

'Where's the other bit gone?' He enquired.

Pat shrugged. With a grin, he said.

'Dunno mate, but I don't recommend you climb out and look for it just now.'

Turning his attention to the others, Pat yelled out to his men.

'Keep your heads down lads! We'll need to find the bastard so stay where you are for the moment. He paused. 'Dusty's hit - but it's only a scratch.'

Dusty looked up with a start from the bloody bandage which hid his missing finger tip, straight into the grinning face of his Troop Sergeant.

'Oh yeah, cheers Pat. Some bloody scratch!'

Over the next few hours, from the safety of their sandbagged embrasures, Pat and his men tried in vain to spot the concealed enemy sniper. Without warning, random bullets cracked overhead, or thumped into the earth beside their fire trenches. It would be a matter of blind luck if any of Pat's elite squad of Special Forces troopers happened to be looking through their binoculars at the precise spot where the concealed sniper lay, at the

10

exact moment when he fired. The sun's bright glare reflecting off the brown rocks on the other side of the border didn't add to their chances of spotting the muzzle flash.

Knowing how good Taliban marksmen usually were, Pat expected he would have used the old snipers 'trick of sprinkling precious water just in front of his rifle's muzzle, to avoid raising puffs of tell-tale dust when he fired. He put himself in the shoes of the sniper, and looked for an ideal place on the rocks around, a crook that afforded a commanding view of their position, but used the rocks and folds in the terrain for the best possible concealment.

Patience was the one true virtue in this sort of situation, and after an hour of slow, careful examination Pat had narrowed his search to three possible locations. To spring his trap however, Pat needed live bait.

'I want someone to break cover and jump into the next trench, so I can spot the sniper when he fires!' Pat yelled. 'John Sheldon, are you awake?'

There was a short silence, before a West Country accent yelled back.

'I've got a bad leg Pat, but I'll do my best.' Laughs erupted from the fox holes.

Pat smiled to himself. 'I'll give you a bloody bad leg, my lad. Get yourself ready!'

He focused on his first likely spot, about nine hundred and fifty yards ahead, up a rocky slope to his right. Pat adjusted his binoculars.

'Standby John...Go!' Pat yelled, intently scrutinising his first likely spot.

John leapt out of his trench, and dashed across the five metres of dry, horribly open ground. As he dived headfirst into the safety of the next trench, the sniper's bullet whip-cracked, and thumped harmlessly into the ground three feet over his shoulder.

'You all right John?' Pat yelled.

As he disentangled himself from the other two grumbling occupants of the fire trench, John Sheldon yelled back.

'Yeah, no problems.'

Pat cursed under his breath; he'd drawn a blank; there was nothing there.

'Right, in ten minutes, I need another volunteer. One of the other two in your new trench can swap places and go to your old trench.'

In a thick Irish brogue, Paddy Murphy called back.

'I'll do it Pat; I need a change of air anyway. Charlie needs a crap and keeps farting. Christ, I'd rather face the bloody sniper.'

When it was time, Paddy Murphy readied himself. As Pat yelled for him to begin his frantic dash, Charlie quickly whispered. 'Paddy, if you don't make it, can I have your watch?'

As Paddy launched himself out of the trench, he yelled back 'Fuck off!' To his grinning mate.

The sniper's bullet cracked overhead and missed Paddy's head by mere inches, smashing into the bank behind the line of trenches in an angry shower of stones and earth.

Pat grinned.

'Got you, you bastard!' He muttered triumphantly.

Sgt Farrell called to his Troop, as they crouched in their foxholes, strung out on either side of his trench.

'Right lads, I've seen him; I'm going to call in an air strike.'

A 500lb high-explosive bomb dropped by a fast air fighter bomber would sort the sniper out, he thought, picking up his map and studying it intently for several moments.

Pat thumbed the microphone of the powerful Tribesman radio transmitter. 'Charlie Mike Four, Charlie Mike Four, this is Alpha one three. Request air strike. Over.'

There was a short pause of static, and then a distant voice crackled from the radio's speaker.

'Charlie Mike Four, Roger that. Send target co-ordinates. Over.'

Pat read the detailed grid reference of the sniper's position from his map into the microphone, and received a curt, 'Charlie Mike Four; Roger that, wait. Out!'

Pat cast his eyes back at the snipers hold out, waiting in silence as the Forward Air Controller at Kandaha double-checked the co-ordinates with his own highly accurate maps.

The radio's microphone crackled suddenly.

'Hallo, Alpha one three, this is Charlie Mike Four, say again target co-ordinates. Over.'

Pat looked quizzically at the radio, shrugged, and pulled the map out of his thigh pocket again. He repeated the eight figure map reference.

There was no delay this time; the reply came almost instantly. 'Alpha one three, that is a negative on the air strike. It's over the border, and a strike has been vetoed

14

by higher command. 'There was another crackle of static. 'Sorry we can't help this time. Good luck anyway. Out.'

Pat was stunned. Fighting the battle-hardened Taliban was bad enough, but to have one hand permanently tied by bloody politicians safe in London made the task a hundred times more difficult. He hurled at sulphuric curse at the silent radio, and sat still on the floor of the fire trench for several moments.

Dusty Miller stared at his sergeant, sharing his gloomy silence.

'What are we going to do now Pat?'

Pat looked up from the microphone. 'I'll think of something,' he breathed.

Counter-sniper fire was usually the quickest way to deal with a rogue marksman, if an air strike was unavailable, but on this occasion Pat had nothing close to matching the range of the gunman. The Afghan was probably using the much favoured lightweight Russian 7.62mm Dragunov sniper rifle, which far outranged anything his SAS Troop possessed. If Pat ordered his men to return fire, the sniper would know his position had been compromised.

'No,' thought Pat. 'If I'm going to protect my lads, and nail the bastard, I'll just have to think of something else.'

Having learnt the trade craft of leadership over the years, Pat always balanced putting in a successful mission, with having to place his men's lives in harm's way. It was a cast iron rule that he would never ask another man to do something he wouldn't do personally, and more than once he had risked his own life rather than asking for a volunteer. It may not have been condoned by those who wrote the big army's leadership manuals, but it had always worked for him.

Pat patiently pondered the situation, still pinned down by the lone sniper, for the rest of the day, planning and systematically rejecting numerous ways of dealing with the enemy marksman. Less than two hundred metres in front of his Troop position, the border crossing was no more than a sturdy rope suspension bridge which spanned a deep gorge. Below it, a dizzying drop of almost 400 feet led down to a shallow but fast flowing river, whose centre marked the actual border between the two countries.

As dusk began to settle over the mountains, Pat Farrell's patience was exhausted - but, at last, his plan was complete. When the blanket of the night had finally fallen, he turned to Dusty and instructed him to pass the word out that he would be back before dawn. Farrell would say no more as he crawled away into the darkness.

He spent several minutes rummaging in the dark through the Troop's ammunition dump. Then, making certain his men knew he was moving in front of the trenches, he passed through their defensive line. To avoid any chance of detection, he ignored the rope bridge - and as the moon disappeared behind a blanket of slowly drifting clouds, he began the dangerous climb down into the deep black chasm.

The long, cold night was uneventful for the other SAS soldiers. There were no incoming shots, no random bursts of gunfire, and the dark hours showed no sign of enemy movement. One man slept as the other kept watch in each of the slit trenches.

Just before dawn's light began to brighten the eastern skies the troop roused itself. With every man alert, they came together with weapons ready in case of an enemy attack as dawn broke.

Minutes later, Pat reappeared from the edge of the chasm, tired but quietly triumphant. Through the early-morning gloom, he grinned: the enemy marksman wouldn't be a problem any longer; the men should all stay in their foxholes, focusing their binoculars on the sniper's lair. Pat wouldn't be drawn any further and, with a wolfish grin, he lay down in his trench, pulled his battered bush hat down over his eyes and told them to be patient.

Hours earlier, Pat had carefully climbed down the sheer granite, manoeuvring around outcrops of razor sharp rock. With several hundred feet still to go, the ancient rock face crumbled where the layer was weak, but Pat managed to hang on by his fingertips, and stopped himself from pitching backwards into the black void. He had to admit to himself that he felt considerable relief when his boots finally crunched on the gravel at the bottom of the gorge.

Farrell crossed the narrow bank, and waded through the freezing shallow waters of the river. Using the cover of the night, he scaled the Iranian side of the gorge. At the peak of the treacherous rock, he lay flat and still for several minutes, recovering his strength and straining his senses for the slightest sign of movement; the place was rife with Taliban, and the Iranian border patrols was never far from his thoughts. When he was satisfied that it seemed safe to press forward, he stood up, slowly drew his 9mm Browning pistol and, holding it ready, began to climb the nearest hill.

After more than an hour of quietly searching the dark mountainside, victory was his. The sniper's deserted firing position was littered with spent 7.62mm cartridge cases. Scooping them aside, he cautiously buried something, just inches below the surface of the sand. Gently scattering some of the spent cartridges back over the concealed booby-trap, he added the finishing touch by gently removing its safety pin. Content that his plan was finally in place, Pat carefully retraced his steps, meticulously brushing away any evidence of his visit. Reversing the descent and climb, he made it back safely to the Afghan side of the border just before the sun rose, re-joined his troop and settled down to watch the fireworks.

As dawn broke, every pair of binoculars the grinning Troop possessed where focused on the other side of the border. Minutes ticked slowly by - but the world remained still. Suddenly, there was a bright flash. A loud boom reverberated across the snow-capped mountains. The small but powerful anti-personnel mine that Pat Farrell had buried exploded and a column of smoke arced fifty feet into the air. The sniper's body hurtled hundreds of feet into the depths of the gorge below.

All around, the cheers and hoots of laughter went up. It was a good day for the enemy to die.

Chapter Two

London - 2006

The rain over London had not relented in hours.

Dark clouds obscured the moon, making the night seem even more miserable. The gutters ran like rivers, lakes of dark water rose and grew in every road, reflecting the bright city lights. Late night partygoers shivered and huddled together under gaudy umbrellas, hoping to find an empty taxi - or else turned up their collars, seeking cover in the dark corners of shop fronts and bus shelters.

Pat Farrell was gloomy, but it had nothing to do with the weather. Since he left the Regiment two years previously, he had felt the deep loss of his comrades. He missed the excitement and adrenaline rush of the life he had led. It was a grief, of sorts, he supposed - but not one he was even beginning to understand.

The society he lived in now was a million miles from his previous world. The big utility companies and banks were motivated by money and greed, and clearly didn't care a hoot for their customers. The country was governed by crooked and incompetent politicians who everyone disliked, and no one trusted. He sometimes listened to their speeches on television, but failed to see how his English culture was being enriched by organised gangs of east Europeans who imported small children to pick-pocket and steal anything their little hands could carry off, or ran vicious vice rings, where their women were treated like cattle. Without consulting the people, the Government had allowed unchecked droves of foreign workers to enter Britain, and then wrung their hands, swearing that they were at a loss to understand why the NHS was more than overloaded. There was a general breakdown in law and order throughout the UK, with decent people living in fear of hooded gangs. Drugs and guns were easily accessible, and violent street murder had become almost commonplace. The bitter war he had left behind in Afghanistan was still being waged - but it seemed to Pat, that decent society was slowly but surely losing the war at home.

He had tried working for a short time in the security industry, but didn't enjoy the prospect of being a permanent bodyguard, at the beck and call of some rich foreigner using the UK as a tax haven for a few months every year. He had sifted through various job options, and had finally chosen to drive a London cab. He needed a permanent job after he left Hereford, and shortly after arriving back in London, over a beer with an old school friend, Pat decided to do 'the Knowledge. When he qualified, he would be his own boss, and could choose his own hours to work. He wouldn't have to be subordinate to some pimply youth with a degree, who lacked any real life experience or traces of common sense. His mate had laughed and winked when Pat had asked him about money.

'You'll get out what you put in, but don't worry mate, you'll do all right.'

Shortly after he passed his knowledge 'finals' at the Carriage Office in Islington, Pat switched to working London's streets at night. He had tried driving through the day, but the traffic made his newly-acquired and intimate knowledge of London's streets almost useless; the shortcuts he had so patiently learnt where just as clogged as the main roads.

He found that driving at night dulled his thoughts. There had been too many doubts buzzing there in recent months, and he was glad of the respite. He had said goodbye to his latest flame only weeks before, but the wound still stung. Since leaving the army, he had suffered a string of bad short term relationships, with girls who failed to fire up the spark he was looking for in a real partner.

With his tall, athletic 6ft frame and rugged good looks, there was never a shortage of willing girls, but they all seemed to Pat to be so self-centred and shallow. He had met one, who was much more than interesting, but her history and background fouled things up for him. Candy was from an extremely rich Devon family, but under a pretty, vivacious and sophisticated exterior, was a very mixed up and unhappy young woman. Pat wasn't sure how it had gone on their first date, but she had asked him in for a coffee in her expensive Bayswater flat at the end of the evening. He found out, shortly afterwards, when she had excused herself for a moment while he sat nursing a brandy. Candy reappeared from her bedroom, wearing nothing more than a pair of sheer black stockings and high heels.

'Coming to bed then?' was all that she said.

It had been fun, at first - but, after six months of being together, she had casually announced she had just been using him to get over someone else, as she calmly scrubbed his back in the bath after work. She dumped him hard, and it hurt him badly. He had let his guard down; owned up to more than a passing interest in her, and that had been a big mistake. She slipped under his radar and got to him, and now he was paying for it.

Civilian life wasn't going very well for Pat Farrell.

One evening, after dropping a late fare at Kings Cross, Pat's night shift took an unusual and unexpected turn. As always, he joined the taxi rank outside the station to wait for another fare. It had been a slow night, and he sat for twenty long and boring minutes until he gained poll position on the rank. A young woman approached the cab, and asked him to take her a short distance, wait, and return to the station.

The girl was clearly on the game, and eager to chat as he drove her through the wet London streets. Surrounded by cheap and sleazy hotels, with easy access by the underground system, the dingy backstreets of Kings Cross were very popular with both the girls and their punters. The girl in the back seat of his cab was in her early twenties, blond, and prettier than Pat had, at first, imagined. She was bitterly complaining about the Arabs, who favoured her blond hair and shapely legs, and made up a large part of her clientele.

'They have plenty of money, but they can be real bastards. They treat us all like dirt,' she said. 'Always want everything for nothing, and haggle over every penny. Look at them the wrong way, and you get a good slapping. A

24

mate of mine ended up in hospital last week, because she wouldn't take two of them on at once… *Bastards!*'

Driving a London cab could be rough at times, and serving in the Regiment had been a tough life, but Pat couldn't help feeling sorry for her and her mates. It wasn't his idea of a good job, and it wasn't a world he could imagine living in. But it took all sorts, he supposed.

Sally continued to complain until they reached her destination, a deserted, poorly lit cul-de-sac just off the City road. Netted scaffolding covered a row of derelict buildings down one side, and along the other parked cars and loaded rubbish skips squatted in the dirt.

'It's down at the far end,' Sally said.

For only a second, Pat paused. Mugging taxi drivers was unusual, but it wasn't unheard of in London. He eased his heavy torch into a position where he could use it to belt anyone stupid enough to try their luck. Watching the dark corners for any sign of movement, he slowed, grinding to a halt at the end of the deserted street. The girl opened the taxi door and climbed out.

Reaching into her shoulder bag, she pulled out a small bunch of keys and unlocked the rear door of a battered Ford Cortina. Pat wasn't blind, and had to admit to himself that she did look pretty good in her very short skirt, as she bent into the rear of the car. As he turned the cab around, he helped himself to another view of her long and shapely legs.

Pat had seen and done a lot of unusual things in his life, but nothing prepared him for what he saw in the car. A small baby nestled in Sally's arms, suckling at a bottle of milk.

Pat shook his head slowly, switching off the cab's engine, and waited in the darkness as the hungry infant finished its bottle. The young hooker lifted her child high, gently rocked it, and patted its back. Rewarded with a loud burp, she slowly and carefully replaced the baby in its carry-cot, tucked it in with a thick blanket, and quietly re-locked the car's door.

'Thanks for that mate,' she said as she climbed back into the cab.

Pat started the engine, but said nothing. There was emptiness in his stomach and he did not have the words. It was quiet in the cab for a few moments.

'It's OK really. 'The girl finally said. 'It's dead quiet down there at this time of night, and I've got to work. I couldn't find anyone to watch her tonight, so she had to come with me. I'll do a couple more punters, and then I

26

can go home. Tell you what though - I could do with a quick warm up. You don't fancy a coffee, do you?'

They stopped at a Greasy Joe all night café close to Kings Cross. Pat bought two coffees, and together they took their seats. Two other girls working the Kings Cross streets were sitting nearby, and made several lewd gestures towards the girl.

'Piss off you two, he's a friend.' She looked a Pat. 'Sorry about that. I know it doesn't look good, but I was really desperate tonight. If I don't come up with the rent money tomorrow morning, me and Jude are out on the street. My girlfriend usually watches her when I'm working, but she had to go and visit her sick mum tonight. If Jude doesn't get fed, she screams the place down. I'm late with the rent as it is, and that old cow of a landlady would call the police if I left her alone. '

As they sipped their coffees, the girl chatted, and told Pat that she had come down to London just eighteen months earlier to get away from her abusive father. She had met up with a young musician who had promised her the earth, but had disappeared in a flash when she announced she was pregnant. With her meagre savings gone, and now with another mouth to feed, she had fallen in with a part-time prostitute while she was staying at a

Women's Shelter. The girl promised to show her how to earn easy money.

Pat Farrell was old fashioned in some ways, but there was such honesty in the way that she spoke that his heart went out to her.

He had to do something to sort it out. He could just have ignored the whole thing, but that wasn't the way he worked.

'How much are you short on the rent?' He asked.

'Oh, I only need another thirty quid,' she said. 'Why do you want to know?'

The girl gave Pat an old fashioned look - but he only grinned back.

'No, it's not what you're thinking; I'll lend it to you if you like.' He looked serious suddenly, and shook his head. 'I just don't like the idea of your baby being left alone like that.'

Sally's eyebrows knitted together 'What, no strings?'

When he said nothing, she looked genuinely surprised.

'Nope, just give me it back when you see me on the rank next time.'

28

Although it had been a slow night, the week had been pretty good, and he wasn't going to miss a measly thirty pounds. He knew he'd probably never see it back, but he knew there was no other choice: he could stop off at the nearest police station and report it, or just bale the poor little tart out. Pat wasn't a knight in shining armour, but it was the least he could do.

The baby was still fast asleep when they arrived in the dark cul-de-sac. As the girl climbed out of Pat's cab, she reached back and touched him on the arm. 'I don't even know your name, but you're different; you're a really nice guy,' she said as she closed the taxi door.

'Pat Farrell will do,' he said, smiling at her.

'Thanks, Pat Farrell.' She stared intently at him for a moment. 'I will pay you back, promise. I owe you one.'

Before she left, she turned and threw him a big smile.

'By the way...,' she said, 'I'm Sally.'

Fares came and fares went. One night bled into the next, until London became only a seething grey mass to Pat Farrell. He did not see Sally the night after, nor the night after that - and, in time, he got to understanding that

that was the way the world turned, that people flitted in and out of each other's lives, never to be seen again.

It was on one of those bleak nights, with nothing to do and even less to think about, that Pat received a telephone call from his old Sgt Major Rover Walsh. Rover was doing some work in the UK, and thought he should look Pat up. Pat knew better than to ask what he was doing in London, especially over the phone. They arranged to meet at a pub just off the Harrow road. Pat was delighted, and felt a surge of relief; at last, he could talk to someone on his own wavelength. Rover had earned the nickname after biting off an opponent's ear during a brawl with some local youths in one of Herefords backstreets when he was a young Trooper, new to the Regiment. Pat didn't care though, Rover was a good bloke, and they were on the same side.

Pat spotted Rover's craggy face almost as soon as he entered the pub. His old friend was wearing the unofficial civilian uniform of the Regiment: a battered leather jacket, tee-shirt, jeans and desert boots. He looked fit and tanned, as if he had just come back from a holiday in the sun.

'Probably not much of a holiday resort,' thought Pat to himself, as he ordered a couple of pints of beer.

30

They settled down in a quiet snug, where they wouldn't be overheard.

'So, how's it going Pat?' Rover asked.

'It's not what I was really expecting, Rover,' said Pat, staring into his beer. 'I needed the change, but I've got to admit I don't like being a civilian much.' Pat sighed. 'I miss being with the Regiment.'

They talked easily for the next hour, swapping news and easy laughter, and chatting about the latest gossip coming out of Hereford. Rover laughed when Pat recounted the story of one fare he had recently.

'I got flagged down by this old gent in Parliament Square. He was smartly dressed in a bowler hat and pin striped suit. He wanted to go to the City, so off we went along the Embankment. Most people like to chat to their cabbie, and I thought nothing of it until he asked me a question.'

Rover took a swig of beer. 'Go on,' he said with a grin.

'The fare asked me if driving a heavy cab had given me my big strong shoulders, and did my girlfriend like them?' Rover laughed and squirmed. 'Talk about being obvious, he was trying his luck!'

Rover shuddered and asked Pat what happened.

'Well, I dropped my voice about four octaves and growled that she did. The bloke just said 'Oh', and that was the end of that..' Pat shook his head. 'Needless to say, I didn't get a tip,' he admitted with a shrug.

They continued to chat, but from what he heard, Rover could see that Pat oozed discomfort.

'If you miss the Regiment so much, why not go back part time?'

Pat looked hard at Rover. 'What do you mean, the Territorial's?'

Rover nodded. 'There's a Territorial SAS squadron based in Chelsea,' he said. 'They're a good bunch of lads, and they've all cracked selection. With your job, getting time off shouldn't be a problem...'

Pat slowly shook his head. 'I don't know Rover, playing weekend warriors doesn't sound much of a fix, not after doing it for real for so long.' He took a long swig from his brimming pint glass. 'No, it's a bad idea. I don't think that would do it for me at all.'

Rover held up his hand, and looked theatrically over his shoulder to make sure no-one was listening. 'Fair enough Pat, but don't draw a line through the idea just yet.' His face was suddenly serious. He lent forward and whispered. 'Things have changed quite a bit since you've been gone mate. What do you know about their new Shadow Squadron?'

Chapter Three

Pat Farrell swept a baleful eye over the young men who made up his new Troop. It felt good to be back in his old uniform, wearing the blue stable belt and winged dagger cap badge on his sandy beret. The Regiments' unique small blue parachute wings sat comfortably on his right arm.

Since Rover had recruited him into the Territorial's SAS five weeks previously, Pat had been working hard to get to know his new Troop; so far from what he had seen, he was quietly impressed with all of them. Like their regular counterparts, they were tough, bright and resourceful, but fiercely maintained their own individuality. No two men were alike, but all of them carried the calm professional aura of the Regiment about them. Between them they oozed a healthy disrespect for 'Big army' discipline and protocols, but carried out their diverse military orders efficiently. They didn't need to be supervised, or told twice. But would they come up to scratch for what he and the Regiment had in mind?

When he had first arrived at the Special Forces barracks in Chelsea, Two Troop were under the temporary command of a caretaker Troop Commander, Lieutenant Nick Pierce. Within the Regiment, officers generally were irreverently known as Rupert's by the men. Nick was a keen bright Rupert, but had only recently been commissioned into the Regiment, and lacked the real depth of experience which a SAS Troop Commander needed. When he had officially handed the reins of command to Pat, Nick Pierce had looked genuinely relieved.

'I hope you have better luck than I did Pat. I'm off to Signals Troop for a while. '

Without another word, he turned on his heal, and beat a hasty retreat.

Weeks earlier, shortly after joining his new SAS squadron and assuming command of Two Troop, Pat had sat quietly in the squadron's office reviewing the personnel files and military qualifications of his new Troop. Pat read each man's file carefully. On paper, there was a lot of talent. The Troop was peppered with ex-regular and Territorial soldiers who had served in an intriguing cross section of other Regiments. Pat noticed ruefully that there were no ex-regular SAS among them, but he understood the anti-weekend warrior mentality in Hereford and the resulting reservations which stopped his old buddies from serving in the T.A. after years of regular service.

Two Troop's diverse backgrounds gave them vast experience of military signalling, engineering and mechanical skills. Some of the men had no previous experience at all, but the Territorial SAS took the view that they could mould a man from scratch into exactly who they wanted, given the intensive training each man received, even before gaining their coveted beret.

When not on duty, his new men lived vastly different lives. Some made a living as skilled manual workers, others held down well placed jobs in the capital's banks and leading insurance firms. As Pat scanned each man's file, he found a plumber, a postman and even an officer of the police, who had managed to gain special permission to serve in the Territorial SAS from the Metropolitan Police Commissioner himself. To Pat's great surprise, one of his new Troop had ominously listed his previous occupation as 'Hell's Angel.'

As he walked into the office, and saw Pat reading the files, his new squadron Sgt Major Sandy Robertson grinned.

'They're a pretty rum bunch, but they're all good lads at heart..' His face clouded over slowly. 'To get the

36

best out of them Pat, especially now, they need some good, old fashioned leadership. '

Pat returned the grin. Perhaps this bunch of misfits might shape up into the razor sharp spearhead of the new Shadow Squadron after all?

As Pat continued to scrutinise the folders, one thing was certain: the following weeks would be a critical time in sculpting the Troop. The door swung both ways; Pat would look hard at his men, but he knew they were going to look even harder at him. These men were the elite, but they needed someone special to lead them into an uncertain and dangerous future.

His mixed bag of soldiers haled from all walks of life; their accents had been forged from the tough streets of London's East End to the far corners of the playing fields at Eton.

Spit and polish had no place in the Regiment. Pat ignored the odd cross section of his men's unique dress code. One trooper's battered camouflage jacket seemed to be held together with masking tape, and another's haircut was long overdue.

One of the four-man teams who belonged to Two Troop lounged in their seats, and were deep in conversation about the merits of a sports car one of them had just bought, and another team was hooting with laughter over the details of a disastrous date one of them had had recently, with a girl whose family had a big estate in the country.

'I think I was just her bit of rough,' laughed Spike Morris, who in civilian life was a trainee British Telecom engineer.

'I'd been feeling bad all day anyway, and that bloody lager and curry mix down at the Bengal Star just finished me off. I thought the Vinderloo tasted a bit dodgy, but it was so hot, I scoffed it anyway. By the time we got to the cinema, I couldn't stop farting. It wasn't just the noise - the bloody smell was awful. The poor girl did her best to ignore everything, but when she started coughing into her hanky, I knew I'd blown it. I was never going to get my leg over.'

The other team members howled with laughter.

Pat cleared his throat and yelled out for his men to quiet down. He waited a moment as they settled.

'Right lads,' he began. 'I'm going to brief you on exercise Bright Star in Denmark, which is coming up in a couple of weeks. Who isn't coming?'

'I'm starting my sniper course at Warminster,' said a cultured accent from the back of the darkened briefing room.

'Yeah, I know about that Frankie, no problem. Anyone else?'

No-one moved, so Pat continued. 'It's a big bridge attack, and the Boss has given me a free hand. I've been kicking it around for a couple of weeks. I've got an idea which might catch the Danes out. '

Bright Star was an NATO exercise involving the Territorial arm of the British army's Special Forces, 21 SAS Regt. Their mission was to enter Denmark clandestinely in small groups, by any means they thought appropriate, and carry out dummy attacks on strategic military and civilian targets. Their job was to simulate Russian army Spetznaz sabotage, which would certainly come just before an all-out Soviet invasion. It was a test of the efficiency of the Danish Home Guard, whose job was to protect their Country's key targets against destruction by the enemy. The Guard's secondary task, whenever possible was to catch the saboteurs. The dice were loaded against the Regiment however, as the attacks were to be carried out over a pre-planned two day period, when Denmark's reserve and regular forces were pre-warned and on full-scale military alert.

Pat turned on a projector, and the white wall screen was flooded with an aerial photograph of a massive steel and concrete suspension bridge, spanning a wide expanse of dark, turgid water.

The Troop whistled in surprise.

'Jesus Pat, it's bloody huge!'

Pat held up a hand to quell any further comments.

'All right lads, settle down, I told you, I've thought hard about this. I've got a plan. Have any of you guys ever blown up a suspension bridge?'

Heads shook around the briefing room, but there were plenty of eager grinning faces staring back at their new Troop Commander.

'We're going to infiltrate the whole Troop into Denmark in civilian clothes, and plant two tons of simulated explosives bang in the middle of the Storstrom bridge. It connects two strategically important islands - Falster and Masnedo in Copenhagen. '

Pat pointed to the picture on the screen.

'We cut this,' he said with a wolfish grin, and Copenhagen is instantly paralysed. '

Nods of approval came from around the room. At last, here was a job, and perhaps a leader, worthy of Two Troops talent's.

'The outline is simple,' said Pat. We'll borrow three mini-buses from the Guards barracks down at Chelsea bridge Road, re-spray them, and change the number plates to make them look civilian. '

Danny Thomas put his hand up.

'I think I can sort the plates out for you Pat, at my dad's garage.'

Someone grunted from the back.

'Not the first set of dodgy plates out of your old dad's garage then Danny?'

Before Danny could reply, Pat held his hand up to quell the sniggers.

'All right, settle down you lot. Yes, that would be good Danny. I'll leave that one with you, but I want three different sets.' Pat paused. 'We all travel over to Denmark on the ferry in civilian clothes. We receive the explosives via a Royal Air Force parachute drop in Denmark, the night before the attack. We drive into Copenhagen and chain two of the vans loaded with the explosives onto the middle of the bridge, then scoot out on our last bus to rendezvous with a Royal Navy minesweeper fifteen miles up the Danish coast. It's pretty simple. Any questions, before I give you the full detailed briefing?'

When Pat had finished, and the evening's other training was over, the Troop changed out of uniform, and back into their civilian clothes. Most of the men settled into the squadron's bar for a quick beer before making their way home. Spike Morris was sitting in a huddle with his friend Danny, and a couple of other mates.

'You worked with the regular SAS when you served in the Parachute Regiment Spike. What do you make of our new leader?'

'He seems to know what he's doing, Danny. He's ex-regular SAS, so he's got to be a hundred per cent better than that bloody idiot Nick Pierce. '

All four young men nodded, and then one of their two companions whispered.

'Someone in the Orderly room told me that Pat got a Military Cross in Afghanistan. He didn't tell me any details, but they don't give gongs like that away for nothing. You can bet he earned his medal the hard way. '

Danny nodded.

'I don't know about you guys, but I reckon he's a pretty good bloke. Let's see how he does on Bright Star.

His plan looks good. I think we can pull the job off without any problems.' Danny looked at each of his friends in turn. 'He certainly knows his stuff.'

There were affirmative nods around the table.

'Fair enough,' said Spike. 'I'll have a chat with the rest of the boys.... '

Chapter Four

It was a strange new life, a life of light and shadow - but Pat didn't resent it, even for a second. It was in those weekends among his new Troop that he felt his life-force surging back. It brought meaning to those long shifts, weaving through traffic from one end of the city to another, gave him purpose in the long nights spent alone.

Standing in the living room of his Paddington flat, Pat leafed absently through his mail. In the corner of the room, the television flared - but, like, always, he paid it little mind.

The news was still full of reports of the horrific attack which had occurred in Holland the previous day. Three cars, packed with high explosives had been exploded by suspected Muslim extremists outside shopping centres in the middle of Amsterdam, killing and maiming hundreds of innocent civilians. Trembling news footage from one of the attacks showed screaming shoppers lying in spreading scarlet pools across the mall's devastated forecourt, the tangled remains of one of the cars embedded at the centre of a deep smoking crater. The car's driver had apparently been intent on driving into the shopping mall before triggering the explosion, but had been mercifully stopped outside by a low security wall.

The report cut to the Dutch Prime Minister. Though the day's events had scored deep lines into his face, he clamoured to reassure his citizens that everything possible was being done to protect them. Pat laid down his letters and studied the images sadly. There had been a time when he would have been on the ground, the smoke curling around him, the children at his feet crying for their mothers. There were some things, it seemed, that he did not miss about the military life.

Pat's first exposure to the after-effects of this type of attack had been in Northern Ireland. Those were the dark days of the IRA, and Pat's memories had been forever scarred. His infantry platoon had been on standby when a bomb wreaked a ruin from a nightclub in the Protestant Waterside district, close to Londonderry's Craigavon bridge. When the smoke had cleared, and the ambulances had taken away the survivors, Pat and the rest of the Standby Platoon had one more job to do.

'Don't bother trying to match up all the bits young Farrell,' his sergeant had said, with a grin. 'That's the coroner's job.'

He had passed Pat a shovel and a big black plastic bag - and so had begun Pat's first grim lesson in what it really meant to be at war.

That night, his fares blurred into the usual pattern: the early evening delivering tired passengers to bus and railway stations; the later hours spent delivering customers with more zeal to smart nightspots, theatres and the cinemas dotted around the bright lights of London's busy West End.

Midnight came more slowly than it had done in the past few shifts. He laboured under the dark starless sky, and even when his passengers tried to spark up conversations, he found that the words would not come.

The rank outside Waterloo station was deserted. Tempted as he was to ditch the cab for an hour and wander the embankment, Pat decided instead to head back over the river and take his chances in the West End.

As he turned onto the approach road towards Waterloo bridge, a man leapt out of the shadows. Frantically waving a furled umbrella, he seemed almost frenzied as he flagged down Pat's cab.

When Pat opened his passenger window to enquire where the fare wanted to go, he was hit by the pungent stench of vodka. The man might have been smartly dressed, a lightweight trench-coat over three-piece suit, but he smelt more like a riverside tramp.

'Maida Vale,' his new passenger croaked.

Pat was used to carrying drunks late at night. He didn't have a problem, as long as they behaved themselves, paid the fare, and didn't throw up in the back of his cab. His current fare looked a little worse for wear, but Pat sensed he would be fine.

After several minutes, the inevitable football talk began. Having been an ardent fan of Arsenal since he wore short trousers, Pat was pleased to hear his passenger also supported the Gunners.

Having chatted for several minutes about Arsenal's defensive line up, the state of UEFA's referees and the Gunners' chances in the F.A. Cup, his fare asked Pat what he did before he drove a cab. Pat was happy to admit he had served in the army, but naturally omitted to mention his connection with the Special Air Service, both in the past and now in the present. Pat couldn't put his finger on it - but, as he chatted, he had the distinct feeling that he knew the man from somewhere. The face and voice were vaguely familiar somehow, but try as he might, he couldn't quite make the connection.

There was a lull in the conversation. Pat began to feel the hairs on the back of his neck prickle. He glanced in his rear view mirror, and could see his fare staring intently at the back of his head. But there was something else, a look of triumphant relief blossoming on the man's face. He wore a peculiar smile - and surely it was not only the vodka making him leer that way.

Pat turned into the narrow street in Maida Vale pulling into the curb outside the passenger's address. On the opposite side of the street, drinkers still gathered around the doors of a late licensed pub, huddling together against the night's cold winter chill.

Pat switched on the taxi's interior lights, lent across and checked the meter.

'That's £9.50 mate,' he said.

Suddenly, the passenger lent forward. 'I don't know if you remember me,' he said. 'But I do remember you. You're Pat Farrell, aren't you?'

Chapter Five

Pat looked at the man's haggard face and nodded.

'But who the hell are you?' he demanded.

The grin quickly faded from the man's face.

'Look Pat, I know this is all going to sound rather strange - but can I buy you a drink over the road?' He stopped, suddenly shamefaced. 'I need to talk to somebody Pat. I need to get something off my chest. '

There had been slower nights, but still Pat was desperate for the break. He looked at the stranger and wondered if the man could take another shot of vodka.

'I could go for one,' he finally admitted.

Locking the cab, Pat followed his fare across the road. Inside, the man felt in his pocket for a cigarette, but stopped suddenly.

'Damn that bloody stupid no smoking law.' He muttered angrily to himself. Pat's fare ordered two large vodkas, and quickly swallowed the contents of one glass down before he asked Pat what he'd like.

'Just a pint would be fine thanks; but no more, I'm driving.'

His companion shrugged, turning to the landlord he said.

'And I'll have the same again Jack. '

Both men carried their glasses to a deserted table in the far corner of the saloon. There were several couples sitting around the bar, but they were intent on each other and their own conversations, and ignored the new arrivals.

Pat lifted the brimming glass to his lips, slowly regarding the man sitting opposite. 'It's time for cards on the table,' he said. 'Where the hell do I know you from?'

The man's face split into a broad grin. 'I'm Cornelius Wilde,' he said quietly. 'You do remember,' he went on, watching Pat's face flinch. 'We met in Somalia about twelve years ago. '

Pat starred at the man, the memories rampaging back. 'Of course I remember,' he breathed, slapping his thigh as the truth dawned on him.

They had met at Mogadishu airport nearly twelve years earlier. Pat had been part of an undercover SAS team on secondment to the SIS, Britain's overseas Counter Espionage Security Service, also known as MI6. Pat remembered in a flash.

The SIS had arranged to 'extract' a valuable terrorist regional leader, who the SIS had 'turned', and was now working covertly for Her Majesty's Government. His cover blown, the man was to be hiding in a specific safe house in Kismayo, the third largest city in Somalia, waiting nervously for an SAS snatch team to spirit him out of the country.

'It was a close call that night,' said Pat, thinking back to the operation which had nearly cost him his life.

Pat and the other SAS men had arrived at the safe house in the nick of time. As they bundled the agent into a car, a terrorist vehicle had screeched around a corner, and opened fire upon them. Across Kismayo they had hurtled, guns blazing on both sides. As they reached the city's outskirts, with bullets cracking and ricocheting past his head, Pat had managed to shoot out one of the enemy's front tyres by leaning from a rear window. The Toyota full of screaming gunmen had slewed violently across the road, hit a wall, and burst into a ball of flames.

'When you and your colleagues arrived, we sat in that awful private lounge in Mogadishu airport for hours waiting for our flight, if you remember?' Cornelius said.

Pat nodded. 'I remember it well. I must admit you didn't really strike me as the secret agent type. '

Cornelius shrugged.

'I was only there because I had the lead on handling the intelligence our man was passing to us. When he was blown, I put together the rescue. Cornelius exhaled and his shoulders began to sag. 'I'm really a back room boy; an intelligence analyst, not a field agent at all. '

Pat sipped at his drink, as Cornelius downed his fourth double vodka.

'Things have not been going well for me recently,' said Cornelius morosely. 'I've been receiving private therapy for depression.' He shook his head sadly. 'The shrinks say it's a result of the intense pressure of work over the years, and has begun to have a profound effect on my state of health. '

According to one of the other spooks at the airport, Cornelius, it transpired, had once been considered an analytical genius by MI6.

'The doctors have put me on anti-depressants, but it's the booze that numbs me out. 'Cornelius paused for a couple of deep breaths. 'It all started innocently enough, with a regular few stiff drinks after work with my colleagues but, as the months progressed, I found that I needed several large vodkas before setting off for work in the morning as well. '

Cornelius sat gazing miserably at his glass as the silence lengthened.

'Things went downhill fast. Finally, my wife left me, taking my lovely children with her. It was the solicitors that told me she wanted the divorce. She even kept my bloody dog…' Cornelius sighed miserably.

Pat nodded. He had seen this happen before; several old friends from Hereford had lost it to alcohol. Their lives had come apart at the seams when pressure and dark memories got too much to handle.

'If the job gets wind of my little problem, I'd be sacked on the spot. They don't do mercy at Vauxhall Cross.' Cornelius hung his head for a moment, and then held up his vodka glass. With a sly, drunken grin, he whispered, 'this has to be the best medicine in the world when I start feeling sorry for myself. '

Pat could see this conversation was going nowhere. Cornelius, he thought sadly, was just another burnt-out, morose drunk. There was nothing he could do.

Pat was about to make his excuses and leave, when suddenly, Cornelius stirred himself and called out in a loud voice.

'One last round for the road, if you please Jack. Couple of large ones over here.'

The landlord nodded, and stopped polishing a glass behind the bar. Pat began to rise, but Cornelius already had his hand on Pat's forearm.

'No, please don't go yet,' he pleaded. There was a new urgency in Cornelius's voice. 'Look Pat, old buddy. There's something else.' He hiccupped again, looking conspiratorially around the barroom. Reaching into his inside breast pocket of his jacket, he handed Pat a dog-eared photograph.

'It's this bastard that's the problem, Pat.'

Pat looked at the cruel hawk-like features of the man who stared back from the grainy black and white photograph.

Pat thought for a moment 'OK, so who is he?' He inquired impatiently.

The landlord brought over two more glasses filled with vodka, and returned to his duties behind the bar. Cornelius snatched up the first glass, spilling some of the clear fiery liquid onto the table. He drained what remained in a single gulp, and leaned forward again, towards Pat.

'He could be real bloody trouble for this country, Pat... Before he vanished during the second Gulf War, this man was a full Colonel in the Iraqi Mukhabarat, Saddam

Hussein's secret police. I haven't found his name yet, but I'm sure he's up to his neck in something really ugly. '

Chapter Six

Kurdistan - Iraq - 1998

Operation Anfal (translated from Arabic, means - The Spoils) was the planned systematic eradication of the Kurdish people, who populated the Northern territories of Iraq. They were considered too dangerous, independent and pro-Iranian to be trusted by Saddam Hussein's ruling Sunni Government. Kurdish Pershmerga guerrilla attacks on isolated Iraqis army outposts in the region had continued to grow in number and ferocity. The problem had grown beyond simply bombing random Kurdish villages in reprisal. The tiny terrorist fly which at first had only irritated Saddam Hussein, now began to bite hard. Between attacks, the fierce Pershmerga fighters simply melted away into sleepy Kurdish villages dotted throughout mountainous Kurdistan. It was decided at the highest Government level that the time had come to implement a decisive, final solution. The plan had been secretly agreed by the Iraqi President and his closest echelon of Ministers several years previously, and was now close to becoming a reality. Saddam and his trusted inner Cabinet proposed that every Kurdish village, town and city within the newly declared north-eastern 'Forbidden Zone' was to be completely cleansed of its population, using mass deportations to death camps, or better still, the Kurds were to be destroyed where they lived and worked

56

using, wherever possible, chemical weapons. The entire Kurdish race was to be exterminated, to provide living space for loyal Sunni Arabs, who although in the minority, dominated Iraqi society and controlled absolute power within the Government of Iraq.

* * * * *

The remote village of Sardasht was about to die.

Concealed five kilometres away, high up on a sandy ridge, Lieutenant-Colonel Jalal Al-Mahdi lay amongst a parched terrain littered with clumps of dry grasses and broken volcanic rock. He swept his powerful Zeiss binoculars slowly across the miserable collection of three dozen mud-brick huts and buildings which danced gently in the heat haze below.

'It is time for these Kurdish dogs to die,' he thought. Smiling to himself, he pressed the send button on his radio microphone.

'Fire!' he barked.

The first salvo thundered out across the slumbering Kurdish hills, shattering their ancient tranquillity, as the Iraqi artillerymen enthusiastically pulled their firing lanyards. The targets' range was relatively short, a little less than nine kilometres; the projectiles' flight time could be counted in seconds. The heavy 152mm shells hit the North-Western quadrant of Sardasht almost simultaneously, with a surprisingly muffled, but distinct crump. There was no explosion at each of the impact points; instead, dense clouds of white smoke billowed up, rampaging quickly through all the surrounding homes. Every nook and cranny within the crude peasant houses was quickly filled with menacing swirls of the sinister fog.

Colonel Al-Mahdi surveyed the village again with his field glasses. A satisfied smile spread across his face. Within moments, he could see people staggering from their houses, collapsing and writhing in the dust. He was always disappointed that he was could see so little detail from this safe distance, but still he relished every vivid image.

Awoken by the sudden whistle and thump of the heavy shells, Abdul Barzani rose sleepily from his straw mattress and rubbed his tired eyes. A simple, poorly educated man, he rarely travelled far from the village where his family had lived for generations. He knew very little about the evils of the outside world, and even less about weapons of mass destruction.

His wife stirred as he yawned, scratched himself and shuffled across the earthen floor. His innocent curiosity would be his downfall. Opening the crude wooden door to see what had caused the noise, he raised his arm and shielded his eyes from the sun's brilliant, if strangely misty, glare. Yawning again, he stepped outside. The first and last thing he noticed was a pungent bitter smell in the air.

Minute droplets of Sarin nerve gas were mixing with the dense smoke as it hissed angrily from the unexploded base of the gas shell, which had landed just thirty feet from Barzani's front door. Tiny, invisible airborne particles of the agent touched his skin - and for Barzani, the attack was almost over.

It was already too late. Without warning, he began to convulse. Powerful muscle spasms suddenly gripped and overcame him. He toppled to the ground, thrashing and shuddering, desperately fighting to draw a shallow gasping breath.

Abdul Barzani's last conscious thought was to save his family. Even as he died, he desperately tried to call out a warning to his sleeping wife, but managed only a gurgled sigh. Flecks of foam dribbled past his lolling tongue as his bowels and bladder opened in a hot steaming flood. In seconds, the nerve gas had shut down his entire body, and there was nothing he could do to stop it.

The sinister mist swirled silently over him, rolling on through the open door. Within moments, his unsuspecting wife and children had joined him on his journey to the next life.

A second artillery salvo was aimed at the North-Eastern section of the village. The same scenario unfolded as the shells crashed home, killing everything that was touched by the lethal fog. One shell screamed over the village, scoring a direct hit on its largest two story building, which disappeared in a thick cloud of choking dust and rubble. The Colonel smiled again, his cruel black eyes narrowing with the pleasure of everything which was happening before him. He couldn't hear the screams from the dying; but from his safe, grandstand view, he eagerly drank in every detail of the horror.

The firing stopped and the respite began. Though the condemned Kurds did not know it, the next batch of shells were already being wheeled up from their armoured carriers and prepared by the profusely sweating Iraqi artillerymen. The protective chemical suits they wore kept the heat firmly locked close to their sweltering skin, as they set the fuses. Their Officers yelled at them to hurry, adding a hard slap or kick to anyone they thought to be slacking.

When the next salvo of shells was finally fused and ready, they were loaded into the hot breaches of the howitzers. The deadly contents of the shells, this time, were just as dangerous - but very different. The long metal cases protecting the lethal cargo carried different vivid markings, showing an ominous corrosive symbol on each of their drab green sides.

During the brief pause for fusing, Colonel Al-Mahdi reflected on the success of his operation. The initial phase of Operation Anfal was now almost complete; Sardasht was scheduled to be the last small village to be tested. The necessary scientific data had been collected, to perfect the execution of Anfal's forthcoming mass chemical genocide. Over the previous months, his unit had deployed and tried different types of concentrated poisons. Cyanide, chlorine and VX nerve gas had all been delivered onto remote, unsuspecting, Kurdish communities using aircraft or artillery, or a combination of both. The effects of each agent had been recorded, but there was no doubt in his mind that the current combination produced the best results.

The Colonel swept his binoculars over to the South-East, where his hidden artillery battery was neatly laid out for the bombardment. It amused him to think of the hot, sweating artillerymen down in the valley, dressed in their clumsy rubber chemical warfare suits, and their sweltering Russian-made SHM gas masks. His men would be extremely hot already, as they nervously lifted heavy shells into the breaches of the howitzers. Each shell was, after all, fully laden with a concentrated payload of the deadly and corrosive agent known as mustard gas.

Although Lt. Colonel Jalal Al-Mahdi had witnessed this scene many times before on the other unsuspecting Kurdish targets, he still felt the same thrill of power course through his entire being.

Grinning, he reached for the radio microphone, which he would shortly use to complete the destruction of Sardasht, and every living thing which thought of it as home.

Colonel Al-Mahdi casually flicked the radio microphone into the 'on' position and spoke to his survey section officer down in the valley, making another check that there was still no sign of any breeze, which might carry the deadly gas towards his own position.

'No Sir, there is nothing, the air's completely still,' came the distant crackling response.

'Good, stand by,' he replied curtly.

Taking one last panoramic scan of the mortally-wounded Sardasht, Al-Mahdi flicked the microphone switch again.

'Major al-Khafaji, are you ready now?' He spat the last words out with every ounce of contempt he could muster; Major al-Khafaji was stupid, incompetent and solely responsible for the irritating earlier delay.

The nervous reply crackled over the background static of his radio speaker and made him smile. 'Yes Colonel, yes ….. Everything is ready.'

Colonel Jalal Al-Mahdi shivered with new anticipation.

When the Colonel had given his final briefing to his officers twenty-four hours earlier, he had instructed them to deploy the same practiced routine they had used on thirty-seven other small Kurdish villages during the previous nine months.

'This operation will be the final field test of the correct concentrations and distribution of Sarin and mustard gas over a known area, delivered in this case solely by the shells of eight 152mm artillery howitzers. '

The earlier trials had been comprehensive, and many combinations of delivery had been tested already - from chemical sprays mounted under helicopters, to cargo planes dropping fifty gallon drums of gas onto their hapless victims. This last method had been abandoned however, after one disastrous test, when a drum was released too high, causing it to drift over a small group of junior Interior Ministry observers; it's content killing them outright when it burst on the ground. The pilot and his family had paid with their lives for the mistake.

As the last howitzer chief signalled that all was ready, Major al-Khafaji snatched up his microphone and quickly reported, 'Second bombardment phase ready, Sir!'

The reply came within moments. From his vantage point, Colonel Al-Mahdi nodded absently at his handset, and pressed the send switch.

'At last!' He hissed. '*Fire!*

Once again, the guns thundered as they hurled their heavy shells towards Sardasht, this time raking the southern end of the village. The clouds of vapour which mushroomed from each of the eight small craters were subtly different from the initial Sarin salvos, the gas clouds much thicker, and tinged with a sickly yellow glow.

A small group of terrified Kurds, several clutching infants, began to flee from the village. Woken by the first salvo of incoming shells, and alerted by the hysterical screams of their neighbours, they ran desperately for their lives, away from their homes along the deserted Kirkuk road.

Someone cried frantically.

'For the love of the Allah - Run!'

As they broke from the cover of the village, eruptions of dirt rose all around the fleeing group, bullets slicing them down. The staccato rattle of the Special Republican Guard's heavy machine guns echoed across the surrounding hills - and then, just as abruptly, the guns fell silent.

Inside the village, hysterical people trapped in the yellow clouds drunkenly emerged from their homes with their eyes streaming, coughing and clutching at their burning throats, staggering forth on their final steps. At last, they were stilled. Their short flight into the open had failed to find them salvation; instead, it had only sent them further into the swirling gas.

Colonel Al-Mahdi's radio crackled once again. Major al-Khafaji's voice reported. 'All rounds now fired, Sir. '

'Very well Major. We will begin Phase Two in one hour. If your gas detectors remain clear after thirty minutes, your men may remove their protective clothing.' Al-Mahdi paused, a fleeting grin flickering onto his face. 'Of course, you may have the honour of personally leading the search of the village. '

'But, but Colonel, Sir! I ...'

'*Silence!*' Colonel Al-Mahdi roared as static crackling his earpiece. 'Perhaps it will ensure you keep better time in future?'

After a moment, he stood up and glanced down at his radio operator, who had lain silent and still beside him during the attack.

'Order my vehicle to meet me at the bottom of the slope,' he said absently, beginning to walk downhill, nonchalantly flicking dust from his uniform as he went.

Colonel Al-Mahdi smoked a cigarette as he stood idly waiting for his jeep. He glanced down at his diamond-studded Rolex and something inside him wrenched - the morning's operation had started one quarter of an hour

66

late. Major al-Khafaji would pay dearly for the delay to his tightly organised schedule. The beautiful Rolex had been a gift from his Uncle, presented to him upon his graduation from the prestigious Baghdad Academy of Army Officers, some six years previously. His powerful family connections, organisational skills and natural cunning had given him a profound head start over the other officer cadets.

The young Al-Mahdi had begun his training at the Academy under a cloud of secret family disgrace - but he was a bright and gifted military student, ultimately graduating at the top of his class. Despite his excellent marks, he knew that his subsequent meteoric rise through the Officer Corps had been helped in no small measure by his Uncle, who held the high office of Secretary General of the Northern Bureau of Iraq's ruling Ba'ath party. His Uncle also happened to be a blood cousin to Iraq's all-powerful dictator, Saddam Hussein.

The young Major Jalal Al-Mahdi had been deeply honoured and excited when he had been ordered from his regular army armoured unit to the Defence Ministry in Baghdad almost a year previously, to be told, during an audience with his Uncle, that he had been promoted yet again, and given overall military command of this

67

experimental phase of the military operation known as *'The Spoils.'*

Operation Anfal was unfolding before him now, and he felt the thrill moving in his blood. Soon, the true horror of the Spoils would be known all over the earth - the whole world would learn the name of Al-Mahdi's ageing Uncle.

General Ali Hassan Al-Majid, the man they would soon dub with a name steeped in the very darkest infamy.

The world would know him as *'Chemical Ali…* '

Chapter Seven

Kurdistan - Iraq - 1998

Colonel Al-Mahdi emerged from his drab command tent, in deep discussion with Dr Tariq al-Numan. As one of Iraq's most eminent civilian scientists, Dr al-Numan normally worked for the Defence Ministry as Chairman of the National Chemical Research Institute.

The ageing Doctor did not enjoy these field trips; far too many flies, and too much dust and heat. He preferred the air conditioned comfort of his laboratory complex at the Institute in Baghdad. Unfortunately for him, he was obliged, from time to time, to clearly demonstrate his utter dedication and loyalty to the Ba'ath party, and personally lead the research team whenever active field testing was in progress.

He didn't like, nor trust the man who now stood beside him, and his face betrayed his reservations.

'But Colonel, if we cut corners with our safety protocols, we face the very real threat of a catastrophic accident. You know how incredibly dangerous these substances are?'

Colonel Al-Mahdi stopped, and turned towards the scientist.

'My dear Dr al-Numan,' he began silkily, 'it is not a matter of cutting corners. It is purely a matter of expediency.' He straightened, and drew himself up to his full height. 'As you are well aware, I have been ordered by my Uncle, the General, on the express orders of our illustrious President himself, to provide you with the various military means of carrying out these experiments. Anfal must sweep clear Iraqi Kurdistan of the disloyal Kurdish scum who infest it. While I appreciate your need for accurate results, it is just taking far too long to achieve them. I have promised Colonel al-Sadun that we will be back in Topzawa before nightfall.'

Dr al-Numan shook his head, but before he could breathe a word Colonel Al-Mahdi cut him off.

'My men are fully trained to detect residual gas of all types, and are perfectly capable of declaring areas ready for your scientific team. I must insist, this time, that they are given the chance to do their job. '

'Very well, Colonel,' said the scientist, sighing deeply. 'You are in charge of the military aspect of these tests, so let us proceed, and see what your men are capable of. '

Twenty minutes later, two specially fitted BMP 60 armoured personnel carriers growled slowly towards the eerily silent village. Outside each Russian built six-wheeled vehicle, special steel baskets were permanently welded to the vehicle's rear doors. Each basket contained dozens of thin metal rods, on each of which fluttered a small triangular red or green flag. The carriers both stopped just short of the entrance to the poisoned village, beside the blood-stained bodies of those who had earlier tried to flee. Inside the vehicle, Major al-Khafaji ordered his crew to carry out the first residual gas test.

Within the cramped confines of the armoured vehicle, one of the operators reached across to his control panel. He switched on an exterior fan, which 'sniffed' the outside atmosphere, drawing a small sample into their hermetically-sealed atmospheric test machine. After a few moments, all five lights on the machine clicked green.

'All clear Sir,' breathed the operator.

Major al-Khafaji nodded. 'Good. Deploy a green flag and continue.'

The operator pressed another button on his control panel, and a muffled pop sounded outside the

71

vehicle, as a rod fitted with a green marker flag was automatically fired into the ground.

The sweating Major turned to the vehicle's driver and ordered him to continue further into the village. He reached for his radio microphone and spoke to the other vehicle's Commander.

'Proceed into the North-Western quadrant of Sardasht and begin testing the area,' he commanded. 'And for the love of Allah, do it quickly!' he hastily added.

For the next thirty minutes, the two sealed BMP 60s continued their slow systematic street-by-street survey of Sardasht.

Despite his crew's best efforts, Major al-Khafaji was becoming increasingly agitated. The whole sweep was taking far too long, and there were too many areas in his northern quadrant which had shown only three or four green lights. In the developing heat of the morning, the non-persistent nature of the gaseous agents should have revealed that they had now fully evaporated, rendering the whole area safe. What worried him was that minute traces of nerve gas still appeared to be clinging to some areas within the village, and that simply made no sense to him. He was an artillery officer, not a scientist, and his technical knowledge of the complex subject of chemical warfare was limited - but his fear of Colonel Al-Mahdi's continued wrath outweighed his natural instinct for caution.

'Incorrect calibration must be to blame,' he thought to himself, and overrode his crew chief several times, ordering green flags instead of red.

While Major al-Khafaji cursed, and urged both his sweating crews to complete their operation, Colonel Al-Mahdi and Dr al-Numan sat in the cool of the Colonel's command tent, nine kilometres away, enjoying hot sweet tea. They had used the time after the destruction of Sardasht to examine the overall effectiveness of Sarin nerve gas and the other chemical agents they had tested. Their conclusions would soon be presented in person to General Ali Hassan Al-Majid himself. The General would then travel to one of the many Presidential palaces in Baghdad, and brief the President in person on their findings.

Dr al-Numan was concerned.

'Although Sarin has always scored highly on the lethal index, its biggest shortfall is the speed it evaporates and therefore is rendered harmless. We have found time and again during our patriotic war against Iran that the day's heat removes its lethal capacity far too quickly. To create Sarin in suitable quantities, the payloads we have used until now have been based on a European formula. They never envisaged its use in temperatures exceeding forty degrees centigrade. '

Colonel Al-Mahdi's head turned from the contemplation of his tea.

'Until now, Doctor?' He asked, his eyes narrowing.

Dr al-Numan's face beamed with pride. '

'Yes, my dear Colonel, the new batch of Sarin you used this morning was the latest in our efforts to overcome the early evaporation problem. We made a significant breakthrough recently, and I believe that the problem is now solved. I will not bore you with the full technical details, but in essence, we have found a very simple solution. We combined liquid Sarin with a very thin, light vegetable oil at a molecular level to provide you with a more persistent agent.'

The Colonel stood up. 'That is very, very interesting Doctor. May I be the first to offer my sincerest congratulations to you and your staff? When he hears of it, I'm sure my Uncle will reward you appropriately, and be truly impressed and delighted with your achievements. '

Major al-Khafaji stood stiffly to attention in front of his Commanding Officer, as he made his report.

'The village is clear of all toxic agents, Sir.'

Dr al-Numan began to rise in protest, but was silenced with a wave of the Commanding Officer's hand.

Colonel Al-Mahdi stared thoughtfully at his nervous subordinate for several moments, and then nodded.

'Very well Major. You may proceed with your men on foot and begin the body count. I want measurements and interrogation of any Kurd scum that still live. Despite your assurances that the village is clear, we will, nevertheless, exercise our usual safety protocols, and full protection will be worn.' He glanced towards Dr al-Numan and inclined his head slightly. 'To avoid any unfortunate accidents,' he added, with only the merest hint of a smile.

The soldiers approached the village casually on foot. They knew, from past experience, that none of its civilian occupants would be in any condition to resist. The Special Republican Guardsmen sweltered in their rubber protection suits, but were spurred on by hungry anticipation of the loot which awaited them. There was always the chance of rich pickings. As they were still obliged to wear their gas masks, it was easy to drop anything of value into the empty case conveniently strapped to their chests.

Survivors were occasionally found, but their summary execution was strictly forbidden. The similarly protected civilian scientists would always promise medical help to anyone still alive, but none of the soldiers had ever witnessed a survivor actually receiving any medical attention. A quick and sometimes brutal interrogation was the most any survivor could possibly hope for.

Inside the village, even Dante's frenzied imagination could not have painted a more horrific scene. Bodies were scattered and sprawled everywhere. Men and women lay curled on the ground, frozen in attitudes of agonising death. Here and there, some still clutched a tiny lifeless infant to them, while most simply lay alone and motionless on the dusty streets. The body of a small girl lay prostrate on the steps leading to her home, where until now she had always felt safe and loved. A dirty rag doll stared blankly into the sky beside her. The deadly nerve gas had done its devilish work, and no living thing had survived it.

76

Behind one house, confined within a makeshift pen of old corrugated iron sheets, a small flock of goats lay unmoving in the dirt. Behind another house, a few sheep lay huddled in a corner of a silent courtyard. Their young shepherd had stayed to protect his flock - but, now, he lay spread-eagled and still among them.

The scientists moved throughout the village, noting impact points, taking measurements, counting bodies. As the scientific data was collected, the soldiers ransacked every house, tipping the lifeless corpses of the old and infirm from their deathbeds, rifling through cupboards and drawers and pocketing anything which might be of value.

As expected, the northern end of Sardasht yielded no survivors. Having loaded the poisoned corpses onto one of their military trucks, the soldiers turned their attention to the other end of the village, where the mustard gas had been deployed. The soldiers moved slowly now, using more caution in their search. Under the harsh eyes of their superiors, missing a survivor here would mean a flogging, or worse.

Somewhere close, faint and pitiful moans drifted from inside a house. Two soldiers kicked the door open, and dragged out an elderly woman. Leaving her lying on the dusty ground, they signalled to their sergeant that they had found a survivor. The frail old woman groaned and was seized by a powerful coughing spasm. Blood trickled from her nose and mouth.

'Please, please help me!' She whispered weakly, as a scientist, alerted by the sergeant strode over and crouched down beside her.

'Be quiet, old woman. The doctors and nurses will be here shortly, and they will tend to you. If you want their help, you must answer my questions. What is your age?'

As the scientist continued to question the old woman, he scribbled her mumbled answers onto a sheet clipped to his mill board.

The old woman was suddenly shaken by more powerful spasms of coughing, and vomited blood and thick yellow pus over her chest. The scientist jumped backwards, and looked down at her with disgust. The old women turned her head towards him. She fought desperately to draw each agonising breathe into her ravaged lungs.

'You two!' He called to the two soldiers who had found her. He looked down at the old woman with a sneer. 'She's dying. I'll get nothing more. Put her in the lorry with the others.'

The soldiers quickly complied, and threw her frail and blistered body into a military truck, which was parked nearby.

As the few disfigured survivors were interrogated, soldiers busily cleared bodies from the remaining streets and houses. When the questioning was finished, other gravely-injured survivors were dumped without ceremony into the same lorry. Their barely audible moans were ignored by the soldiers, who were interested only in boasting to each other of their recently looted spoils.

The emptied village now stood silent and still. Standing orders stated that it was to be left intact. Once Anfal was completed, the town was to become the home of Arab Iraqi citizens. To eventually re-colonize the now deserted region, the rich reward of free land and houses would be offered to encourage its rapid re-population by poor but loyal Sunni Muslims drawn from the slums of the southern Iraqi cities.

The small convoy of covered trucks containing the dead, and the few severely injured survivors, were driven from the village to a large pit a few kilometres away. One by one, the vehicles backed up to the edge of the deep, gaping trench - and there the dead and the dying were dumped. All evidence of today's slaughter would soon be gone, and the population of Sardasht would be publicly listed as 'missing' by the Iraqi Interior Ministry.

When the last lorry was emptied, Colonel Al-Mahdi nonchalantly dropped his cigarette onto the ground, crushing it beneath his beautiful hand-tooled leather boot. He smiled. From within the pit, he could still hear feeble moans, and faint cries for help.

'It will do these scum no good to be helped,' he thought. Very soon, they would be silenced forever.

Al-Mahdi turned. He signalled to the idling bulldozers driver with a curt nod of his head.

'*Bury them!*' He ordered, gesturing vaguely to the tangled mess of the dead and the dying.

With a leer, the driver crashed the gears home. Enveloped in a cloud of black exhaust smoke, the bulldozer slowly began to rumble forward as its huge blade lowered and bit into the ground, pushing a wall of dry earth towards the waiting pit.

When the Colonel returned to Sardasht, he ordered Major al-Khafaji to his command vehicle, following a heated discussion with Dr al-Numan.

'You declared the village clear of all toxic agents, Major. That is a most interesting report. The good Doctor believed that traces of residual toxins should have been found, and yet you reported finding nothing at all?'

The Major blanched. Should he continue the lie that nothing poisonous remained in the village, or should he admit that he had ignored the real findings of both crews and perjured himself to his Commanding Officer? He deeply feared this man, and his mind churned as he searched for a plausible reply. If his falsehood was exposed, it wasn't only he who would face the death penalty.

'Well Major?'

Major al-Khafaji's sweating palms balled into fists as he stood rigidly to attention.

'The village was clear, Sir, no doubt of it. I would stake my life on it.'

Dr al-Numan began to protest - but the Colonel silenced him with another imperious wave of his hand.

'If what you say is true, these months of research and development carried out by Dr al-Numan have all been for nothing - but, if you are lying to me, Major, you are guilty of sabotaging this operation's results. That is treason. There can be only one punishment for such a serious crime against the state.'

Major al-Khafaji palled as Colonel Al-Mahdi turned to the scientist.

'I think we need to conduct one final test Doctor, to determine the real truth in this matter.'

Major Al-Khafaji began to twitch and die after walking only one hundred meters into the empty village, without even the protection of a rudimentary gas mask. Al-Khafaji knew that the Colonel would have him court-marshalled if he refused, or more likely Al-Mahdi would have him summarily shot for disobeying his order. He also knew that his wife and children would suffer the same severe consequences; their lives would not be spared if he disobeyed. If he was to survive, there was only one chance: comply, and walk alone into the village.

He managed to successfully cross the area contaminated earlier by the mustard gas, which in the growing heat, had now fully dissipated. He almost believed he was safe - until he stooped to pick up the small bundle of discarded newspapers in the area touched by the deadly Sarin. Much had indeed already evaporated, but pinhead traces still lingered. The good Doctor had been right all along.

Using his binoculars, Dr al-Numan watched the violent, convulsive death throes of Major al-Khafaji. As he slowly lowered them, the Colonel looked at him and smiled.

'Well done Doctor. It would appear that the Major's report was incorrect. Your new Sarin formula is a complete success.'

Chapter Eight

Ignoring the muted conversations of the pub's other late night drinkers; Pat looked again at the faded photograph.

He shrugged. 'OK, he was a Colonel in the Iraqi secret police,' he slowly began. 'We've seen his sort before. But Iraq's dead. It's history, Cornelius. What makes him so important?'

Cornelius rocked slowly, trying desperately to find the words to explain. His fingers whitened as they strained at the table.

'Have you ever heard the word Gilgamesh, Pat?'

Pat sat back. 'Outside of cheap Saturday matinees?' he questioned.

Cornelius's eyebrows furrowed.

'It was the deepest layer in their program to weaponise their nuclear program. The Iraqis called it the Gilgamesh program. We'd been aware of it for years; there was plenty of chatter on the agency's...'Cornelius paused. Pat watched him yawn deeply as his head began to fall. 'Al-Mahdi was involved. Only, when Gilgamesh disappeared, so did Al-Mahdi - and so did the bomb. He's my prime suspect in its theft, Pat. That's what makes him so bloody important!'

Pat lifted his palm, as if in apology - anything to quell Cornelius. The other drinkers in the pub were staring at them now; it was attention Pat could live without.

He stared in silence at the semi-conscious drunk. Surely, this man was delusional? Iraq had never had an atomic bomb; nothing had been found after more than two years of fruitlessly searching the countless abandoned scientific and military facilities over there. The allies had invaded on the back of the fear of Iraq's weapons of mass destruction, and to the US President and British Prime Minister's considerable embarrassment; they had only found little more than a few rusty shells full of mustard gas.

He smiled grimly at his sleeping companion, as the landlord walked over to his table.

'You'd better get him off home, I'm about to call last orders…'

Pat nodded and winked back at the licensee. 'Yeah, I think you're right mate,' he said, 'He's had enough.'

Across the table, Cornelius emitted a wild, bestial snore.

Careering out of the path of an oncoming bus, Cornelius weaved across the road, Pat at his shoulder. Mumbling incoherently as Pat half guided and half carried him to his door, the words 'Gilgamesh' and 'Al-Mahdi' were never far from the tip of MI6 man's tongue.

'Where are your door keys?' Pat demanded, propping the hapless Cornelius against the wall.

With his head rocking, Cornelius mumbled again, but already Pat knew that he would get no more sense out of him tonight. Frisking him with a military expertise, Pat was rewarded when he found the keys in the drunk's jacket pocket.

'You ought to be more careful, Cornelius. I could be anyone. '

As he opened the door, Cornelius slid down the wall, crashing into a rack of empty milk bottles that showered him in glass. On the other side of the street, someone opened a window and started to yell.

'Will you keep it down for Christ's sake! There's people trying to bloody sleep over here!'

With a supreme effort, Pat hauled Cornelius back to his feet, and pushed him inside. At the end of a darkened corridor, the sitting room was a mess. Bathed in streetlight shining in through the window, Pat could see ghostly white papers scattered across the floor, strewn upon the sofa and armchair both. He let go of Cornelius, who slid slowly down to the floor, and snoring loudly, curled into a ball, his knees tucked into his chin.

Pat had been in the same state too many times himself after riotously celebrating some victory during his time in the regular SAS, to judge Cornelius harshly. The difference between the two of them was that for Pat, it had been only occasional; surrounded by other tough men, who understood that booze and comradeship made the tension and bad memories slip away. Alcoholism was a cruel but velvet-gloved master, and it had taken over Cornelius like master's always do. With no-one to unwind with, here he slumped every night, his trousers round his ankles, his bottle in his hand.

Pat reached out and turned on the light. At first glance, the mess in the living room looked like an explosion in a paper factory - but, as Pat looked around, he noticed a suggestion of chaotic order among the piles of papers. There were maps of Iraq and photographs of sunlit buildings and swarthy men in Iraqi military uniform pinned against the walls, narrow cleared areas between the folders and heaps of documents. Pat looked down at the nearest pile, and his eyes widened. The uppermost sheet of paper was diagonally stamped with a broad red slash, and at its head, in red capital letters, it bore the legend 'MI6 - Top Secret.'

Pat froze for a moment, and then whistled to himself. The same markings were everywhere in the room. Here was a treasure trove of top secret documents, which surely should be under lock and key in the heavily guarded dungeons of MI6's headquarters at Vauxhall Cross, not scattered across the drunken Cornelius's living room floor, for all to see.

Pat slumped down and surveyed the wreckage. He had once carried a high security clearance himself - but surely even that would have not been enough to sneak a look at most of these files. As he listened to Cornelius murmur contentedly in his sleep, he spied a lone buff folder, lying on a low coffee table in front of the silent television. It appeared to be thick with papers. At its top the letters leapt out:

'Gilgamesh Project Intelligence Briefing
Final Conclusions'

Pat thought for a moment longer, and looked down again at Cornelius, blissfully asleep on the carpet at his feet. There were too many unanswered questions here, but intelligence gathering had been Pat's business for too long to let this go. Pat grinned to himself as he recalled those halcyon days. Some years earlier, shortly after Pat had finished his Senior NCO course at Hereford, he had been given his course report in a sealed envelope, and told to hand it straight into his squadron office. None of the course instructors would tell him how he had done, but with a true SAS disregard for the rules, Pat had steamed it open and read it, before resealing and delivering it. He had been pleased to see that he had scored an overall 97%, and been passed as top of that intake.

Smiling as he relived that memory, he picked up odd documents from different piles, and saw that many were imprinted not with MI6, but with the title NSA. Pat had dealt with the US National Security Agency once before - and though he had no wish to travel that road again, perhaps he had no choice. Beneath each sheet, was a document printed in Arabic. Languages had been an important part of his Special Forces training, and Arabic was the first he had learned at the army's school of languages at Beaconsfield. Keenly, he thumbed through the papers. The top sheets were clearly English translations of the Arabic documents below.

For more than an hour, Pat carefully studied the contents of the folder. Inside, there lay a thorough appreciation of Iraq's geography and a series of arguments as to why each region in turn should be discounted from the search for the atomic bombs' construction facility. Cornelius had gone into considerable depth in deciding on whether the facility might have been above or below ground, and the security implications of both. There were points concerning the lack of positive allied satellite surveillance across Iraq, which had, several years previously, first betrayed Iran's hidden nuclear program to the West. Electrical power was also considered, or more specifically, the lack of it to most remote parts if Iraq. To refine the raw uranium ore into weapons grade material, Pat read, huge amounts of electricity were required to run hundreds, if not thousands of complex centrifuges, which distilled the necessary and highly radioactive material. As he read more and more of the report, Pat marvelled at the intense detail that Cornelius had used as he built up, then discredited the case for the numerous locations as to where the bomb might have been developed.

90

Half way through, Pat broke off, and helped himself to coffee from the kitchen. There was a lot to take in, and a short break was in order, while he thought about what he had read. When the steaming cup of instant was finished, Pat walked back into the living room. Meanwhile, Cornelius snored fitfully on.

It was still dark outside when Pat finished the report. Outside, an early morning bus rumbled past the ground floor flat. He rubbed his eyes, and yawned. It seemed to him that Cornelius's report asked more questions than it answered - but, for Pat, it had an ominous ring of truth. There seemed to be enough evidence here that the case was at least worthy of more research and investigation.

Cornelius, it seemed, was on to something. And yet, there he lay, curled and bedraggled on the living room floor, sweating out alcohol from every pore. Would the powers at MI6 take notice of him, or his opinions? Pat had a nasty feeling that they wouldn't. His bosses at Vauxhall Cross were not blind.

Pat needed more information, and there was only one person who could give it to him. He looked down at Cornelius for a moment, stepped over him and headed for the kitchen. Once again, he set to work brewing a fresh pot of strong black coffee. Filling a cup from the kitchen tap, he strode back into the living room and, without ceremony, dumped the cold water into Cornelius's face.

With a spluttering shout, Cornelius woke, a string of foul language frothing on his lips. When he finally rose, rubbing the water from his bloodshot eyes, Pat handed him a mug of steaming coffee.

'Drink it,' he ordered.

Cornelius scowled up at Pat.

'Bastard!' he snarled - but, all the same, he began to sip from the mug.

'Drink it all down, Cornelius. I need you sober. I've seen all the top secret stuff you have here, and I've just finished reading your report on the Iraqi Gilgamesh project. There's enough top secret information here to get you thirty years in prison under the Official Secrets Act. Why on earth have you brought all this home?'

Cornelius held his head.

'How about a quick hair of the dog...?.For Christ's sake Pat, I need a drink!'

Pat turned on his heel and left the room. Returning moments later, he brandished another cup of strong aromatic black coffee.

'Sorry, no more booze Cornelius. Finish the first mug, and then get this one down your neck as well. You've got me involved, so come on; it's time for some answers. '

Cornelius took a big gulp of black coffee, and cleared his throat. Still not trusting himself to stand, he remained squat upon the floor.

'When I showed a preliminary report on Gilgamesh to my immediate boss Piers Ingram, he just bloody laughed at me. I only had the name to go on, and a few scraps of information. I've crossed swords with the little shit before, and since I've been out of sorts, he's done his best to discredit me, and dismiss everything I've put in front of him. '

Cornelius downed the rest of the coffee.

'I've been working up the report in secret ever since.'

He waved a hand across the room, and with bleary eyes, looked up at Pat.

'I've been copying and smuggling out files ever since, and now the report is finished. That's why I'm feeling in such a state. I'm absolutely positive I'm on to something Pat. '

Still undecided, Pat looked coldly at Cornelius

'Your report is shot through with guesswork, Cornelius. I'm assuming that no other National security agency, including the Yanks has come up with any of this. I didn't see any hard facts or concrete evidence anywhere. Why the hell should your bosses at MI6 believe you?'

Cornelius's face was morose.

'Before I started to drink, I was the best MI6 had. I've been working for them for nearly thirty years, for God's sake. Call it a gut feeling, call it intuition, call it whatever the hell you want - but I'm convinced there is a live Iraqi atomic bomb out there, and the guy in the photograph is linked to it. 'Cornelius lent forward, his head in his hands. 'I've got to make them listen to me Pat. But how on earth am I going to make them believe? With a head start of over two years, the bomb might be anywhere by now. It could have been sold into the hands of some political madman or religious fanatic. '

Cornelius's anguish was real. He was on the verge of tears. Pat went to him and laid a hand upon his shoulder. His shirt was sodden with alcohol and sweat, but still Pat rest it there.

'Don't you see? I think there's a powerful atomic bomb out there somewhere. It's been missing for over two years.' He stopped, unwilling to go on. His words might make it real.

'It could already be in London,' he breathed.

Chapter Nine

Baghdad - Iraq - 1998

An aide sat at his desk at the far end of the room, typing out the minutes of an earlier meeting. Dr al-Numan nervously ran his finger around the inside of his limp collar. Although the beautifully furnished anti-room where he currently sat was air conditioned, he could feel sweat slowly trickling down his back. He removed a handkerchief from his trouser pocket, and mopped his brow. He and Colonel Jalal Al-Mahdi had been waiting for over two hours for an audience with the Colonel's uncle, General Ali Hassan Al-Majid. They had arrived promptly, but now had no option, but to wait patiently until the General called them both into his inner office. The full scientific results of eight months research and testing, for the full and final implementation of Operation al-Anfal, were contained in the Doctor's battered leather briefcase.

Inside his office, the Secretary General of the Northern Bureau, and Lt. General Nazar la-Khazraji; the Commander of the Fifth army Corps were deep in conversation. Seated around them were senior members of the Northern Bureau of the Ba'ath party, and high ranking members of General Nazar la-Khazraji's personal staff. The meeting's theme had once again been the on-going deportation of thousands of Kurds from the North, the seizure of their lands, and the arrest and mass execution of hundreds of suspected spies and saboteurs. They had filmed Kurds being well treated in a 'resettlement' camp near Topzawa. Footage of this fantasy was shown on Iraqi national television, and reported through the heavily censored, and tightly control national press. The real truth was that Topzawa was a fully operational concentration camp, built and run along the lines of the Nazi death camps of Auschwitz, Sobibor and Treblinka. It was a state run tool ruthlessly committed to the Iraqis Government's own 'holocaust', and remained to the everlasting shame of the Iraqi people; a dynamic factory of death.

Pacing slowly across his office's richly carpeted floor, General Ali Hassan Al-Majid spoke.

'But what am I to do with these….goats? They are merely the families of the men we have already executed. Where am I supposed to put such an enormous number of people? Do we take good care of them? No, of course we don't. We bury them with bulldozers. One day they claim to be Arabs, but the next, they are Kurdish fighters and agents of Iran. Transporting that many people wastes our time and resources. I have had to send bulldozers hither and thither.......but we will shortly hear a full report of the final solution to our problem. Soon, we begin our first large scale assault on the Kurds in the city of Halabja using our special chemical ammunition.

He nodded to his secretary.

'Send in my nephew and Dr al-Numan. '

Smartly dressed in his drab green Ba'ath Party uniform, the anti-room aide had done his best to ignore the Doctor and the Colonel. Although he knew them both to be important men, his orders were always the same. He was to treat them with the same arrogance and distain which befitted this high office. Visitors were almost always made to wait for long periods, as it increased their tension, and humbled them before their meeting with the General. A buzzer sounded on his intercom. Startled, the Doctor jumped as the aide stood up.

'The General will see you now. '

He nodded to the two armed guards, who stood stiffly to attention, with their backs against the closed doors of their Secretary General's office. At his signal, they turned smartly, and opened both heavily soundproofed doors. Al-Majid passed the trembling Doctor, marched through, and saluted his Uncle, who was now seated behind his desk. Dr al-Numan followed, nervously clutching his briefcase to his chest.

'Ah, Jalal, … Dr al-Numan . Welcome, welcome. Please forgive the delay, affairs of state weigh heavily on my shoulders.' He smiled at his nephew 'Please, begin your report. '

'General… Gentlemen,' began Colonel Al-Mahdi with a slight bow towards his uncle, 'It is my honour to present Dr Tariq al-Numan , Chairman of the National Chemical Research Institute. He has directed the scientific research project for Operation al-Anfal. During the last eight months I have organised and commanded all the military aspects of the trials. '

Al-Mahdi then began an in depth explanation of his role within the project. He spoke with occasional reference to his notes for a full thirty minutes, outlining in great detail how he had organised the logistics of the operation, used different delivery means for the chemical weapons, arranged security, and dealt with survivors. He paused only occasionally to sip water from a glass, and then answered numerous questions from his uncle and the other members of the meeting. When he finished, he handed over to Dr al-Numan , who explained the technical aspects of what they had achieved, their latest chemical developments, and which materials would be required to proceed to the next massive up scaling of al-Anfal; the annihilation of thousands in the northern Kurdish city of Halabja.

When their briefings were finally finished, General Ali Hassan Al-Majid rose to his feet and thanked them both. Clearly impressed, he said.

'Dr al-Numan, I shall mention your part in this project to the President, our great Father. I am sure he will shower you with rich rewards. This is the greatest thing you have done for your country.'

The delighted scientist bowed his thanks.

'That concludes our meeting comrades,' said the General.

As the attendant military officers and senior members of the Ba'ath party began to leave, General Al-Majid caught his nephew's eye.

'Jalal, indulge an old man, and wait a while. '

As the last official left the room, the General directed his nephew into a smaller anti-room, where two comfortable leather bound armchairs had been arranged beside a low and highly polished coffee table. An elderly white coated steward was pouring coffee.

'Please Jalal, sit down and drink coffee with me, I have something very important to discuss with you. 'When his duty was done, the servant bowed to the General and left the room.

'I have been monitoring your progress closely during your military career Jalal. You have been loyal and very efficient in every task which has been set for you. I have had regular reports from comrade Barzan Ibrahim al-Tikriti, our Head of the Mukhabarat, about you. '

Al-Majid's eyes widened at the dreaded name of Iraq's secret police.

The General smiled, and lifted his hand, as if to wave away the shadow of fear which fell across his nephews face.

'There is nothing to worry about my dear nephew. I am not concerned by minor indiscretions in the past.'

The young Colonel's mind flashed back to memories of Paris a decade earlier, when he had been hastily removed from the Sorbonne University under a cloak of diplomatic immunity. He remembered the vivid mental snapshot of the bloodied and beaten body of the naked prostitute, lying tightly bound and very dead on her luxuriously perfumed and softly quilted bed. She still had the remnants of beauty about her, but plying her particular trade in the notorious red light district of Paris had already begun to take its toll on her young body. When his dark and sadistic demands exceeded even her considerable pain threshold, he pushed her even further and in genuine fear of her life, she panicked. He had already beaten her repeatedly, but then choked the life from her to stifle her terrified screams.

His two Iraqi Mukhabarat minders, who were guarding the front door had heard her desperate cries for help, and had broken down the door, and quickly entered the girl's flat. They had taken the scene in, in an instant, and had rapidly got the young Al-Mahdi dressed. They quickly removed him from her flat behind the Boulevard Haussmann in the 9th district. He was driven through the evening's chaotic Parisian traffic straight to the Iraqi Embassy, where he was ordered to stay, until matters had been resolved. Al-Mahdi was alone and afraid, but he learnt two valuable lessons. He must never again allow himself to be without a means of escape. He must be sure that he could always save his own skin, if things ever went drastically wrong again.

Secret and intense political exchanges between the French Interior Ministry, Ministere des Affaires Estrangers, the Ministry of French Foreign Affairs and Baghdad followed. A huge nuclear Technology for Oil deal was balanced at a critical stage between the French and Iraqi Governments, and it was decided by all parties that the life of one little whore was not worth potentially destroying months of intense and highly detailed commercial negotiations. The resulting lost sale worth billions of U.S. dollars was simply unacceptable.

As a remote member of the President's family, it was agreed that Jalal Al-Mahdi would immediately cease his studies of ancient Arab antiquities at the world famous Parisian University and was quietly declared persona non-grata by the French. Agents of the Renseignements Generaux (R.G. - French internal police/security service) escorted him onto the first available plane bound for Baghdad, and the French Interior Ministry ordered, in the sovereign interests of France, that the local authorities hand over all records and forensic evidence to the R.G., and the murder case was quietly buried.

Al-Mahdi's aging uncle stared intently at his nephew.

'It was I who arranged that you would command the first phase of al-Anfal, because I needed to know that you were a truly capable officer, and could be relied upon to carry out such an important and complicated task. You have shown no mercy to the enemies of Iraq, and I was extremely pleased with the report you have just given me. Your conduct during your time with al-Anfal will be of vital importance to the future of Iraq. '

General Al-Majid paused for a moment, and sipped his coffee. 'My position as Secretary General of the Northern Bureau of Iraq's Baath Party means that I am the keeper of many secrets. I will shortly reveal the greatest of them to you Jalal, but such a secret comes at a very high price. 'Colonel Al-Mahdi leant forward, and stared intently at his uncle. 'What I am about to tell you is the most closely guarded secret in all of Iraq. The hangman's noose waits for any of those who comrade Barzan even suspects of betrayal….. Even the fact that we are related by blood would not save you if there was any doubt of your loyalty. 'The General leant forward, and gently patted his nephew's hand. 'Are you ready to learn the great secret Jalal?

104

Colonel Al-Mahdi sat rigid in his chair. He knew that he had reached a crossroad in his life; one that would change it forever. He smiled, and his tongue flicked across his lips in anticipation.

'Yes Uncle, yes...... I am ready.'

General Al-Majid nodded, and stood up, walking slowly to the bullet-proofed French windows. He drew the net curtain aside and gazed across the Islamic spires of Baghdad.

'Recently, in the western press, there have been many words written about Iraq, and its weapons of mass destruction. You have seen the power of the chemical weapons we have developed, with the help of people like Dr al-Numan. When we used them against the Iranian massed infantry attacks during our patriotic war with them, we won many battles because we had the courage to use such things.'

Al-Mahdi nodded. His uncle paused. He decided it was inappropriate to mention that Iraq's ground forces had been almost overwhelmed by the suicidal waves of thousands of fanatically loyal Iranian infantry soldiers, who crashed a human wall of flesh and blood into the Iraqis battle formations. He had pressed the solution into the hands of Saddam Hussein, as Iraqis military Intelligence had predicted to him, without the use of chemical weapons, Iraq could well lose the land war against Iran.

'Yes Uncle, many glorious victories.' General Al-Majid let the curtain fall away,. He turned and opened an ornate box on a small side table. The General withdrew a cigarette and lit it. He exhaled slowly. 'What do you know of our biological weapons program?'

'Well Uncle, I know we did look into the feasibility of using Anthrax during al-Anfal, but it is too difficult to control; it poisons the ground for many, many years afterwards. All who enter an area infected by it will perish.'

The General nodded

'Ah yes, a terrible weapon. Quite un-usable. Smallpox and Bubonic Plague have also produced disappointing results. Although our tests on condemned prisoners taken from Abu Ghraib prison have proved effective, germ warfare is something to be used for retaliation, not as a first strike weapon. It is prudent to stock pile these things, but for now, we must look elsewhere for more powerful weapons to protect the motherland, and to threaten Zionists and all other enemies of Iraq.'

The General paused, and looked quizzically at his young prodigy. Something in his smile alerted Al-Mahdi.

'There is another option nephew, perhaps the greatest of all, is there not?'

'Nuclear Weapons?' The Colonel whispered, with a distinct tone of awe.

'Yes nephew, the ultimate weapon of mass destruction, the atomic bomb! We have already spent billions of U.S. dollars on research and development on our nuclear program, because having an atomic bomb will greatly increase our prestige in the Arab world. It would make the West tread more carefully in their dealings with us. We will be able to threaten Iran and be a constant thorn in their side. They would fear us Jalal. Iraq would rightly take its place as the greatest of all Arab states, and perhaps one day we will lead our Arab brothers in the annihilation of Israel.'

Colonel Al-Mahdi nodded but said nothing. What was the old man leading up to. he wondered? What was the real purpose of this private meeting? His Uncle continued.

'We will never openly admit to making a bomb, because as you are well aware, the United Nations Atomic Energy Commission monitors our research closely. We carefully hide the truth from them where we can, and they believe us to be perhaps ten years from taking our place as a nuclear power.' The General's eyes glittered with amusement. 'The fools; they have failed to find the real truth, that we are less than two years from completion.'

Colonel Al-Mahdi's mouth fell open with astonishment.

'But uncle, how?'

The General sat back and slapped his thigh with triumph.

'We have used the results from our admitted research in a highly secret duel program codenamed *Gilgamesh*. Many counties around the world seek to produce their own nuclear weapons, and we have deliberately shown that we suffer the same problems of refining the uranium necessary to produce such a weapon. We are currently very close to finishing the construction of a nuclear reactor at the Al-Tuwaitha Nuclear Centre, which as you know, is close to Baghdad. The French are providing us with boundless technical help of course, but we should be capable of producing enough plutonium for a bomb within two years of commissioning the facility. This is our showcase nuclear project, but it will always be vulnerable to attack.

Pausing for a moment to light another cigarette, the aging General exhaled and continued as he watched its curling smoke.

'We are currently quadrupling its air defences because already, the Iranians have sent two phantoms jets, and tried to bomb it just a short time ago. They did only minor damage, but the threat is very real.' The General paused again, and leaned towards his nephew. 'The Al-Tuwaitha Nuclear Centre is really only a smoke screen however.'

The General stared hard at his nephew. 'Iraq has been covertly buying the special steels and aluminium alloys on the world market, necessary to build the gas centrifuges with which to produce enriched uranium 235, which is at the heart of an atomic bomb. We have used third parties, shell companies within shell companies and a complex maze of purchasing agents to secure the supplies we needed. A 20 kiloton atomic bomb requires around fifty kilos of enriched uranium to explode properly. It has been necessary to build thousands of centrifuges, as refinement is a very slow business, and each one harvests the correct quality of uranium in minute quantities.' The old General's eyes narrowed as he began to deliver his conclusion.

'Within Gilgamesh we are currently refining nearly ten kilos of weapons grade uranium each year. It means that as a fall back, within the next five years, whatever else happens at Al-Tuwaitha, Gilgamesh will provide the atomic weapon we seek.'

Al-Mahdi slumped into his chair, staggered with the enormity of what he had just been told. The influence that Iraq could wield in the Arab world would be enormous. Never again would Iran dare threaten their borders. The West would have to recognise Iraq as a nuclear power, and tread very cautiously in their dealings with Iraq. The General smiled at his nephew.

'We now come to you, dear nephew. I have decided to promote you to full Colonel, and transfer you to the Special Security agency, within our secret police. A small number of them are already protecting the operation. You will be charged with the overall responsibility for the security of Gilgamesh, and must defend it against spies from Israel, Iran and the rest of the world. You must root out any disaffection from the people working within Gilgamesh, and deal with them accordingly. Show no mercy. I hope you understand the importance of your role?'

Colonel Al-Mahdi's mind whirled as his staff car drove him to the Ministry of Internal Affairs; headquarters of the state's dread secret police - the Mukhabarat. The Mukhabarat were at the top of the State's security pyramid, and were responsible for watching other internal police networks and controlling the activities of all the great state institutions; the military, Government departments and even non-governmental organisations (youth, women and labour etc.) The Mukhabarat had its own dedicated Brigade of paramilitary troops, the Special Republican Guard, who were drawn from the most loyal and trusted tribes, which were linked with a blood tie to Saddam Hussein. Although theoretically, on paper the Mukhabarat fell under the jurisdiction of the Ministry of Internal Affairs, in practice it was literally a law unto its-self, reporting directly only to the very highest echelons of the Iraqi Government; the National Security Council, which was headed by the President himself. Mukhabarat agents and informants were in place throughout Iraqi society, but their reach did not stop there. They were also charged with international counterespionage operations and to ensure the complete loyalty by close observation of the Iraqis Diplomatic Corps in their embassies abroad.

Although now promoted to full Colonel, Al-Mahdi knew that his real power lay in the fact that he was in command of an offshoot agency of the Special Security department of the Mukhabarat, and answerable directly to his Uncle for all matters relating to Operation Gilgamesh. As a result, his power was almost unlimited, as he had been given carte-blanche to act as he saw fit to protect the program. He would have full access to the facilities at Abu Ghraib prison, where information could be extracted by beatings and torture, or any other means thought necessary by its interrogators. He also now possessed his Uncle's full authority to execute anyone he considered to be even the slightest security threat.

His briefing at the Mukhabarat Headquarters revealed that their Special Security department was already responsible with hiding 'weapons of mass destruction.' Security around the location and development of enhanced Scud B missiles was also a part of their remit, and hiding them from the United Nations teams of observers who were authorised to search almost anywhere in Iraq for them. Special Security constantly played a game of cat and mouse with the U.N. officials. They would delay entry at the main gates of various vast research facilities, while a secret police team drove lorry loads of documents, computers and equipment out of a concealed rear entrance.

Colonel Al-Mahdi was introduced to his second in command, Major Talabani, and the other senior members of his personal staff, and then began reviewing the security files, which were piled high on a desk in his new office in Mukhabarat Headquarters.

Chapter Ten

Jordanian Airspace - 1998

After secretly planning the bombing mission for nearly three years, with Israel's very future hanging in the balance, failure was not an option.

Major Ilan Ramone made the slightest adjustment to the throttle setting of his Israeli single engine fighter bomber. There was absolutely no margin for error, leading his tight formation of eight F16 attack aircraft, flying at only 50 feet above the dull brown Sinai desert.

The formation had taken off only a few minutes earlier from a top secret airbase in the South-eastern corner of Israel, close to the Jordanian border. Each aircraft in the top gun squadron was carrying almost twice the manufacturer's recommended take-off weight. To complete their mission, the ground crews had fitted two extra fuel-laden drop tanks and two one tonne high explosive bombs to each aircraft. Under normal conditions, in-flight refuelling would be used to feed the hungry jet engines voracious appetite for aviation fuel. But this mission could afford neither the time involved, or, more critically, the altitude and space needed to conclude the task. Every drop of fuel was vital if the pilots were to complete the raid on the Iraqi's Osiraq light-water nuclear power station near Baghdad, and return home safely.

The heavy F16s had roared down the runway when the signal to take off had finally come, but each pilot passed the normal point when their nose wheels should lift, and the aircraft would usually begin to climb. Even with their afterburners set on full throttle to extract every last ounce of thrust, the struggling aircraft left the runway just a few short metres from its sandy end.

Israel's powerful Intelligence agency Mossad had spent the last six months desperately trying to stop the final commissioning of the new Iraqi nuclear power station at the Al-Tuwaitha Nuclear Centre. Across five continents, they had quietly liquidated eleven key members of the Iraqi project. They had also attempted to blow up the warehouse in France, where the radioactive core was being stored, prior to its shipment to Iraq. Although the attempted attack on the building was only partially successful, Mossad had managed to cause a considerable delay to making Iraq's first plutonium producing nuclear reactor fully operational.

Because the Israeli flight would cross Jordanian, Saudi and ultimately Iraqi airspace, the aircraft had to hug

115

the ground, and fly under the formidable radar defences of each of their Arab neighbours. Surprise was a vital element of the plan, and early detection would have disastrous repercussions on the mission's conclusion. Because their take-off weight went way beyond critical, the aircraft had been stripped of their defensive anti-radar jamming pods and were, as a result, utterly defenceless from radar-guided, ground-launched enemy missiles. It had even been necessary to 'hot fuel' the F16s on the edge of the runway, a technique which had never been tried elsewhere. With their jet engines running in a throttled back state, waiting for final take-off clearance, ground crews continuously topped up the aircraft's fuel tanks. As they waited, each of the Israeli pilots whispered a silent prayer to his God. One pilot pressed his gloved finger gently to his lips and tenderly touched a photograph of his wife and children.

'For you, my loves,' he whispered.

When the head of Mossad had finally reported to Israel's Prime Minister Menachem Begin that all their efforts to stop the commissioning of the Iraqis atomic plant at Al-Tuwaitha had met with only partial success, the Prime Minister ordered his Air Force chief to carry out the planned bombing mission codenamed 'Operation Opera.'

Five years of diplomatic efforts had failed to halt the building of the French-designed 40 Megawatt light-water reactor in Iraq. The fundamental question raised and constantly repeated by Mossad, weighed heavily on Bergin's conscience. Why would a neighbouring Arab country, who was the sworn enemy of Israel, need a nuclear power station, which produced weapons grade plutonium as a by-product of energy production? Iraq enjoyed a huge abundance of oil, and could generate electricity for centuries to come, simply by using a tiny fraction of its own crude oil reserves.

Plutonium, Mossad maintained, was the key. They remained convinced that Saddam Hussein planned to use it to build an arsenal of thermo-nuclear hydrogen bombs and ultimately, that Israel would be the target. Naturally, Menachem Begin deeply feared another holocaust. The Israeli intelligence service had reported the systematic mass murder of the Kurds in northern Iraq to him only a few months earlier. If the Iraqi President could use non-nuclear weapons to slaughter thousands of his own people, what choice did Israel have but to take drastic military action, and destroy the reactor from the air? His military chiefs had looked into using paratroopers or helicopter borne troops for a ground assault, but the spectre of the

117

recently-failed American rescue attempt of their hostages in Iran ultimately led to the rejection of both strike options as viable plans. The Air force strategy was daring, and riddled with risks, but the time to act was at hand. The vital reactor core was due to be shipped from France in a matter of days, and commissioned shortly thereafter. If the bombing plan was implemented after the uranium fuel rods were inserted into a working reactor core, the attack would cause a huge, deadly plume of radioactive fallout, which could drift across the entire Middle East. The ultimate consequences of that scenario were just too terrible to contemplate. Israel was simply out of time.

As the flight of F16s sped over the flat desert plains of Jordan, none of the pilots could know that their mission had already enjoyed a huge piece of luck, within minutes of take-off. The flight plan had been carefully scripted to avoid Arab villages and cities where they might be discovered by casual observers. Leaving the comparative safety of Israeli airspace, the jets roared across the blue waters of the Gulf of Aqaba in tight formation, closely hugging the waves at an almost suicidal altitude. They had suddenly flown over a large and beautiful yacht which, until then, had been lost in their radar's background electronic clutter of the Jordanian coast.

Calmly anchored inshore, King Hussein of Jordan was enjoying a short cruising holiday. He had been on deck with his wife when the jets roared over him, and he had clearly seen the blue Star of David markings on the aircraft, and the huge bombs and drop tanks slung beneath their wings. He immediately ordered his startled Captain to radio Jordan's capital Amman, and alert his own defence forces, and his Arab neighbours, that the Israelis were launching an air strike somewhere into Arab territory. For some still unexplained technical reason, the warning message was lost somewhere in the ether of the ionosphere. It was never received in Amman, and unaware of their good fortune, the Israeli attack flew on unchallenged.

Observing strict radio silence, the pilots continuously monitored their flight systems, as they thundered across the featureless Jordanian desert. Their on-board radars and computers constantly scanned the area for miles around them, searching for patrolling enemy fighters, but no hostile blips appeared on their screens. As the aircrafts' fuel consumption was of the utmost concern to the attack's planning team, the pilots were forbidden to engage in air to air combat with enemy aircraft, which would very soon consume the tiny margin of reserve which had been factored into the operation. They had been warned during their final briefing that those who engaged in dogfights wouldn't make it back. Their commanding officer had briefed them all that the mission was of absolutely critical importance to Israel's future as a nation. Most of the pilots had lost fathers, mothers or grandparents during the Holocaust, and they were set with grim determination that their own families would not suffer the same fate.

With no sign of detection during their flight through Jordanian airspace, the border with Saudi Arabia was approaching fast, which added new problems for the F16 flight. The Saudis had recently bought the formidable airborne radar warning system known as AWACS. This American 'Airborne Warning and Control System' could look down during its long flight, and see 400 kilometres in all directions. It was designed to detect and identify even the smallest aircraft, which flew within its invisible radar net. The flat revolving radar was fitted on top of an adapted Boeing 707 airliner, and was at the time regarded as the best airborne early warning radar system in the world. Once again, the Israeli pilots enjoyed a stroke of pure good fortune. As Saudi Arabia covers such a vast desert land mass, and neighbouring Jordan to its west was considered a close friend and ally, the Saudi AWACS aircraft were currently busy watching the North and Eastern sides of the country, and carefully observing Iraq, the Persian Gulf, and particularly Iran, following its recent, and violent Islamic revolution.

To compound the problems at this halfway stage in their flight to Baghdad, it was approaching the moment when, to reduce drag on the superbly aerodynamic F16, and improve fuel consumption, the spare drop tanks would have to be jettisoned. This was certainly not advised by the manufacturers under the present circumstances, because strapped only a foot from each temporary fuel tank was a one tonne high explosive bomb. All other aspects of the mission had been rehearsed many times, but this manoeuvre was considered too dangerous to try before the operation. It simply had to work.

If an empty drop tank fell away from its wing pylon and collided with a bomb at 500 miles an hour, the chances were that the entire tightly packed flight would be destroyed in an instant by the resulting blast.

Lieutenant-Colonel Ze'ev Raz, the squadron's leader, signalled to his other aircraft by waggling his wings that the time had come. The aircraft slightly adjusted their relative positions to each other to avoid a mid-air collision. Demand increased to each pilot's oxygen supply as they all involuntarily took several deep breaths before punching the jettison button. All sixteen empty drop tanks fell away harmlessly, and the flight flew on.

The attack had been planned to take place on a Sunday, because the Israelis wanted to minimise the death toll among the French technical personnel working inside the facility. Their help and assistance was part of the $200,000,000 trade package to build the reactor, which had been signed between Iraq and France five years earlier. The seconded engineers had followed the western religious custom of taking Sundays off, rather than the Arab tradition of Friday being the day of prayer and rest. Mossad had correctly assessed that the foreign technicians would be as far as possible from the reactor site.

Ninety minutes after take-off, the Israeli squadron crossed the shining blue ribbon of the Euphrates River and flew into Iraqi airspace. They now began to assume their final attack formation. Accelerating to 540 knots, the flight broke into four wings of two aircraft each, with just three seconds of flying time between each pair. It remained a vital part of the mission to stay low until the last possible moment, to avoid alerting not only the reactor complex air defences, but also the Iraqi capital's powerful anti-aircraft screen.

Just sixteen miles short of the target, each pair of F16s ignited their afterburners to full power and began to climb. The pilots' breathing rates began to raise, as each aircraft executed a slow roll through the clear blue skies. Having identified the target, they began to angle into a steep 35 degree dive towards the main reactor building.

It had been calculated that at least eight direct hits by one tonne bombs were necessary to completely destroy the entire building. Because of the numerous pitfalls and dangers involved, with the expected loss of aircraft en-route, a 100% redundancy had been factored into the plan. Through good fortune and meticulous planning, all sixteen bombs were still available to the F16 squadron. To further ensure the destruction of the building, delayed action fuses had been fitted to each of the bombs, to allow them to impact the surface, and then bury themselves deeply beneath the building before detonation.

The huge silver dome of the main reactor building was clearly visible to each of the first two pilots, as they made minute final adjustment to their attack run. The first pair of aircraft reached the bottom of their dive, and released their bombs at a pre-determined altitude of 3,500 feet. Both pilots immediately pulled back hard on their controls and began a left turn, and a punishing high 'G' climb to 30,000 feet. Their four bombs smashed through various parts of the main reactor building's dome, instantly disappearing inside. A moment later, four titanic explosions erupted deep inside the complex, and huge chunks of the gleaming dome were blown from its steel skeleton. The anti-aircraft guns protecting the reactor opened fire as the second pair of F16s screamed in towards the target. Columns of angry black smoke appeared everywhere in the skies above the reactor complex, as the Iraqi gunners threw up a thick curtain of anti-aircraft fire. Glowing tracer bullets hosed skywards in all directions, accompanied by the staccato rattle of heavy machine guns. The F16s were flying into the target at just under the speed of sound, and the Iraqi gunners couldn't traverse quickly enough to lock onto the fleeting targets.

All need for radio silence was gone, and the Israeli pilots yelled warnings to each other. The second pair both scored direct hits on the target, as did the third.

Suddenly, rapid warning beeps were heard in the pilots headsets, as a SAM missile streaked past a frantically climbing F16, leaving a white exhaust trail in its wake. Another anti-aircraft missile roared from its launching platform, quickly followed by another, as the machine gunners continued to fire a wall of deadly bullets into the clear skies above. Even before the impact of the last bombs, the once proud Osiris class reactor had been reduced to nothing more than a volcanic hole in the burning ground. The silver dome was gone, completely collapsed by the second salvo of bombs. Thick black smoke issued from its devastated centre, and jagged chunks of masonry rained down on the heads of the frantic gunners.

Each pilot's headset crackled for a moment. They heard the message 'Everybody Charlie'- which was the coded phrase indicating that all bombs had been successfully released.

The last two F16s levelled out and re-joined the rest of the squadron in the cold blue skies at 30,000 feet. The exit strategy called for an even tighter formation, which assumed the same single electronic radar blip as a commercial airliner. This part of the plan was designed to confuse land based gunners, and avoid further missile attacks from the ground.

In his cockpit, Lieutenant-Colonel Ze'ev Raz waved to his wingman, and clicked the transmit button on his throat microphone.

'Well done everyone, it's time to go home…'

Chapter Eleven

Pat awoke with a start, his bedside alarm screaming a warning. He had left Cornelius to sleep off the vodka, but he was due to make his formal presentation concerning Gilgamesh, to his superiors at Vauxhall Cross later in the morning. He had pleaded with Pat to ensure that he made it to MI6's riverside headquarters on time. Pat focused tired eyes on the clock. He had managed only four hours sleep, but it was better than nothing. He sat up, threw the duvet aside and sleepily headed towards the shower.

After continually ringing the doorbell for several minutes, Pat finally heard movement from somewhere inside Cornelius's flat. He had expected to wake Cornelius, who he thought must be suffering from a killing hangover, but was horrified at the man's appearance when the door finally opened. Cornelius stood swaying in the doorway, glowering at Pat, clearly trying in vain to remember who it was that had disturbed him. Recognition suddenly flooded across Cornelius's face, and he smiled feebly at Pat when his heavily bloodshot eyes eventually focused.

Pat glanced at his watch. It was 10.00, and the presentation was due at noon. Pat pushed past Cornelius, and marched into the living room. To his disgust, he saw an empty bottle of vodka lying discarded on the floor beside the armchair. Cornelius shuffled into the room behind Pat, but said nothing.

Pat rounded on Cornelius, his face flushed.

'What about the bloody briefing you're supposed to be giving in two hours at Vauxhall Cross?' He snapped.

Cornelius rocked back and forth. 'What briefing?' He asked in a heavily slurred voice.

The stench of vodka hit Pat once again. 'Don't you remember a thing about what we said? Gilgamesh, Cornelius! *The bomb!*'

'Don't worry about it,' said Cornelius with a vacant shrug, slumping awkwardly into the armchair and trying unsuccessfully to light a cigarette.

Pat wasted no time in arguing with the drunk. Time was short, and this whole business was too important to consider Cornelius's feelings. Pat marched out of the room, and having found the kettle in the kitchen, brewed another large pot of strong black coffee. He spent the next five minutes pumping as much of it into Cornelius as he could manage to make the man swallow.

Suddenly, Cornelius jumped shakily to his feet and announced that he was going to be sick. Pat quickly steered him towards the toilet, and was rewarded when Cornelius threw up most of the coffee in a wave of stomach-churning heaves. Pat suspected he also dumped a considerable part of his liquid breakfast at the same time.

The first part of Pat's emergency sober-up plan had worked spectacularly, but now it was time for stage two. Ignoring the awful stench of vomit, while an ashen-faced Cornelius remained bowed with his hands on his knees. Pat lent across and turned the shower onto its maximum setting. Judging that Cornelius's stomach must surely be empty by now, Pat pushed him without warning, still fully clothed under the freezing spray of water. Cornelius howled and struggled, but Pat held him under the pounding ice with a grip of iron.

'I'll sober you up if it kills you, you stupid bastard!' Pat thundered, above the loud hiss of rushing of water.

Firmly pinned down, Cornelius suddenly stopped struggling, and slumped defeated into an untidy heap on the floor. Pat wasn't in any mood for compassion this morning, and he lifted the shower's head from its cradle, directing the powerful spray into Cornelius's pathetic face. Cornelius weakly put his hands up to defend himself, but to no avail. Pat immediately redirected the ice cold water onto the back of his neck.

His face stone, Pat continued the cruel treatment for several long minutes, until Cornelius began to shiver uncontrollably. Only then did he know that Cornelius was back in the world of the living.

'Now strip off, and get yourself dry.' Pat ordered, dragging the hapless analyst from the shower. Pitching forward, he thrust his menacing face inches from Cornelius. 'Or I'll do it for you...'he growled.

Cornelius dripped but said nothing, holding up his hands in surrender. As he did so, Pat threw him a towel, and set off into the kitchen, determined to find something other than vodka with which to line Cornelius's empty stomach.

Five minutes later, Cornelius reappeared sheepishly, looking shaken but dry, and dressed in a pair of brown corduroy trousers and a clean shirt. His hair, still damp, hung wildly around his bloodshot eyes.

Pat stared at him coldly. 'How do you feel now Cornelius?' He asked, buttering some toast, the only food he could find.

Despite his soaking, Cornelius managed a faint smile.

'Terrible,' he admitted.

'You've got five minutes to eat this, and finish dressing.' He passed the warm toast to Cornelius who pulled a face but continued to remain silent. 'If we're going to make it, you had better be ready. '

The morning traffic was heavy and sluggish, roadwork's carving the centre of London into a tangled maze. In the back of the taxi, Cornelius sat sullen and quiet. Before they left the flat, Pat had gathered up the all-important folders containing the final analysis of Gilgamesh and, having checked that Cornelius had his wallet, keys and Vauxhall Cross security pass, bundled Cornelius into the cab. He sat there now, buried deep beneath the avalanche of his own investigation.

The sky was grey, and dark clouds threatened rain. Pat crossed the Harrow road, and drove through Paddington towards Hyde Park, knowing that he could use its inner ring-road to bypass the gridlocked roads around Marble Arch altogether. Pat glanced at his watch. If he dropped down past Buckingham Palace, and then cut through Victoria, it was going to be tight, but unless there were unforeseen problems ahead, there was a chance they would reach Vauxhall Cross on time. He glanced into his rear view mirror.

'Still alive in the back then, Cornelius?' He asked with a grin, staring at his passenger.

Cornelius still looked dark-eyed and a little shrunken around the edges, but at least he was awake and sober.

'Yeah, I'll live. It was touch and go for a while in that damned shower, but I'm OK.' Cornelius thought for a while, staring out at the rolling green expanse of Hyde Park. 'I'm sorry Pat, I dragged you into this, and let you down last night. After you had gone, I felt pretty miserable. I woke up a couple of hours later, feeling like shit and thought I'd have a vodka to wake myself up, but...'He thought again before going on. 'The trouble with being an alcoholic is that the first one's always one too many, but always never enough. I got the taste again, and ended up drinking what was left in the bottle for breakfast.
'

An uncomfortable silence passed between them as Pat skilfully guided his taxi past buses and cars. His anger was fading, now, but that did not mean it was gone completely. Cornelius was a fool for risking something so important - but at least he was now ready to make his pitch at Vauxhall Cross.

Since he first joined the Regiment, Pat had lived by an unwritten code of reliance. If he said he'd be at a specific place at a specific time, he was always there, ready to go, without issues raised or questions asked. His SAS comrades shared the same code and, come what may; the circle of reliance on each other was complete. Cornelius had broken the code but, then again Pat thought, Cornelius had never been SAS material.

As Pat steered them along Vauxhall Bridge Road, Cornelius pitched forth.

'Can you drop me on this side of Vauxhall Bridge, Pat? I'm OK for time, and a quick walk over the bridge and a breath of fresh air will do me good I think, before I go in. '

Pat shrugged. 'I'll park up somewhere close by,' he said. 'Give me a ring on my mobile, and I'll pick you up outside the building when you've finished. '

Leaving Cornelius behind, Pat turned the cab left onto Millbank. After the earlier let-down, Pat decided to drive around the block, and then head back across Vauxhall Bridge, if only to make doubly certain that Cornelius kept his appointment.

Cornelius walked briskly over the bridge, tightly clutching his briefcase. The mournful waters of the Thames flowed silently beneath him, and at last he looked up to see the glaring windows of the headquarters of Britain's overseas security service. It was an ugly building, known locally as Legoland and also as Babylon-on-Thames. Turning left onto the Albert Embankment, he ascended the steps, nodding gravely to the security guards as he came. For the first time, his head felt clear, the cool morning air and smell of the river bringing him, at last, back to his senses.

Swiping his pass at the inner security barrier, he approached the elevators and stepped through the doors.

Cornelius cleared his throat and turned to the assemblage of senior MI6 Targeting and Reports officers, who assessed threats to the security of the United Kingdom. Sitting in their midst was his immediate boss, Piers Ingram. Ingram remained highly sceptical of his initial report on Gilgamesh, but Cornelius hoped that his new detailed briefing might now inspire confidence. At his side, his analyst assistant, Julie Wallace, widened her eyes. The simple gesture spurred him on.

'Ladies and Gentlemen,' he began, 'it is my firm belief that, shortly before his overthrow, Saddam Hussein used project Gilgamesh to finish refining sufficient uranium ore into weapons grade material, and that at least one viable Iraqi atomic bomb was produced. '

Gasps rose around the room. Flanked by his men, Cornelius noticed Ingram shaking his head as he whispered something to a colleague sat at his side. Cornelius raised his hand for a moment. When, at last, the muted conversations diminished, he was free to continue.

'I have based the following report on the assumption that the Iraqis put all their eggs in one basket, and centralised their efforts secretly in just one location to avoid snippets of information trickling out. I should point out that I have found absolutely nothing in any of our databases which refers to Gilgamesh. GCHQ did find reference from intercepts concerning two calls made on mobile phones in Iraq before the invasion, which included the name, but both calls had been terminated immediately, when the name was spoken, and revealed only that both phones belonged to Saddam Hussein's Interior Ministry. '

Cornelius walked over to the wall map of Iraq, and drew an imaginary circle around it with his hand.

135

'I would like to open by looking at Iraq's geography. Iraq covers a huge area, nearly 450,000 square miles which, for the purposes of my briefing, can be broken down into three separate land masses. The biggest area is over to the west, and is predominantly featureless desert, with little water. This is the area where that SAS chap Andy McNab was operating, searching for Scud missiles during the first Gulf War.' Several heads nodded. 'He described the desert as a brown, flat billiard table. Population can be classified as relatively thin, and made up from mainly nomadic tribesmen. The centre and south of Iraq is a mixture of desert and marshland, which has the highest population density. Finally, the North and North-eastern areas are primarily mountainous in nature. Again, population is extremely thin - but I'll come back to that point shortly.'

Cornelius paused, and sipped coffee from a plastic cup.

'As you are aware, the Iraqis have always had a talent for deception and camouflage. During the first Gulf War, for example, they were transporting their Scud B missiles in gutted civilian coaches, making the missiles invisible, although the vehicles were in plain sight, for all to see. As a result, aerial reconnaissance and satellite imaging failed to spot the Scuds being openly moved around western Iraq. It demonstrates the Iraqis propensity to hide things in the open. I mention this as our search has been multi-layered, and I need you to think accordingly. I have looked in great detail at the logistics of building and hiding a complex big enough in all three geographical areas. I discounted building or excavating in the west, because any disturbance of the ground would be picked up immediately by western surveillance satellites, much in the same way that we first spotted Iran's nuclear program. Having checked carefully, no new facilities on the scale we are talking about exist in western Iraq. The centre and south of Iraq, as I mentioned, are densely populated, and it would be difficult to build a high security complex without it being noticed by someone on the ground, let alone from space. The North and North-east regions are mountainous, and would require enormous engineering to build and hide a nuclear production facility. The population density per square mile is naturally extremely low, however, and has been further diminished with the large scale ethnic cleansing of the Kurds before Saddam Hussein was ousted. '

Cornelius sipped from his coffee cup again, wishing he had more aspirins with him. The hangover was returning with a vengeance.

'The complex would need huge amounts of electrical power to continuously run the thousands of centrifuges required to produce enriched uranium 235, in sufficient quantities to produce an atomic bomb. The complex would also need to be, in my opinion, in a remote location, which would be easier to guard from the prying eyes of the United Nations inspectors, and anyone else. My assistant and I have thought about over-ground and underground facilities, and concluded that underground is the most likely. The question, clearly, is how to hide such a big construction?'

Cornelius scratched the stubble on his chin. Grimly, he imagined what the morning might have looked like if he had tried to take a shave.

'It occurred to me that it couldn't be done, with any certainty, given that security must be an overriding factor. So what is the answer?' Cornelius looked up at his audience and shrugged. 'It's incredibly simply really: concentrate the search on somewhere which has already been constructed. '

Perhaps he was losing his way, but some of the eyes in the room were wandering. Cornelius risked a glance at Julie Wallace, who needled him with her gaze.

'It would be necessary,' he went on, 'to protect this project in depth, to avoid any chance discovery, so I imagine that the Iraqis would have created a wide exclusion zone. That has been their normal practice in the past. This led me to the conclusion that it was likely they would use somewhere remote, already devoid of population, to avoid arousing suspicion or interest from the West, or their Iranian and Turkish neighbours. Word would have spread, and we - that is you - would have heard of it, if they had suddenly begun evicting thousands of people from their land. If the area was already clear, why not use it?'

Cornelius Wilde yawned again, and continued his briefing.

'The next obvious problem they had was electrical supply. In order to run a refinement complex of this nature, the Iraqis would need to consume huge amounts of electrical power. They had the capacity to supply, but they needed a physical connection from power station to refinement facility. Clearly, there are two ways open to supply: first, of course, are underground cables. I looked into that, but discounted the option, because it would, again, require a huge engineering operation to run high voltage cables for hundreds of miles to a remote location, and bury them along the way. The other option was overhead cables, supported by pylons. Again, there is the problem of construction, and being seen. We come back to using a long chain of pylons and overhead cables which are already in situ. '

Julie Wallace rose and handed Cornelius a photograph. 'Last little piece in the jigsaw?' He said, smiling as she went back to her seat.

Walking over to the map, he pinned the satellite image to the wall. 'This satellite photo of an existing pylon chain led us to a remote spot, devoid of population in the Northeast of Iraq. The entire search parameters I have outlined are met at just this one location.'

With real conviction, Cornelius thrust his index finger at the green circle on the map.

'Ladies and Gentlemen, you should concentrate your search at a place called Bakhma. '

When Cornelius returned to Pat's cab, he looked on the edge of tears, his face a death-mask of dissatisfaction.

140

'Christ, I could do with a drink,' he said as he fell into a back seat.

Slamming his foot on the accelerator, Pat suppressed a growl.

'It's even worse than I thought,' Cornelius murmured as he scowled at the floor of the cab. 'Ingram and the rest of those overpaid idiots didn't believe a bloody word I said Pat, they told me I needed a rest. Not one of them will face up to what's coming our way. And by the time they know they made a mistake, it will already be too late…'

Chapter Twelve

Northern Iraq - 2003

Colonel Al-Mahdi's carefully scripted plan was now very close to completion; he had already planned how and where, but the flurry of urgent messages to the Gilgamesh project's head of security, via the secure microwave link from Baghdad's Defence and Interior Ministries, had finalised the schedule. Time had run out. The allies were crawling all over Iraq, and the bomb had to be moved soon.

The Americans had already penetrated Iraq's border, and sent in a large armoured 'flying' column, which was currently speeding across mainly open desert, straight towards Baghdad. Saddam Hussein had ordered that it be stopped, at any cost. The covering screen of Iraqi armour had so far proved ineffective against the formidable American Abram's main battle tanks, which swatted away the dug-in Iraqi armour like flies. Their rush unchecked, the Americans would be on the outskirts of Baghdad in a matter of days. In a crisis war Cabinet meeting, Iraq's President had made his decision, and ordered it implemented.

'They seek our weapons of mass destruction? Then we shall give our atomic bomb to them. They will feel the power of Iraq out in the open desert, and the dogs will die there, in their thousands. '

Saddam Hussein was taking the greatest gamble of his life. If he exploded his nuclear weapon under the American armour, he was sure it would check the allied advance. While the Americans recovered from their shock, they would need to re-evaluated Iraq's nuclear arsenal. It was true that only one atomic bomb existed, but the Americans wouldn't know that for sure, and couldn't risk another strike. The resulting causalities and political fallout would surely cripple them for years to come. It would also declare to the rest of the world that Saddam Hussein was nuclear armed, and afraid of no-one.

Colonel Al-Mahdi had already meticulously planned the removal of the bomb from Bakhma. His encoded plan had been received and approved by his Uncle weeks earlier. Although it had been prepared before the allied invasion, the bomb's transport plan remained in place, and was due to be implemented when the final movement order came through from Baghdad.

The allied invaders clearly didn't know of the installation's existence. Heavy bombing was being reported by military installations all over Iraq but, as yet, no attempt to attack the Bakhma complex from the ground or air had materialised. He had immediately placed the Special Republican Guard who surrounded the complex on a war footing, and ordered the vehicles and personnel which had been prepared for the bomb's movement brought to one hour's readiness.

There were to be four identical convoys of vehicles. Three were for deception, and would carry dummy devices, and the fourth would guard and transport the real bomb. The Colonel had considered the transportation issue carefully. Too many vehicles might attract unwanted attention from the unmanned allied reconnaissance drones which were criss-crossing Iraq in search of targets of opportunity, but too few vehicles would not carry sufficient firepower to protect the precious cargo.

He had decided on six vehicles per convoy. Three lorries would carry his heavily armed Republican Guards, one vehicle would handle command and control, and the remaining two lorries would carry a device, real or otherwise, or act as its counterpart's backup. He had considered providing extra armoured protection but, ever mindful of the allies' reconnaissance capabilities, had

144

decided that the elements of speed and surprise far outweighed the enormous amount of dust which tanks threw up. Full air cover was not an option, as allied radar would instantly pick up circling fighters, and inevitably lead to an inspection and assault. He had been allocated a heavy lift helicopter as an emergency back up, which would remain on standby at Bakhma until delivery was completed.

The Colonel briefed his convoy commanders, and their accompanying Mukhabarat secret police minders. He outlined the mission, and told them exactly what was being transported. The look of disbelief on each of the Republican Guard Major's faces pleased Al-Mahdi. They had all been concerned with guarding the exterior of the facility at the Bakhma dam, but none of them had ever been told exactly what they were guarding, and they all knew better than to ask.

'The future of our beloved country hangs in the balance comrades, and you will shortly hold that future in your own hands. You must defend the convoy with your lives. Nothing must stop you from completing your mission. Do not tell your men what you are guarding; simply tell them that it will be the most important service they will ever have to do for our beloved Iraq. '

The assembled officers nodded gravely, as the true magnitude of their task sank in.

'I will now brief each of you individually, with details of your routes and destinations. I will begin with you Major al-Jaafari. The rest of you will wait outside. '

When the last officer had received his detailed briefing, Colonel Al-Mahdi checked his Rolex. His plan was progressing well. He now needed to place four static sentries along the initial route, to guard the two long tunnels which all the convoys must pass through, before they fanned out, and began their own individual routes. He also needed to plant a package of his own in the second tunnel - which was a key part of his own, secret plan.

The four tunnel guards sat in the back of the civilian Toyota Land Cruiser, as Colonel Al-Mahdi drove quickly to the entrance of the first tunnel.

'Remember,' he said, 'at the first sign of trouble, you will alert the convoy Commander, but do not delay the convoy if everything is OK. The first convoy will arrive within the next three hours. Do not leave your position for any reason. Do you understand?'

The guard snapped to attention. 'Yes Sir!' He barked.

146

The second guard was placed at the far end of the tunnel, and Colonel Al-Mahdi continued along the lonely road through the mountains for another three kilometres until he reached the second, where he stationed the next guard, at its entrance.

The Toyota's wheels kicked up dust as the Colonel entered the second tunnel. He switched on the headlights, and sped through the dark, the grunting of the engine echoing all around. Months earlier, he had inspected this tunnel carefully, and not a thing had changed. It was ideal for his purpose. Slowly, it curved and wound its way through the belly of the mountain, descending over sixty metres before reaching its end. The natural updraft that this caused would suit his purpose admirably.

The Toyota slowed as it reached the mouth of the second tunnel. Colonel Al-Mahdi called back to the last guard.

'I have a special vantage point for you. It will give you an excellent view of the tunnel, and the surrounding area.' The Colonel stopped the vehicle outside the entrance, and ordered the guard to follow him. Climbing the steep slope, he quickly reached a flat, narrow plateau. 'This is your position,' he said, with a sweep of his arm.

147

The young Republican Guard had felt privileged to have been chosen for this mission. He turned his back to the Mukhabarat Colonel, and carefully surveyed the tunnel entrance, the Kirkuk road, and the surrounding mountains. He didn't hear the shot, and felt no pain, as the Colonel's 9mm hollow nosed bullet suddenly exploded in the base of his skull.

The dead soldier dropped instantly, like a discarded rag doll. Colonel Al-Mahdi holstered his pistol, quickly dragging the lifeless body several metres across to the back of the plateau, where it would not be seen. He didn't bother checking for a pulse; the bullet had left a bloody, fist-sized hole in the front of the man's forehead.

Colonel Al-Mahdi returned to the Toyota, and set the milometer trip counter to zero. He began to drive back through the tunnel, watching until the meter registered eight hundred metres, which was exactly half way through the tunnel. Having spotted what he was looking for, he stopped his vehicle, opened the door, and climbed out. Quickly, he walked to the back of the Toyota, opened the rear door, and carefully removed a large steel ammunition box, which the guards had used as a footrest during their journey.

In the glow of the headlights, he paused. His plan, at last, was coming together.

'What the hell do you mean, he's not there?' yelled General Ali Hassan Al-Majid into the telephone receiver.

Far to the Northeast, in the Kurdistan foothills Colonel Al-Mahdi's second in command Major Talabani blanched.

'He is out making a final check that the convoy route is secure, Sir. We don't have any radio contact with him, not this deep into the mountains.'

General Al-Majid fought to control his rising anger.

'It is imperative that I speak with him Major. The President has authorised the immediate movement of the package!'

Major Talabani breathed in sharply. 'Yes, Sir, I understand. We are currently at one hour's readiness, and I will inform the Colonel as soon as he returns. I expect him back at any moment.'

'See that you do, Major,' the General seethed. 'Your life depends on it!'

Major Talabani ran to the Toyota as it stopped.

149

'Colonel, the General has ordered the convoys to leave Bakhma immediately!'

Colonel Al-Mahdi regarded his subordinate calmly. 'Very well, Major. Give the order for the first convoy to leave in five minutes. The others will go at ten minute intervals, exactly as planned. I will leave with the real bomb in the last convoy.'

The Mukhabarat Major saluted. 'Yes, Sir, I will see to it immediately.'

As the first convoy began to roll out of the unfinished Bakhma dam complex, Colonel Al-Mahdi calmly walked into the restricted control area, deep inside the complex.

'You are relieved Lieutenant,' he said, approaching the officer on duty. 'Take your men, and get out. I will take personal control of the complex, until the first three convoys have left. Give me your keys.'

The Lieutenant looked confused. 'But Sir, standing orders forbid...'

'I know what standing orders say,' sniped Al-Mahdi. 'But I am countermanding them.' The Colonel's eyes narrowed to slits and his voice hissed like a Cobra. 'Are you daring to question my authority?' He demanded.

In breathless silence, the Lieutenant handed the Colonel his keys, snapped at his men to follow him, and beat a hasty retreat, closing the control room door as the last of his technicians left.

Swiftly, Colonel Al-Mahdi approached one of the large electrical panels bolted securely to the concrete wall. Unlocking the panel, he turned off the warning siren before it could activate. He dialled in a one hour delay, and set the four master switches to '*Arm*. 'In quick succession, he was rewarded with four green lights, which electronically confirmed the Bakhma dam complex was fully set to self-destruct in sixty minutes.

Closing the panel's steel door, with the butt of his pistol, he hammered the key and snapped it in the lock, making it impossible to open again without cutting the panel with an acetylene torch. Satisfied with his work, he left the control room, locked the door and repeated the process, snapping the key in one of the three locks which secured the room.

Moving swiftly down the concrete corridor, Colonel Al-Mahdi made haste towards the exit. Resisting the temptation to run, after two minutes of brisk walking, he clambered back into his Toyota and slammed his foot on the accelerator. Moments later, he had covered the short distance to reach the huge Iraqis Air force Mil Mi-24 Helicopter, which sat silently on a landing pad south of the complex. The pilot and co-pilot stood talking beside the front of the aircraft, while the flight engineer busied himself with his pre-flight checklist.

Both the pilots snapped to attention when they recognised the Toyota's driver.

'There has been a development,' Al-Mahdi began. 'My plans have been changed. I have a map in my vehicle. I'll show you where I want you to go.'

The pilots followed the Colonel over to the Toyota, as he spread a map of the Bakhma area across the bonnet. Pointing to a corner of the map, he indicated an area a kilometre beyond the second tunnel entrance.

'One of my guards thinks he saw movement in the hills above the tunnel mouth here...' Al-Mahdi used the point of a pen to indicate the exact spot on the map. 'The convoys should be safe between here and the second tunnel, but I'm concerned that I have no back up air cover beyond that point, and no way of calling for your immediate support if we are attacked. '

Both pilots nodded their agreement. If their helicopter remained on the ground at the Bakhma dam, the surrounding mountains blocked any chance of getting a radio message through from the convoy.

'I want you to fly to this point, land, and keep your engines running. You will be four kilometres beyond the second tunnel mouth, but we should have excellent radio communications again. If I can't get through for any reason and need your support, I will fire a red flare. You will take off now, and go to the tunnel mouth immediately. Do you understand?'

The senior pilot stiffened. 'Understood, Sir!' He announced.

The Colonel's eyes narrowed and he pierced the Air Force Major with his cold stare. 'This is a top secret mission,' he warned. 'The very survival of Iraq depends on it. My convoy will be the last to pass, and will be carrying an atomic bomb. We plan to stop the Americans with it. Speak to no-one, and do exactly as I have ordered you.'

Stifling their shock, the pilots saluted and hurried back to their aircraft.

'Fire it all up Ali!' The co-pilot thundered. 'We're taking off right now!'

The third dummy convoy was just beginning to roll away from Bakhma as Colonel Al-Mahdi's Toyota arrived beside his own small line of vehicles. Summoning the convoy Commander and his second in command, he allowed himself a faint smile. Behind him, the Mil Mi-24 took off in a cloud of dust and a growing roar.

Al-Mahdi turned and spoke to Major al-Jaafari. 'Your convoy has the real bomb Major, and I want you to carry the trigger device in your command vehicle. Guard it with your life. Without it, the bomb is useless.' Al-Mahdi waited for an acknowledgement before ploughing on. 'I will lead, you will follow, and the bomb will be third in line. The guard vehicles will come after that. We now have air support after the second tunnel, but I cannot stress too highly the importance of this mission. It must not fail.'

Major al-Jaafari straightened. 'We will not fail you, Sir.'

The Colonel looked at Major Talabani. 'Load the trigger device into Major al-Jaafari's vehicle, and get everyone who is staying here underground into the complex, and under solid cover. Our activity today will almost certainly bring an American airstrike.'

As the two officers hurried away to carry out their orders, Al-Mahdi could not suppress another smile. In the end, all men were fools he thought. Their patriotism would destroy them all, in the end.

154

As the last vehicle of Colonel Al-Mahdi's convoy drove out through the heavily guarded gate, the Lieutenant who had been on duty in the control room looked up to see Major Talabani approaching.

'May I return to the control room, Sir, now that Colonel Al-Mahdi has left?'

Talabani looked puzzled. 'Why have you left your post Lieutenant?' He demanded.

'The Colonel ordered me to leave the control room until the last convoy had left, Sir. He countermanded standing orders, and just ordered me out.'

Major Talabani's face contorted with confusion for only a second. He knew Colonel Al-Mahdi to be a meticulous planner, and he wouldn't have ordered the Lieutenant out without a reason. The Colonel had always briefed his second in command on every aspect of an operation, and had informed him of any changes as soon as he made them but there had been no mention of leaving the heart of the complex unmanned and unguarded during this critical time.

'Get back to the control room, and make sure everything is as it should be!' Snapped Major Talabani.

'Yes Sir,' answered the soldier meekly. 'But what about the keys?'

The convoy passed through the first tunnel quickly. The static tunnel guards were picked up by the last lorry, which slowed sufficiently to allow them time to scramble on-board. As the entrance to the second tunnel came into view, Colonel Al-Mahdi signalled to Major al-Jaafari to stop. The other vehicles slowed and stopped in their dusty wake. The tunnel guard ran over to Colonel Al-Mahdi's Toyota, as he climbed down from his vehicle.

'Well, have you anything to report?'

The guard came to attention. 'No Sir, I have seen no-one. '

The Colonel nodded. 'Very well, get onto the last truck, and join the others.'

Colonel Al-Mahdi called to Major al-Jaafari, whose command vehicle was now parked just behind the Toyota.

'I'm going on ahead,' he said, 'to make sure everything is well at the other end of the tunnel. Follow me inside. When I give the signal to stop, hold there until I return.'

Major al-Jaafari nodded. He saw the wisdom of it. Waiting inside the tunnel would conceal the convoy, protecting it with millions of tons of solid rock. It eliminated any possibility of detection or air attack, while the Colonel went on and checked ahead.

Colonel Al-Mahdi set his milometer to zero, switched on his headlights, and drove into the darkness, closely followed by the rest of the convoy. As the milometer registered six hundred meters, he put his arm through the open driver's window and held up his hand to stop the convoy. Major al-Jaafari saw the signal and ordered his driver to flash his lights in acknowledgement.

Behind Al-Mahdi, the convoy ground to a complete halt. Smiling contentedly to himself, the Colonel drove on, disappearing around the next curve in the tunnel, all the time closely watching his trip meter. When it showed eight hundred meters, he stopped the Toyota, jumped out, and ran back a few yards to a partially concealed culvert grate. Opening the grate, he carefully removed two long fat metal canisters. Gently, he placed them down on the road surface, with their nozzles pointing in the convoy's direction.

Licking the palm of his hand, he held it above his head. He could feel the breeze blowing slowly over his hand, towards the convoy. Donning a service gas mask, he quickly broke the seals on both canisters, and unscrewed

157

the valves. The contents of the canisters hissed noisily from both, and began to drift in a dense but invisible cloud towards the unsuspecting convoy.

'I don't care what it takes, get that damned door open!' Yelled Major Talabani as two of his men frantically hammered on the hinges of the steel control room door with their rifle butts.

'It's no good, Sir,' said one of the profusely sweating soldiers. 'We need to cut through it with a torch.'

Major Talabani ground his teeth with anger.

'Then go and get one…' he seethed.

Talabani watched the Lieutenant go, and willed him to return as swiftly as he could. He had known, as soon as the Lieutenant admitted that Colonel Al-Mahdi had his keys, that something was seriously amiss in Bakhma. Al-Mahdi was Chief of Security - and he already had access to every key in the complex. There was only one reason to take the Lieutenant's set.

The Major pressed his hands against the doors, as if he could discern in the sensation of the cold metal exactly what Al-Mahdi had done on the other side. Frantically, he ran through every set of controls in the room: the electrical power grid, the air conditioning, water

158

supply, radio communication and telephone systems, security cameras. Inwardly, he cursed. Every single thing was controlled from that one room.

He looked up to see the Lieutenant returning, cutting torch in hand.

Every single thing - including, of course, the means to make the complex self-destruct...

Chapter Thirteen

Pat Farrell sat on the taxi rank just off Park Lane, reading a newspaper while he waited patiently for his next job of the morning. Lost in stories of what his fellow soldiers were doing in the farthest flung corners of the planet, he didn't notice the smartly dressed young woman approaching his cab, and was quite startled when she spoke to him.

'Hey Pat Farrell, I thought it was you. How are you doing?'

For a moment, Pat didn't recognise her, but his eyes widened as the penny dropped

'Blimey! Hallo Sally. Nice to see you again.'

Since the incident months previously, Pat had switched to working during the daytime, and had not seen any sign of Sally plying her trade in the back streets of Kings Cross.

'You're looking good,' he said. 'How's the baby?'

Sally smiled, and climbed into the rear compartment of his cab. 'Jude's doing well.' Perhaps she saw the way Pat was regarding her, but she punched him playfully on the shoulder. 'She's with my child-minder at the moment. How have you been?'

Pat pulled a face. 'Yeah, OK, you know, keeping busy,' he said.

Pat had only returned from Hereford two days previously, after two weeks of intensive CRW training with his Troop. The Counter Revolutionary Warfare wing at Hereford was charged with providing its elite SAS commandos with anti-terrorist training, specialising in hostage extraction. The successful release of nineteen hostages in the 1980 Iranian Embassy Crisis had been carried out by thirty heavily armed members of regular 22 SAS Regiment's crack CRW team. Because Pat's Troop was being inducted into the Shadow Squadron, CRW training was considered a vital part of their development. Pat had taken his boys to Hereford for their annual two week camp, and they had been put through an intensive schedule of training, endlessly practicing entering buildings with explosives, close quarter battle shooting, releasing hostages from improvised situations. The training had culminated in a drill to rescue real 'hostages' from the dark, tear gas filled rooms of the Regiment's infamous Killing House using live ammunition.

161

'Oh yeah, I owe you some money,' chirped Sally happily, opening her expensive Gucci handbag. Pulling out a crisp new £50 note, she handed it to Pat.

'There you go mate, paid in full, with a bit left over for a beer.'

Pat thought for a moment and smiled. Taking the note, he said. 'You look like you're doing well at last.'

Sally beamed. 'Yeah, I've teamed up with a Maltese bloke in Mayfair. I'm still doing Arab work, but it's a different world now, believe me. I've got my own place just up the road off Grosvenor Square, and I've even got a maid. Trade is strictly by appointment only, my man sees to that. I did an old Arab oil sheik last week. He was over for some high powered oil meeting or something. I thought that lot couldn't drink, but we managed to polish off a bottle of Jack Daniels between us.'

Pat laughed. 'Strictly medicinal, eh?'

Sally pulled a face. 'I suppose it was, but he paid me a nice bonus, and gave me this afterwards.' Sally showed Pat a sparkling diamond bracelet. 'Spoils of war mate,' she giggled.

With a click of her high heels, Sally was gone, passing Pat a business card as she went.

As he watched her go, Pat looked at the card. It bore her flat number in Grosvenor Mansions, a prestigious and expensive apartment block off North Audley Street. The card bore Sally's name, phone number, and the legend 'At your service' embossed in gold leaf.

'Yeah, I'll bet,' thought Pat raising an eyebrow.

The Troop's intensive training at Hereford had ended late on the last afternoon in the main lecture theatre. The CRW wing co-ordinator Tanky Smith addressed Two Troop.

'Your training is coming on well boys, but never forget that this is a deadly serious business. You have to practice, practice, and practice until those drills are second nature. Once you go in, you've got just seconds to save the hostages. Always keep the Regiment's Mantra in the back of your mind: SAS -Speed, Aggression and Surprise. All right, now the big boss wants a word...'He nodded towards the door at the rear of the lecture rooms. 'Sit up!'

The SAS Brigade's Director, Brigadier Charles Lethbridge strode into the room.

'Thank you, Tanky,' he began. 'Sit easy, Gentlemen.

163

Brigadier Lethbridge was greatly respected within the ranks of the SAS. He had begun his career with the Regiment during the secret, vicious war against the Communists in the North African state of Oman, years before. As a young Squadron Commander, towards the end of the campaign, he had led a brilliant assault on the Communist headquarters high up on the Jebel Akhdar Mountain. It had been considered an impossible climb by the Communist guerrillas and, as a result, they had left the only single narrow goat track on that side of the mountain lightly guarded. Each of the Regiment's men had been weighed down with well over 100lbs of weapons and ammunition, and had climbed several thousand feet during the night in preparation of the attack. As dawn broke, the SAS men poured over the ridgeline, completely overwhelming a disbelieving and confounded enemy. A natural leader, after promotion - and a tedious attachment to the army's General staff - Charles Lethbridge was offered the Directorship of the SAS Brigade.

He surveyed the occupants of the room, and said gravely, 'Gentlemen, I must begin by informing you that this briefing is classified Top Secret. Its SAS eyes only, and you may not discuss its subject matter with anyone outside this room at any time unless so authorised.' He paused. 'I

164

cannot overemphasise the seriousness of what I am about to reveal.'

The Brigadier paused for a moment and regarded the faces looking up at him. He continued

'Over the last year, Two Troop has been singled out as the best in 21 SAS. I have been liaising closely with your Troop Sergeant, Squadron Commander and CO, because you now have a new, vitally important role to play in the defence of London. If Al-Qaeda is planning a spectacular here, it is you who will be called on first to meet the threat. '

He clasped his hands behind his back, and stared thoughtfully out of one of the windows for a moment. He turned back to the silent men.

'The regular SAS are spread too thinly on the ground, Gentlemen; most of them are deeply committed, serving overseas in Afghanistan and Iraq, or elsewhere in the world. As you are all well aware, we won't drop our selection standards, and currently, we simply do not have enough regular Special Forces manpower to cope with all the operations we are involved in. Indeed, we will shortly be looking for volunteers from the two Territorial SAS Regiments to bolster our numbers, and serve on attachment with the regular SAS squadrons overseas.

165

Hereford's CRW team cannot be quickly reinforced and, should the need arise, due to say, multiple simultaneous incidents within the UK, we intend to activate you, as our immediate CRW reserve.'

He paused for a moment

'You will now become our other line of defence Gentlemen, responsible particularly for London. With immediate effect, you are all seconded into our new Shadow Squadron active service unit. You will continue with your civilian jobs, but are liable to full activation at any time in the future, with only one hour's notice.'

A hand went up. 'What about our civilian jobs Boss?'

Brigadier Lethbridge smiled. 'Ah yes. Your employers have received a friendly visit from our people this week. I can assure you, your employment is absolutely secure while you serve in the new force, no matter how often we need to call on you. '

No one else spoke or moved within Two Troop. Suddenly, the whole point of their training had become apparent. In their chairs, they sat stunned and silent.

The Brigadier nodded to Pat, who stood up beside him.

'Well there you have it,' said Pat. 'Now you know why I was talked into coming back to the Regiment, and why I have been working and training you so hard. The Boss needs someone for the job - and congratulations boys... You're it!'

He paused. 'Spike,' he grinned, 'hand out those bleepers. '

Chapter Fourteen

Northern Iraq - 2003

Colonel Al-Mahdi had calculated that twenty minutes should be ample time before he could move forward and retrieve the bomb and its detonating trigger. He had allowed at least ten minutes for the gas to drift the two hundred meters to the nearest convoy vehicle, five minutes to kill every man within it, and an extra five minutes set aside as a contingency. During his time as military Commander of Operation Anfal, he had learnt much about toxic gases. He had considered using nerve gas, but had rejected it as too dangerous. He doubted that he could remove all residual traces of it from the large wooden packing case which contained the atomic bomb. It would also linger on every surface of the tunnel, and would kill him if he made even the slightest mistake. Mustard and chlorine gas posed similar problems, and had the added disadvantage of being highly visible; a drifting yellow or green cloud would alert the convoy before the gas could do its work. Although almost as dangerous and lethal as nerve gas in the confined space of the tunnel, their traces would linger for hours, and he could not allow

168

himself the luxury of a long wait, while the toxic chemicals evaporated naturally.

On balance, hydrogen cyanide seemed the ideal gas to use. Under the commercial trade name Zyklon B, the Nazis had used it to kill millions of Jews during World War II. Invisible, extremely lethal and with no residual after-effects, it would stay in a dense, highly concentrated and very toxic cloud as it drifted silent and unseen. The natural breeze that blew continuously through the tunnel would force it to flow through every vehicle in the convoy until eventually it dispersed into the atmosphere beyond the tunnel's mouth. Using the authority of the Mukhabarat, it had been a simple matter to procure the canisters of cyanide. Dr Tariq al-Numan, from the National Chemical Research Institute, who had worked so hard during Operation Anfal, had been only too pleased to co-operate.

Carefully avoiding the white hot edges of the still smoking hole, Major Talabani quickly stepped through into the deserted control room. It had filled with thick black smoke from the superheated torch flame, but he knew that the panel he wanted was mounted somewhere off to the left. Coughing as he groped his way towards the wall through clouds of dense acrid smoke, his fingers finally touched the cool concrete wall. He felt his way along it until he was rewarded with the touch of a cold steel casing.

The access handle was locked, but he had expected that. He felt in his pocket for the spare key to the panel. Through a haze of smoke, he could just see the outline of the keyhole beside the handle, and he stabbed the key into it. The key stubbornly refused to slide into the lock, and he bent forward to see why it wouldn't fit. He cursed. Al-Mahdi must have blocked that as well.

Precisely four seconds later, the electronic timer finished its sixty minute countdown, and the panel sent out the first of a series of powerful electric pulses, instantly detonating the first two hundred pound Semtex demolition charge.

The solid rock was the only barrier that held the mighty Zab River at bay, and the millions of litres of water which flowed through it every day. A massive, foaming torrent burst into the first great turbine hall, smashing and sweeping centrifuges, workbenches and laboratory technicians before it. Moments later, another huge explosion destroyed the second turbine hall, adding to the chaotic flood waters; destroying everything in its path.

Rocked by the subterranean explosions, Major Talabani yelled to his men to get out. As they groped through the smoke, more explosions shook the complex, and part of the control room's ceiling caved in, adding to the terrified soldiers confusion and panic. With blood streaming from a deep head wound, Major Talabani found the door, and climbed through the freshly cut hole. Technicians and soldiers surged past him, racing up the corridor towards the surface.

Overhead, the lights flickered suddenly, and went out.

'*Run!*' Roared a dazed Mukhabarat Officer as he careered, wildly, through the dark passage.

Major al-Jaafari glanced at his watch, and wondered what was keeping the Colonel. It had been more than ten minutes since he had driven towards the other end of the tunnel, and there had been no sign of him since. The Major was tempted to drive down the tunnel, but the Colonel's orders had been quite explicit. Slowly, he walked around his lead vehicle, and absently kicked a tyre. As he turned back towards the front of the convoy, he raised his head, suddenly noticing an overwhelming smell of almonds.

Too late, his chest began to tighten, and he found himself gasping for breath. He clutched his throat, struggling to remain upright, and then his stomach heaved for the first time. Doubling up, he vomited onto the dry concrete road. The men behind him were also starting to show the same symptoms, staggering and vomiting as they tried in vain to draw oxygen into their poisoned lungs. Several had already fallen to the ground, grimacing as the invisible, lethal cloud of hydrogen cyanide overwhelmed them.

As the lights of the tunnel appeared to dim, Major al-Jaafari fell to his knees, and pitched forward. He twitched violently for several seconds ...and then was still.

The men at the rear of the convoy were startled and confused. They could clearly see their comrades at the other end coughing and vomiting, plunging to the ground from their vehicles.

Seconds later, they understood only too well what had happened. The bitter smell of almonds was curling around them as well...

The canisters lay on the road quiet and empty, but Colonel Al-Mahdi remained where he was, with just the sound of his own slow breathing inside the gas mask to keep him company. He wondered what was happening at the dam, although he knew they were doomed. The destruction of the complex had been a risk - but a necessary one. It would help to hide his tracks, and confuse the Iraqi authorities, or the Americans, whoever got there first. He saw no reason to advertise what he had done. The last thing he needed was every security agency in the world looking for him before he had a chance to make good his escape. His prize was worth a king's ransom, and he did not intend to squander it. When the Americans found out about Gilgamesh, as he knew they eventually would, they would have to search the flooded underground ruins of Bakhma to confirm the story, and see if the bomb, if it existed at all, was still there. He smiled ruefully, and wished the infidel scum the best of luck.

Colonel Al-Mahdi glanced down at his beautiful watch. At last, it was time to move. He decided to leave his gas mask in place, as there was no need to risk walking into a lingering pocket of cyanide further up the tunnel. He kicked the two empty canisters to the side of the road, and climbed into his Toyota. Driving back to the convoy, picked out in his headlights he nodded with satisfaction at the grim scene ahead. The convoy was exactly where he had left it, but the Republican Guardsmen lay sprawled everywhere. Leaving his lights on, he parked in front of Major al-Jaafari's staff car and, drawing his pistol, walked slowly to the far end of the convoy. His own breathing and footfalls were the only sounds he heard as he walked cautiously along the line of silent vehicles. With the toe of his boot, he rolled one of the fallen soldiers onto his back. The man was clearly dead; his glazed eyes stared blankly at the tunnel's roof. White foam dribbled slowly from his mouth.

The Colonel holstered his pistol, and walked back to the middle of the convoy. He stopped beside the lorry which had the large wooden crate securely strapped to its cargo floor. A dead sergeant was slumped across the driver's door, with his head and arm hanging from the open window.

Al-Mahdi stopped and considered another dead soldier for a moment. Picking up the man's AK47 assault rifle, he returned to the lorry, cocked the rifle and pushed its safety change lever down to the 'auto' position. Aiming from the hip, he fired a long raking burst into the door of the lorry, ensuring that some of the bullets hit the dead driver's body. The noise was deafening inside the confines of the tunnel, but he thought the effect would be well worth such a small effort. The high velocity bullets ripped through the soft steel skin of the lorry's door and riddled the lifeless corpse which lay behind it. Discarding the rifle, Al-Mahdi opened the passenger door, and dragged the blood spattered body across to the passenger seat. Satisfied, he thought to himself. 'If you wanted something doing properly, you should always do it yourself. 'With a smile at his own cunning, Al-Mahdi checked his watch again. Everything was going according to plan.

Deep underground, in the Bakhma complex, Major Talabani clawed desperately through the rising water as it filled the pitch black corridor. The gash in his head still wept thick blood and, with arms outstretched, he groped blindly through the air, fearful of walking into more jagged debris. The rising water sloshed around his knees

He knew he had not gone far, and must still be well below the water line of the Zab River. His leg touched something soft, and he heard a female voice cry out.

'Who's there?'

Reeling from the shock of finding someone else in the dark, he replied, 'it's me, Major Talabani.'

'Oh thank God it's you Major!' At once, her voice faltered. 'I saw you a few minutes ago, before the lights went out.'

'It seems more like an hour,' he said. 'Are you good to get out of here?'

The woman paused momentarily. 'Get out?' she said, her voice twisting into a cruel laugh.

'Major, the roof fell in. The passages out of here - they're all blocked!'

Satisfied that all was ready, Colonel Al-Mahdi started the lorry's engine and pulled away from the silent convoy. He was uncomfortable having the small crate containing the trigger device resting on the dead sergeant's body but, during his briefing months ago at Bakhma, the Professor had assured him that it was safe to transport, so he considered it an acceptable risk.

In under a minute the lorry left the tunnel. Discarding the gas mask, Al-Mahdi's cruel eyes narrowed for a moment as they adjusted to the bright sunlight. He pulled off the road, stopped and quickly climbed down from the vehicle.

'Those dogs had better be awake,' he thought savagely, as he loaded a fat cartridge into his pistol.

Pointing it skywards, he fired the heavy signal gun, and was instantly rewarded with an impossibly bright red flare, which arced high into the blue skies above.

Within moments, he heard the distant clatter of the Mil Mi-24 Helicopter's rotor blades. The Colonel allowed himself the luxury of a broad smile. The Mil Mi-24 hugged the ground as it flew low towards the tunnel mouth, its massive rotor blades threw up a thick cloud of dust as it landed noisily, close beside the lorry.

When the pilot approached, the colour drained out of his face. He saw the bullet riddled cab, and its blood splattered windscreen.

'My God Sir, what happened?' he cried.

Al-Mahdi's face twisted in mock horror. 'We were ambushed…'he gasped. 'I want this lorry lifted away from here, quickly, before they come after us.'

The pilot's eyes flicked nervously from the lorry to the tunnel's mouth, and then back to his helicopter. 'Yes, yes Sir. It can be done,' he said, darting back to the aircraft and shouting instructions to his crew as he ran.

The flight engineer looked at the pilot, yelling to make himself heard over the noise of the idling engines.

'It will be heavy, but we have carried heavier loads before. I'll get the cables out.'

177

The big Mil Mi-24 was designed to carry cargo internally or alternatively, heavy loads could be slung beneath it, suspended via a thick steel cable. The flight engineer and co-pilot quickly attached a shackle to each of the reinforced strong points on the lorry's chassis. Normally used for towing purposes, they could be utilized in emergencies for an airlift.

While they made the attachments, Colonel Al-Mahdi used his map to show the pilot exactly where he wanted to be taken and, as the pilot climbed back into his cockpit, the Colonel turned and shouted for the crew to hurry. 'Quickly men, we are running out of time. They could be here at any moment!'

Spurred on by the thought of imminent attack, both men worked with frantic haste. When the heavy cables were firmly attached to the lorry, the flight engineer connected them to the main lift cable.

'That's it Sir, we are ready to go!' He shouted, and began to run back to the helicopter, closely followed by the co-pilot.

As he scrambled aboard, Al-Mahdi slapped the flight engineer on the shoulder. 'Tell the pilot to lift off *NOW!*'

The engineer nodded vigorously and relayed the order, via his throat mike to the Captain. Slowly, the helicopter began to rise as the pilot fed power into his collective control. Now wearing a long safety tether, the flight engineer hung precariously from the open cargo door, intently watching the steel cable beneath the aircraft. As it became taut, he warned the Captain, who increased power into the huge rotor blades.

The aircraft shuddered, straining to lift the heavy lorry and its cargo.

'This is going to be close!' Yelled the pilot, over the deafening roar of the straining engines.

Imperceptibly at first, each of the lorry's wheels left the ground, and the helicopter and its deadly cargo slowly began to climb away from the tunnel's mouth.

On the surface, thick black smoke poured from numerous air vents, and hung like a dark shroud over the Bakhma dam complex.

'It's no good Sir; every entrance is blocked,' said a junior Republican Guard Officer to his Commander, as sirens wailed around them. 'If there's anyone left alive down there, they're finished, we can't get them out.'

Alerted by the explosions, the perimeter guards had rushed through the main gate.

'It must have been the Americans and their damned cruise missiles,' somebody cursed - but their shocked Commandant was not so sure.

'Perhaps you are right, but there was no warning.' He shook his head and looked sadly at the nearest blocked entrance. 'Those poor devils,' he whispered quietly. 'Bakhma is no longer just a dam to them. It has become their tomb.'

The Mil Mi-24 and lorry stood silently beside a worn track almost forty kilometres from Bakhma. As the flight crew busied themselves recovering their lifting cables, Colonel Al-Mahdi spoke to the pilot

'I want the sergeant's body put into your helicopter, and flown out of here. He is to be buried with full military honours.' Colonel Al-Mahdi looked grave. 'He died to save the bomb during the ambush. Without him, there is no question that we would have lost it.'

'I will see to it, Sir,' answered the pilot. No man wanted a corpse aboard his aircraft, but the Mukhabarat Colonel was not a man to argue with.

180

The bullet-ridden body was respectfully loaded into the cavernous cargo bay, and covered with a blanket. Colonel Al-Mahdi knew he must make this last act convincing so, climbing into the aircraft, he knelt beside the body. Pulling back the top of the blanket, he lent forward, and gently kissed the dead soldier's forehead, muttering a short prayer over him.

None of the aircrew noticed him crushing the acid ampoule inside a time pencil, which he had fitted snugly into a hand grenade in the dead sergeant's greatcoat pocket before he left the tunnel. The acid would slowly eat through a thin copper wire inside the pencil, releasing a spring loaded plunger, detonating the grenade within thirty minutes. Colonel Al-Mahdi wanted no witnesses, and the crew would die before the helicopter cleared the mountains.

Standing up, he saluted the dead man - and the men soon to be dead. Climbing down from the helicopter, he turned to the pilot for the last time.

'It is done, Captain. Be sure that my orders are carried out. You and your crew have served me well. I will mention you favourably in my report. Maintain radio silence until you are close to Mosul. I must go now, and

181

meet my standby force who will escort me for the rest of my journey.'

He offered his hand, which the Air Force Officer shook enthusiastically.

'Well done Captain,' he breathed 'And good luck...'

The light was beginning to fade as Colonel Al-Mahdi arrived at his final destination. It was just as he remembered it, from many years ago. The dry, rocky gorge showed no sign of being touched by the hand of man since his last visit, while he was still a young archaeology student. He had discovered the hidden gorge while studying the nearby remains of an ancient Assyrian settlement on his last field trip, before he left Iraq to further his studies at the Sorbonne in Paris. The surrounding hills were riddled with ancient caves, a few of which would be deep enough for his purpose, but the Colonel had one particular cavern in mind. The gorge was angled into the rocky mountain side, and impossible to notice by a casual observer. Al-Mahdi had stumbled upon it by accident. On his party's return to Baghdad University, he had classified his search area as being of no archaeological interest. While the academic faculty accepted it to be valueless, Al-Mahdi had subsequently considered it to be an ideal spot to hide his valuable prize. The neck of the rocky entrance was narrow, but just wide enough to drive through. It opened out into the narrow gorge, and a series of further caves, which cut deeply into the mountain side. Years before, one in particular had caught his attention. He drove into it now, and disappeared completely from view.

'We'll get rid of that stinking corpse as soon as we land,' muttered the pilot as they rose into the air.

His co-pilot grinned, and nodded his agreement. They had been tempted to jettison the body as soon as they were out of sight of the Colonel - but disobeying Mukhabarat orders could have the severest consequences. The pilot maintained radio silence, and kept the big Mil Mi-24 flying low. He was keen to avoid detection by the allies airborne radar net, which he assumed had by now been cast over most of Iraq.

His tactics hid him from friendly Iraqi radar as well. As a result, no-one on either side registered the disappearance of a stray electronic blip when, three hundred feet above the barren and lonely foothills of

North-Eastern Iraq, the helicopter suddenly became a massive fireball of flaming fuel and burning debris.

Chapter Fifteen

Pat's duties with the Regiment seemed to be swallowing up more and more weekends, as well as one or two evenings for training and administration at his Chelsea barracks. Paperwork, he thought ruefully, was the curse of all Troop Commanders.

Now that Shadow Squadron was fully operational, the need to keep the Troop's skills up to date and razor sharp was more important than ever. The Troop's bleepers had gone off several times recently but, each time, he had been disappointed when he arrived at the barracks, to find that the alarm calls were merely training drills to test the Troop's ability to be ready for action within an hour of mobilisation.

During this current shift, Pat had dropped an American tourist off at the Cumberland hotel, close to Marble Arch, and decided to join the back of the stationary line of taxis waiting for their next jobs outside the hotel's imposing main entrance. Time seemed to drag as the line of black taxis gradually shortened. After twenty wasted minutes, Pat was at last sitting in poll position, ready to take the next job that came along. Several porters began to pile suitcases at the curb outside the hotel's luggage door, which usually meant one thing: an airport run to Heathrow or possibly even Gatwick. It was a good fare, and worth the wait.

Overcoming the roar of the passing traffic, the head porter whistled, and waved at Pat to drive forward, so that loading the luggage could begin. As Pat's engine roared into life, his bleeper suddenly started to sound. Shrugging disappointedly at the uniformed porters, he accelerated away from the taxi rank and, turning left, disappeared into the traffic.

Pat arrived at the Territorial barracks in the Kings Road ten minutes later. Parking his taxi in the secure area allocated to the Troop, he headed straight towards his operations room, to find out what was happening. Chalky Palmer, an old friend of Pat's, and currently one of the regular SAS instructors attached to Shadow Squadron, nodded to him as he walked into the building.

'You're wanted upstairs, Pat. There's something going on up there mate - sounds urgent...'

Pat felt his pulse quicken as he took the stairs two at a time. Was this just another training exercise, or had a real mission surfaced for the Troop at last? Walking into the operations room, Pat spotted the duty officer. 'You just cost me an airport job Ian,' he grinned. 'What's the score then, another bloody drill?'

The SAS Captain shook his head. 'Not this time, Pat,' he said gravely.

Pat froze, raised an eyebrow as if to implore him to go on.

'There's been a multiple shooting incident on the other side of the river. During a routine raid, Special Branch attempted to arrest some suspects at a Muslim college in Dulwich half an hour ago. Two of the officers have been shot dead, more than that wounded. There's a hostage situation on. The Troop is to go in as soon as you're assembled. 'The Captain paused. 'What's wrong, Pat? This is what your lads have been waiting for, isn't it?'

Pat nodded, slowly and deliberately. 'You'd better tell me everything you know. '

'Come with me to the Troop Room - we've got the street plans laid out. You'll have to start thinking about how you want to play it, while we wait for your boys to arrive.'

Pat nodded, and strode off down the corridor to the Two Troop ready room. Behind him, the Operations Officer carried a rolled bundle of large scale street maps and building diagrams tucked tightly under his arm.

187

The briefing room lights flickered as they came on, illuminating a large room filled with chairs, neatly laid out in two rows of eight, facing a long table and briefing dias. The room doubled as the Troop's storage facility, and was lined with tall grey metal lockers, each one crammed with his men's uniforms, body armour and equipment.

Pat spread the maps out on the table in the centre of the room, and began to assess the ground, and plan the assault. As he did so, picturing routes of attack and retreat, the Operations Officer fed him the most current information he had. It quickly became clear that, given the lack of time, and the orders for immediate action, there was only one course of action open to him. When Pat was satisfied, he opened his own locker, and began to pull on his black fireproofed boiler suit.

'Pat!' Came a voice from behind. Turning, Pat saw Danny and Spike piling into the room. 'Is it for real this time?' Danny asked hopefully.

'It's for real,' Pat answered. 'Get your body armour on, lads. It's time to show what we're worth. '

'The Home Office has authorised the use of deadly force - two Special Branch Officers have already been shot and killed this morning, and two more

188

wounded. We're working on the assumption there are up to five gunmen. We're going in hot lads, so it's going to be a smash and grab immediate entry. There's no time for surveillance, finesse or detailed planning. '

Pat knew that this was the most dangerous form of assault, but had no other viable option. The longer it took to mount the assault, the more entrenched the terrorists would become, and the more difficult it would be to dislodge them. The time for talking had come and gone. Blood had been spilled; now the gloves were off.

'The Government wants this incident dealt with swiftly, before it escalates into something even worse. One copper is still missing, and the police think he was grabbed and taken inside the building. There is also some civilian staff in the building. They will be used as hostages, no doubt - but that's why we're here.' Pat looked up at his men 'To avoid a bloodbath. '

Pat paused, and looked around at each of his troopers. They looked back at him with anticipation. After a moment, he continued.

'The plan is simple. We go in hard and fast. If there's an opportunity, we put men on the roof before the assault kicks off. We drive up to the entrance, bail out, and the main assault team blow the doors with their shotguns.

189

The front support team lob in as many flash bangs and tear gas grenades into the building as they can. While that's happening out front, exactly the same thing is happening at the back of the building. I'll lead the front assault team, with Alpha one, with Bravo one as my support team. Dickie, you'll lead the rear assault group with Charlie one and Delta one doing the bombing.

Corporal Dickie Spencer nodded. 'Roger that, Pat.
'

Pat looked at his watch. 'We draw weapons and ammunition from the armoury in five minutes, and I want everyone down at the motor pool ten minutes later, fully loaded and ready to rock. We'll use standard vehicle deployment, so take all five Range Rovers. I'll update vehicle commanders by radio on the way with any new information, as I receive it from Special Branch over the secure link. I'll take the lead Rover. We'll have a police motorcycle escort, so don't worry about having to stop at junctions and red lights. It's foot down all the way. Any questions?'

The men were silent. As chairs scraped, and Two Troop prepared to leave for the armoury, Pat watched them go. 'You've done this hundreds of times in training boys,' he called after them. 'And you're bloody good at it.

I'm one hundred per cent confident that we are going to conquer today.' Pat smiled wolfishly and paused for just a moment. Adrenaline surged as he raised his hand as it balled into a fist. 'Trust me boys, we'll do this right. The bastards won't know what's hit them.'

Fifteen minutes later, Two Troop paraded beside their vehicles, dressed in their boiler suits and black body armour vests. Most carried sinister-looking snub-nosed MP5A submachine guns. A few carried powerful short-barrelled semi-automatic shotguns, loaded with fat solid shot rounds to deal with the buildings doors. Every man carried a Browning high powered pistol - chosen by the Regiment for its excellent stopping power at close range, and the fact that thirteen 9mm rounds were carried in each magazine, whereas other comparable pistols usually housed only eight. The handguns were worn in a thigh holster, carried as a backup weapon, in case of a sudden cataclysmic stoppage with the MP5.

Pat thumbed his radio mike, and checked communication between each of the vehicles. When the last Rover checked in and Pat was satisfied, he nodded to the police outriders and gave his men the order to mount up. The Troop disappeared into the green Rovers, hidden behind dark, smoked windows. With sirens blaring, the convoy began its high speed dash towards Dulwich.

Following the flashing blue lights of the police escort, Pat's mind churned with thoughts and worries about the mission, and his men. His Troop knew their jobs; they were tough, fit and highly motivated. They had proved themselves to all concerned by exceeding the high standards which the regular SAS instructors had demanded of them. There were no weak links. However, now it was the moment for the Troop to finally step up to the plate.

There was something fundamentally different in the minds of the Shadow Squadron troopers, as the convoy raced towards Dulwich. One final act would be their unholy baptism into the ugly, bloody world of counter terrorism.

It was time for the men of Two Troop, to kill…

Chapter Sixteen

Spike Morris carefully began to lift the building's rooftop maintenance hatch. His number two, Danny Thomas had several minutes earlier carefully dripped penetrating oil over the iron hinges to avoid the rusty metal from squeaking, as it was raised. Once opened, Spike gently lowered the heavy hatch, and quietly eased it down onto the flat asphalt roof. When a hostage release demanded immediate entry, timing was everything. If charges placed covertly around the building failed to detonate simultaneously, or vehicles delivered the assault teams even a split second late the critical element of surprise was blown, in one disastrous instant.

Pat Farrell and the rest of the troop were in their vehicles, hidden strategically in the streets surrounding the college, waiting for the moment to initialise the main assault.

From behind his respirator Pat's eyes flicked to his watch. A thin bead of sweat trickled slowly down his forehead. Sitting hunched in the front of the lead Rover he counted the seconds on his watch as they ticked down towards the moment. His mouth was dry as a desert. The rush was coming, like an old friend. It always felt like this, just before an op. kicked off.

His men sat quietly and gripped their weapons. Pat knew they felt worse than he did. But they were ready, he knew that too. Soon now, Pat thought. Under a minute, and he must order his men into harm's way. Their lives were in his hands.

Pat breathed slowly and moved his hand to his throat mike. He forced his voice into calm and level mode.

'All stations, this is Zero Alpha…30 seconds…*Stand by.* '

The message crackled in their ear pieces. Restricted by respirator and body armour, Spike peered down inside the darkened room. It seemed deserted, but that meant nothing. He looked up at Danny and gave a nervous thumbs up signal. Danny chewed his lip and nodded. Breathing deeply, he quietly removed a fat stun grenade from his pouch, laying it gently on the flat roof beside him. Reaching into his pouch again, Danny extracted a CS grenade, and passed it to Spike. Danny looked at his watch. On a nod from Danny, both men gripped their grenades tightly, and eased out the safety pins. Swallowing hard, Danny whispered.

'Any second now! '

Inexorably, the countdown continued on Pat's watch. He forced himself into deep rhythmic breathing. As the second hand ticked the last seconds towards the dials zenith, Pat cleared his throat and spoke into his mike again.

'All stations. Stand by…. Stand by. *Go! Go! Go!.* '

Pat's driver floored the gas pedal. With a roar the Rover surged forward, closely followed by its twin. The Rovers screeched round the corner in a cloud of exhaust as they broke cover.

'Come on Dave, faster!' Yelled Pat from behind his mask.

The Rovers cannonballed through the open iron gates. The drivers slammed on the brakes as they reached the college's main entrance.

'Out! Out!'

Vehicle doors gaped, as heavily armed troopers leapt from each carrier. Sprinting to within feet of the building, two of Pat's men armed with shotguns took aim and fired point blank into the entrance doors hinges.

As the troopers stormed the building below, Spike's head bobbed in time with Danny's countdown.

'Three, Two One DROP!'

Both fizzing grenades disappeared into the open hatch, and clanged on the concrete floor below. Seconds later, both exploded. Stun grenades were designed to temporally blind their victims with a brilliant flash, and stun their senses with the powerful concussion and deafening bang. The CS grenade instantly filled the room with thick, choking tear gas.

Around its exterior, other explosions rocked the building. The front door and several windows were instantly blown in by solid shot or explosive frame charges, which had been shoved into place moments before by other members of the Troop.

Danny and Spike quickly dropped into the smoking room, and wrenched its door open. Spike lobbed another stun grenade into the corridor, which exploded with an incredibly bright flash, and a deafening roar.

Downstairs Pat and the main assault party stormed through the shattered doors, shooting a staggering terrorist who appeared through an internal passageway. At the rear of the building, two troopers swung in through blasted window frames, having abseiled down from the roof. Within moments the building was a whirl of deafening noise and smoke filled chaos, but it was a critical part of Pat's assault plan. Noise and confusion were friends, not foe.

'Keep it tight boys, and watch out for the civvies'

The assault teams quickly and systematically cleared each room. Door kicked open, flash bang lobbed in. Wait for the blast and immediately enter and clear. Missing a room could be fatal, and invited a bullet in the back of the head.

Having finished their sweep through the empty rooms upstairs, Danny yelled.

'Bravo three, top floor clear,' into his throat mike as both men took cover, and with chests heaving, set guard to the stairs.

One of the troopers who had come in through an upstairs window fired a full 30 round magazine into an armed terrorist who suddenly appeared in front of him through the smoke. Stepping over the riddled body, his number two opened the door, and both men quickly disappeared through it.

Pat kicked opened the door of the room where he believed the hostages were being held. With hinges blasted, the stun and gas grenades had already filled the dark room with drunken staggering shadows. Somewhere in the smoke, a woman screamed. The small torch clipped to

Pat's submachine gun barrel illuminated a coughing man holding a grenade. Without hesitation, Pat fired half his 30 round magazine into the target. The man fell lifeless, his chest ripped apart and bloody. Behind the corpse, Pat saw more movement. A figure rushed towards him through the smoke. Pat swung the smoking muzzle of his MP5. A voice screamed inside his head

'NO!'

The figure was one of the women hostages.

'Save me!' She screamed hysterically, as she staggered towards him, blinded with gas and stomach churning terror. Someone moved in the dark fog behind her and shouted.

'Allah Acka..... '

Pat fired past the woman into the shadows, a split second before his opponent. The nickel cased 9mm bullets found their mark, and the terrorist fell backwards, never to finish his battle cry.

Behind Pat, other members of the Troop were hunting the darkened corridors. When their quarry was identified, there was no time for mercy. The enemy were eliminated, with withering bursts of fire from the deadly snub-nosed SAS machine guns.

The firing stopped abruptly as the last terrorist was dropped. There was a moment's silence. With his heart pounding Pat yelled

'Get the civvies out!' He cast his eyes across the bodies he could see. 'I want a full body count done, quickly!'

The coughing, cowering band of terrified civilian hostages were pushed and dragged from the room by the SAS men. One of the masked troopers helped a sobbing girl with a torn blouse past the shattered remains of the door. Once outside, there were troopers waiting to cuff them all, until positively identified as innocents.

Through the swirling clouds of chocking gas Pat scanned the room again. Satisfied, he reached for the switch on his throat mike.

'All stations. Check the bodies. One more sweep.' He ordered.

The count was short. Seven gunmen were believed to have been in the building, but the hasty count revealed only six lifeless corpses.

Pat's voice carried a ring of new urgency. 'There's one Tango still alive and hiding somewhere. Fan out and for Christ's sake boys, find him!'

Throughout the building, his men retraced their steps and returned to their victims, and began the hunt for the missing gunman. Somewhere above, guns chattered suddenly, then abruptly fell silent.

With weapons ready, Spike and Danny crept towards the body of the last terrorist, who had made the fatal mistake of trying to flee up the stairs and escape across the building's roof.

'Fuck!' Said Danny, staring down at the bullet riddled body. He gave it a tentative push with the toe of his boot. Both young men looked at each other, but remained silent. Ashen-faced, they heard footfalls on the stairs below. Crouching in the gloom, they raised their weapons.

'All right lads. It's me, Pat. *Hold your fire!* '

Both troopers relaxed, the tension in their shoulders visibly disappearing at the sound of his voice. Pat saw their faces behind the masks. Their skin was pale, their eyes wide. The three men stood in silence until Pat's firm voice broke the silence.

'You both did well.'

Neither young man said anything as they stared at the bullet-ridden body lying in a pool of dark blood at their feet. They heard him but somehow Pat's praise didn't cut it. His words had no effect.

And Pat knew why. Their deadly apprenticeship was over and now, there was no going back. He understood the turmoil which was coursing through them, the bitter blend of pride and shame. He had tasted it once. But this was their time to deal with what they had done, and they needed the slap of stark painful truth from someone they trusted and respected.

'So you killed a man today. You'll both get over it.'

The truth stung them. It hurt. Was that regret he saw in their eyes?

He turned and headed back down the stairs. He had other men to talk to.

Pat stopped suddenly halfway down and turned to face them. He fixed the troopers with dark, cold eyes.

'Don't worry about it. We're soldiers. Killing is what we do… '

Chapter Seventeen

Washington D.C.

When 3-star Admiral Patrick 'Tubby' Church had first received the phone call, he had to admit to himself that he was intrigued. As Director of the U.S. Defence Intelligence agency he was responsible for acquiring and co-ordinating foreign military intelligence, which his agency disseminated to the relevant civilian and military defence policymakers and force planners, whose powerful committees sat on Capitol Hill, in Washington D.C. The intelligence the DIA provided helped the U.S. Government's defence planners to assess potential future threats to their military, and allocate millions, and sometimes billions of tax payers' dollars for weapons and equipment research and development, to counter the impending threats which Admiral Church's people had detected.

He was intrigued because the call had come from David Summers, a personal assistant of Derek Cordell III, the Director of America's ultra-secret National Security Agency, at 4am on a Sunday morning. The aide had politely requested that he make himself available for a top level meeting at the Federal Bureau of Investigation's J. Edgar Hoover Building at 935 Pennsylvania Avenue, in Washington D.C. at 10am that morning. During his two years in office, Admiral Church had become accustomed to occasionally receiving an urgent phone call during the night. It was always something important, but had never come from the Director of the NSA. This must be something very, very important he thought. The aide finished the call by telling Admiral Church that a car would be sent, and would arrive at his home in Washington's leafy suburbs at 9 O'clock. It would take him directly to the FBI's headquarters. As the Admiral replaced the receiver and climbed out of bed, his sleepy wife asked him what the matter was.

'Oh it's nothing Honey, just the office calling.'

Pat Church took his seat around the vast oval table in the spacious briefing room. He was flanked by the Heads of the other fifteen security agencies which carried joint responsibility for the security of the United States of America. Earlier, as the delegates had assembled in the large anti-room next to the room in which he now sat, he had chatted with several old friends who had made their way up the chain during the cold war, to head some of the most powerful security agencies in the world. The usual suspects were all there. Peter Marshall, Director of the Central Intelligence Agency, Paul Timmins Jnr., head of the Federal Bureau of Investigation, and Peter Brown, head of the new Department of Homeland Security. The Intelligence chiefs of the Military were also present; army, Navy, Marines and Air force were there, with the heads of the Treasury and State Department, plus the Coast Guard and the high tech. National Geospatial-Intelligence agency. Admiral Church also recognised Dr Solomon Manstein, head of the U.S. Department of Energy.

The meeting began, when Derek Cordell cleared his throat and hammered his gavel onto the table. Conversations around the table stopped abruptly, and all eyes turned to the Chairman.

'Gentlemen, thank you for coming here at such short notice. A situation has arisen during the last few days which may become a major threat to the safety of the continental USA.' Cordell paused, and looked around the table. His Ivy League New England accent held their attention, and all eyes were focused on him, 'An intelligence report provided by the Marine Corps was received a week ago from Baghdad Iraq, which although unverified, suggests a threat of cataclysmic proportions may now exist to the free world, and particularly to the United States. '

Cordell paused again, and looked towards the seated Marine Officer. 'Perhaps you could explain how the information was recovered, before I continue General Morrison?'

The lean, hard faced Marine General nodded, and spoke in a slow Texan drawl.

'Mr Chairman, Gentlemen. During a routine sweep for weapons and improvised explosive device materials seven days ago, one of my Marine infantry patrols in Baghdad found an Iraqi army lorry loaded with documents, in a deserted garage close to the army Canal district in the east of the city. The patrol Commander judged from its condition, the vehicle had been locked away for several years, and had probably been there since the time we invaded Iraq. The patrol searched it for booby traps, but found nothing, which suggests the lorry had been abandoned in a real hurry. The patrol opened several crates of documents, which all had Iraqi Secret Police seals on them, and the patrol's Iraqi interpreter scanned a few of them. He reported to the patrol Commander that the papers were stamped 'Ultra Secret' and were concerned with something called Gilgamesh…..'

The NSA Director held up his hand.

'Thank you General, I'll take it from there. The documents were taken away and scrutinised in detail by the in-theatre Central Marine Intelligence unit. They were deeply concerned with what they found, and after a call to General Morrison, faxed several hundred pages over to us in the NSA. We looked at them, and immediately passed them on to Dr Manstein who most of you know heads up the U.S. Department of Energy. Perhaps you will give a synopsis of what you found Doctor?'

The scientist cleared his throat with a slight cough, looked down at his notes.

'Yes, thank you Mr Chairman... Well Gentlemen, we have a problem. We looked at the faxed documents, and have now finished sifting through the originals, which were flown direct to the United States, specifically to our research facility at Los Alamos, New Mexico. There has been a delay, because everything was of course written in Arabic, and we have had to have every document interpreted, and re-written into English. It has been a massive task, and I am grateful for the huge assistance of the NSA.' He inclined his head towards the Chairman.

'What could have taken months, has taken just days to achieve. The documents overall are a complex and mixed bundle, ranging from equipment requisitions and shipping documents to personnel files and technical data. The most important items we have deciphered so far are a series of blue prints, mathematical equations and some very specific and accurate calculations, which lay at the heart of the Iraqi Gilgamesh project. I have no hesitation in verifying that the documents are quite genuine. '

Dr Manstein looked up from his notes, and turned his head towards the NSA Director again.

'Yes, thank you Mr Cordell. Your people have worked very hard on this, please pass on my grateful thanks to all of them.' He looked around the table again, knowing from the grim faces of the assembled security chiefs that they already suspected the conclusion he was about to make. 'Well Gentlemen, there we have it. The documents have given us absolute proof that unknown to any of us, Saddam Hussein had an on-going ultra-secret project to build an atomic bomb, which as far as we have deduced from the hoard of recovered documents.........was successfully completed just before we invaded Iraq. '

There was stunned silence in the briefing room. After failing to detect the 9/11 attack on the twin towers in New York, every security agency in the U.S. had undergone a dramatic and soul searching review of why each of them in turn, had failed to detect and foil the plot, which had so convincingly slipped under their collective radar. Tubby Church looked across the briefing room and winced at his old friend Theodore Frost, Rear Admiral in charge of Naval Intelligence. The NSA Director continued.

'I briefed the President on Gilgamesh last night Gentlemen. On one hand, he is delighted that his decision to press for the invasion of Iraq because of the threat of weapons of mass destruction has in part at least been vindicated.' Derek Cordell paused once again, and scanned the faces sitting around the table. 'On the other hand however, he is deeply concerned that we have only just found out that the bomb appears to have actually been built, and he wants to know why, despite a combined annual intelligence budget of billions of dollars, we have never even heard of project Gilgamesh until now, two years after the invasion?'

Derek Cordell cleared his throat, and continued 'The President is right of course, and has a perfectly valid point Gentlemen, but I don't think it is appropriate for recriminations or investigations at this time. Due to the gravity of the situation, the need for full co-operation between our departments has never been greater. The President has authorised the release of all our information on every aspect concerning Gilgamesh, to our closest allies, Gt. Britain and Israel. He considers this to be a direct threat against all three countries. Should this weapon, if it exists, fall into the hands of Al-Qaeda, then he believes any of the three are most likely to be the intended victim. I should stress however, he considers the United States of America to be the prime target.'

Derek Cordell paused, and sipped from a glass of water. 'As I see it, we have three immediate tasks to accomplish. First, we need to find the development facility. Second, we need to confirm that the bomb has actually been built. Finally Gentlemen, if it does exist, we need to find out who has it, and where the hell has it gone?'

Chapter Eighteen

'It's a real mess down there Sir,' said the SEAL team Commander to Rear Admiral Theodore Frost, via his satellite phone. 'We got in there by climbing down a vertical air shaft; the normal entrances are blocked with tons of rock. The corridor beneath the shaft was full of water, so I had to put in a full diving team.'

When Admiral Frost had originally taken the call from Derek Cordell, he knew that to search an underground complex, which would probably be flooded was a job for the Navy's specialist SEALs. Expert in underwater reconnaissance, and highly mobile, he ordered the U.S. Navy's Special Forces team flown in to Bakhma as soon as helicopter transport and gunship escorts could be arranged. The helicopters now stood silently nearby as the SEAL Lieutenant John Murphy continued his report.

'My guys found evidence of human remains down there Sir, lots of them in the flooded tunnels near the surface.'

Admiral Frost closed his eyes for a moment, putting aside the horror of their last moments, trapped like rats in the dark water.

'What else did they find down there Lieutenant? He demanded impatiently.

'Well Sir, they found tons of smashed metal tubes and pipes down in the lower levels. There were two big caverns full of water, and the debris was all in there. We are uploading some pictures now Sir, of exactly what they found down there.'

Admiral Frost was relieved, and proud of his men. His Marines had located the first evidence of the Gilgamesh project, and now the SEALS had confirmed it.

'Good, well done Murphy, pass my thanks on to your men. Make sure you bring up some samples of the smashed equipment, and get them to Baghdad ASAP.'

With a crisp 'Roger that. Sir.' Lieutenant Murphy clicked the off button on his phone, and called across to his exhausted divers.

'Hey guys, the Admiral says well done.'

None of the tough wet suited SEALS said anything as they lay in the hot sun. Dive conditions had been hellish in the tunnels; dark, claustrophobic and deep. It had felt somewhere between cave and sunken wreck diving. They were all well practiced at both techniques of course, but never at the same time. There was a constant danger of snagging on some sharp metallic object, or

211

breaking a safety line and getting lost in the maze of flooded tunnels as their air tanks ran dry. Murphy knew his men, and grinned to himself. He wasn't annoyed in the least by their lack of enthusiastic response to the Admirals commendation. Right now, he knew every man jack of them would have swapped all the praise in China for an ice cold beer.

The American NSA signal handed to the Director of MI6 by his most trusted personal secretary Mrs Grey confirmed Cornelius's analysis and report had been right all along. Sir Alex cursed himself for a fool for accepting that damned idiot Ingram's conclusions, when he red lined almost every deduction Cornelius had submitted. Sir Alex usually made a point of reading anything from his brightest analyst, but Ingram had assured him that there was no need, as the latest submission concerning Bakhma was nothing more than the ramblings of a burnt out drunk.

Sir Alex anger grew when he realised that to compound the debacle, a golden opportunity to steal the march on the NSA and CIA had come and gone. With their almost limitless money and resources, it was always extremely satisfying to put one over on his colleagues on the other side of the pond. He couldn't undue the

American's being first past the post, but there was something he could do within his own organisation. Sir Alex lent across his desk and depressed the call button on his intercom.

The man would be lucky to collect his pension. Sir Alex would personally see to it that he spent the rest of his career counting paper clips in some backwater civil service department, far from SIS. His silken voice hid the deadly venom of a trap door spider.

'Mrs Grey, would you be kind enough to ask Piers Ingram to come to my office immediately please?'

Thinking about Cornelius, the SIS Director stood at his bay window, contemplating the magnificent view across the Thames. Abruptly, he turned on his heal and returned to his desk. The SIS chief read more of the highly classified intelligence signal.

The Americans had found clear evidence that the Bakhma dam complex had been used to produce uranium 235, but their divers had been unable to find anything remotely resembling a finished atomic bomb during their initial examination of the site. A further detailed search was under way, but early estimates suggested it would take weeks, possibly months to bring in enough equipment to clear the tons of rock and twisted metal from the dark warren of submerged corridors and caverns. The bomb might still be there Sir Alex mused, but if it existed, what was he going to do if it wasn't?

His intercom buzzed, his secretary said. 'Mr Ingram is here Sir Alex.'

The chill in his voice betrayed the outcome of the meeting to Mrs Grey, but she said nothing to the visitor.

'Ah yes, thank you Mrs Grey. Please ask Ingram to step in, will you?'

When he had finally struck the deal with the Al-Qaeda agent, Al-Mahdi had expected complications, but he had not expected to have to deliver the bomb to its target. He wanted to be rid of it, by selling the location of the bomb and trigger to the purchaser, but that wasn't what his customer would agree to. Al-Mahdi had refused to haggle over the price. He considered his asking price to be a bargain, considering that the bomb had cost the people of Iraq more than eight billion U.S. dollars in research, development and production costs. He would not budge on the asking price, but he had been forced to agree to the condition of delivery. The agent had explained that it was felt by his leader that any man capable of

214

successfully stealing such a weapon was also capable of moving it across international borders without detection. The other factor was security. The plan was known only to a few men, and Al-Mahdi would in effect become an ultra-secure one-man cell, which could not be betrayed by accomplices.

It was agreed between them, for a final price of $50,000,000 U.S. dollars that Al-Mahdi would recover the bomb, and find a way to move it to its final destination. There, he would also hand over the trigger. Only then would the balance be released to his account in Switzerland. It was a hard bargain, but Colonel el-Majid had accepted it. They had also agreed that the projected time scale was six months which Al-Mahdi had reluctantly agreed to, on the provision that his study would prove it feasible. His biggest gamble had been making first contact with the leaders of Al-Qaeda.

He had begun worshipping at the Great Mosque of Paris, located in the Ve arrondissement, shortly after arriving in France as an Iraqi political refugee, masquerading as a man whose family had all been slaughtered by Saddam Hussein's secret police. He had provided the names of the Alhassen family, who he had

had executed shortly after joining the Mukhabarat, save the persona he had assumed. When the overworked officials of the French immigration service had checked with the new Interior Ministry bureaucracy in Iraq, the names had eventually been found, and confirmed as murdered by the Mukhabarat. They had failed to note the name of Abu Alhassen, who wasn't on the search list. The French authorities had granted him a work permit, and permission to stay until a decision was reached on his future. That had been two years previously, and he had heard nothing more. He wasn't concerned, as French television regularly ran news pieces on the tidal wave of illegal immigrants and bogus refugees flooding into France from North and Central Africa. One legitimate refugee who could prove his identity and support himself without asking for hand-outs was definitely at the bottom of their files to action.

Built in the Mudéjar style, the beautiful Great Mosque of Paris was founded after World War I as a sign of French gratitude to the Muslim colonial soldiers who had fought against the Germans, and died in their thousands. Its many splendid rooms offered the opportunity for prayer and Islamic study, but also to listen to the teachings of various visiting clerics. Al-Mahdi visited the Mosque regularly, and had waited his moment to speak to one particularly vociferous Saudi cleric, who was well known for his criticism of America and her allies, and his sympathy with Osama Bin Laden and Al-Qaeda. Fearing that his conversation might be overheard by R.G. French Security Service bugs, he placed a message written in Arabic into the cleric's hand at the end of his stormy sermon. It read:

'I must talk to someone in Al-Qaeda urgently. In the name of the Prophet, peace be upon him, I have something of supreme importance to discuss, concerning the war against the infidels, and a means for you to punish them even more harshly than New York. God is Great!'

Attached to the note was his business card showing the address of Alhassen's Antiquities. Al-Mahdi's eyes narrowed as he held his finger to his lips, left the Mosque and waited patiently for contact.

Several weeks later, the Alhassen's Antiquities telephone rang, and a voice enquired after a small Neo-Babylonian idol which sat in the window of his shop. The caller spoke to him in fluent French. He informed Al-Mahdi that he had noticed the idol as he passed the previous evening, and wondered if it was still for sale. Al-Mahdi assured the caller that it was, and arrangements

217

were made to hold the piece until later in the day, when the customer would call in and view it more closely. It would please Al-Mahdi to be rid of it; he had picked it up for a handful of Euros from a junk stall, in the Latin Quarter's flea market several months previously. It was a convincing fake, carefully weathered and aged sufficiently to fool an inexperienced amateur collector, but it was a fake, never the less.

Customers occasionally browsed, and Al-Mahdi took little notice of an Asian man who entered the shop several hours later. In his late fifties, the man was greying, and his tired face looked older than his years. Walking with the aid of a stick, he crossed over to the counter and quietly said.

'I phoned about the idol this morning, may I see it?'

Al-Mahdi picked up the piece and handed it to him.

'Ah yes, this is an interesting item, late Babylonian perhaps?' He thought for a moment as he glanced around the otherwise empty shop. 'Perhaps you will permit me to buy you coffee in the café next door, where we can sit and discuss its price like civilised men?'

The café was empty of customers, the morning breakfasts were finished, and the lunchtime rush was not expected to begin for another hour. The man ordered coffee for two, and sat with his back to the counter, at a discrete corner table. When the café owner's wife had served them coffee and returned to her cup washing duties behind the counter, the man spoke quietly to Al-Mahdi in Arabic.

'Now Mr Alhassen,' he said, producing the letter from the Mosque. 'I believe you have something you would like to discuss with me?'

Chapter Nineteen

Helmand Province - Afghanistan

Mutaleb Latif and his family sat miserably under guard, with their backs resting against one of the thick mud walls of their family compound. Dawn was breaking as British soldiers and Afghan Police officers continued the search inside for hidden weapons, and caches of raw opium.

With his younger brother, Latif farmed five acres of fertile valley floor in Helmand province, in southern Afghanistan. He had faced a critical dilemma months ago, when armed Taliban had come to his compound late one night. Two disastrous years of drought had left him without enough money to buy the seeds to grow their next crop of wheat, and Mutaleb's family faced starvation during the coming winter months. The Taliban said they would provide him with new seeds and money, to be repaid when the harvest was in, providing he switched his crop from wheat to opium. They had explained that if he grew wheat, he could expect no more than $121 per acre for any meagre surplus he had left, but if he grew the Opium Poppy he could earn perhaps $5,200 per acre. They had also offered to protect him against imprisonment, if he paid protection tax, when he sold the milky opium gum to the traders who dealt in such things. It was a simple and easy choice; he could let his family face starvation, or prosper growing the poppy, and become a wealthy man.

In the late summer of 2000, when the Taliban still controlled Afghanistan, their supreme leader Mullah Mohammed Omar had decreed that growing poppy plants to produce opium was against the strict teachings of the Koran, and anyone caught would be punished or imprisoned. Latif's Uncle, who farmed further up the valley, had chosen to ignore the edict, and was discovered growing poppy plants on his wretched three acres. The Taliban used heavy iron bars to break both his legs, and cut off four of his fingers as punishment.

After the Northern Alliance, backed by the Americans, had overthrown the Taliban Government of Afghanistan, the area where Mutaleb Latif lived and worked came under the control of the powerful warlord General Hazrat Ali. General Ali was much favoured by the Americans; he had provided thousands of his fierce fighters in the war against the Taliban. Unknown to the impoverished farmers of Helmand province however, General Hazrat Ali had now come to a very secret but agreeable financial arrangement with the ousted remnants of the Taliban, where both parties made huge profits by feeding the world's army of addicts, cursed with an insatiable hunger for heroin. There were two reasons why the Taliban policy against cultivation of the Opium Poppy had changed. Firstly, they needed a constant supply of money to buy arms and ammunition, and now, Al-Qaeda secretly needed to raise $50,000.000 U.S. Dollars.

'Bingo, found something Sarge!' Shouted Private Dave Manning, as he searched an outhouse within Mutaleb Latif's compound. The hut was crammed with the paraphernalia used to refine the raw opium gum which would shortly be harvested from the poppy plants, and process it into almost pure powdery heroin. On-site refinement made sense to both farmers and traffickers; raw opium gum was bulky and heavy. Refined heroin was much lighter and easier for the smugglers to hide and transport out of Afghanistan. Sergeant Watts, of 'C' Company, 1st Battalion Royal Anglian Regiment surveyed the contents of the gloomy hut. Five battered fifty gallon oil drums, a crude pressing machine, cotton filters and jars of what he assumed to be an acid called acetic anhydride, which he knew was used in the refinement process.

'Nice one Manning, well done. Now where's that bloody interpreter gone?' Demanded the tall sergeant, as his eyes scanned the dusty inner compound.

'Mohammad, tell those fucking weasels outside, they're under arrest. Manning, I want you to smash and burn all that gear in the hut, then join the others outside. '

Sgt Watts strode through the compound, stopping when he found one of his rifle section commanders.

'Corporal Kennedy, when they've finished the sweep, get all the lads outside, and cover the Afghan fuzz while they start chopping down those bloody poppy plants. '

As his men assembled outside, Sgt Watts knew that the army's anti-drug sweeps looked good on paper, but accounted for the destruction of less than 2% of the 500,000 acres of land now being used to produce raw opium. The Boss had said previously that there were political arguments against using something like Agent Orange to kill the poppy plants. 265,000 civilian families were now involved in the growing of opium Poppies throughout Afghanistan, and surely faced starvation if their fields were poisoned. The Americans had used the powerful herbicide in Vietnam, to defoliate vast tracts of jungle from the air, removing the cover which the Viet

Cong used so effectively. Something to do with losing the 'Hearts and Minds' war; at least, that's what his Major had said before the op.

'Our bloody Government probably can't be arsed to spend the money' he thought angrily. He had seen good men die because the body armour had been slow in coming, and when it did, there wasn't enough to go round. Whatever the reason behind not using defoliants, in a technological age when millions could die at the press on a button, the Afghan Police were reduced to the stone age tactic of chopping off the gum bearing heads of the poppy plants by slashing at them with wooden sticks. It was an inefficient and painfully slow process, which laid them open to sudden ambush by the guerrillas. The Battalion had lost six men so far to snipers and roadside bombs on the current tour, and Sgt Watts didn't want to lose any of his platoon, before the Battalion finished its tour, and flew back to the UK in five short weeks.

'Come on lads,' he shouted. 'Hurry up before the Taliban start slinging bloody mortar bombs at us again. '

When the Afghan interpreter kicked Mutaleb Latif, and told him with a broad grin he was under arrest, Latif shrugged his shoulders. He wasn't particularly worried, and had expected it. As a reward from the grateful interim Afghan Government, for his priceless help against the Taliban, General Hazrat Ali had not only been granted control over Latif's valley as the new and all-powerful Governor, he had also, incredibly, been made Helmand Province's Chief of Police. Mutaleb Latif knew, because he had paid his protection money, he would be released from the dank confines of any Afghan jail within a matter of days. Corruption was so rife throughout Afghanistan society that provincial prosecutors and judges, who earned as little as $100 per month, were easy targets for hefty bribes, especially when they came from the ruthless Taliban, or an equally ruthless Chief of Police.

Al-Mahdi sat quietly thinking in the small office which adjoined his antiquities shop. He had spent the last few days outlining in his mind how to move an atomic bomb weighing almost half a ton from its hiding place, to a target which he would be told of shortly. He had formulated a basic idea on how to conceal the device during its shipment, but it would probably take him at least a day to prepare it for movement, before he dared take it out of its hiding place into the open, and begin its final journey. When he had its delivery date, and ultimate destination, he would arrange for its transportation overseas.

He saw the operation falling into seven distinct phases. First would be his return to Iraq. Second, would be gathering the necessary items of equipment and stores, then returning to where the bomb was hidden. The next phase of the operation was to prepare the device for transport. During this phase, he would need to camouflage it in such a way, as to be invisible to anyone who looked at it during a routine Customs or security check. He had that matter already calculated. Next, would be transporting the device to a seaport, and loading it aboard ship. The sea journey to its destination would be the penultimate phase, and finally, delivering the bomb and its trigger to his Al-Qaeda customers.

His train of thought was broken when his telephone rang. The caller introduced himself as Herr Otto Borgman, Deputy Manager of the Banque Cantonale de Basel in Switzerland.

'Following your instructions, I ring to inform you that we have just received a deposit into your account of five million U.S. dollars Mr Alhassen.'

Al-Mahdi could not help but smile.

'Thank you Herr Borgman. Goodbye.'

When he had flown to Switzerland and opened the account some months previously, Herr Borgman had initially asked too many questions. It was only when Al-Mahdi mentioned the fact that he eventually expected fifty million U.S, dollars to pass through the account, that Herr Borgman had immediately stopped asking questions, and assured his new client that although the bank was not one of the larger private banks in Switzerland, the Banque Cantonale de Basel enjoyed a well deserved reputation for absolute discretion when it came to their customers private business.

'Money is the true language spoken by all men,' thought Al-Mahdi smiling, as he went back to the serious business of planning.

Chapter Twenty

It was 2am GMT, and the slipstream roared and screamed like some terrible wounded beast outside the metal skin of the low flying C130 Hercules. The lumbering four-engined aircraft was making its final approach towards the tiny island Drop Zone. Pat Farrell stood in the aircrafts open side door, with his eyes firmly fixed on the red light beside it. He and his Troop had been ordered to make a simulated attack on a remote Royal Air Force station at Saxa Vord, which formed part of the forward radar chain protecting NATO's northern flank. Situated just outside the Arctic Circle, it had been built on the tip of the most northern of the British Shetland Islands. The strange twilight at such high latitudes clearly demonstrated that inside the Arctic Circle the sun never fully set at that time of year. Ignoring the screaming slipstream, Pat momentarily pulled his eyes away from the red warning light, and glanced through the open door. A sombre curtain of grey clouds hung in the dark forbidding skies, meeting rows of deep ocean breakers somewhere in the blur of the distant horizon. Massive white capped waves undulated and foamed their way slowly underneath the aircraft, in a rolling and never ending chain.

As his eyes swept the frothing grey waters 800 feet below him, it occurred to Pat that from where he stood braced in the doorway, there was no sign of land anywhere, and the red warning light beside his head heralded that his exit from the aircraft was imminent. Never an enthusiastic fan of low level static-line parachuting, Pat offered up a silent prayer that their RAF pilot was still sober, and the island's DZ was somewhere just in front of the aircraft. Tightly packed behind him, were seven more of his Troop, also heavily weighed down with steel helmets, parachutes, military equipment and weapons. The opposite side door was similarly crowded with the other half of the elite Two Troop. It was the second line of eight part-time Special Forces soldiers counting the seconds, waiting for the order to jump.

Further thoughts of the pilot's sobriety vanished from Pat's mind when the red light suddenly changed to green. The Royal Air Force dispatcher slapped Pat's shoulder, and yelled into his ear above the roaring slipstream.

'GO!'

Without thinking more about it, Pat drove himself forward into the screaming void outside the aircraft. Behind him, the rest of Two Troop was rapidly being dispatched at one second intervals from alternate doors. The slipstream turned each of them as they stepped out of the aircraft, and each man dropped for several seconds before their parachutes automatically opened with a loud and profoundly satisfying - *Crack!*

Pat looked up and checked his parachute had deployed properly. After a moment, when he was happy with its uniform shape, he looked around to make sure no-one else was on a collision course with him. Satisfied, he dropped his heavy bergan backpack, which fell beneath him, until the connecting suspension rope stopped its further decent with a distinct jolt. He looked down in search of his landing point. Hundreds of feet below, in the eerie half light the ocean frothed and boiled against the islands narrow rock strewn shoreline and he could hear the huge waves, as they crashed into the base of the ancient granite cliffs far beneath him.

Pat could now clearly see the cliffs, and the tiny Drop Zone beside it, but he was drifting inexorably straight down into the raging seas. Reaching up, he grabbed a forward lift web, which connected his harness to the parachute rim, and pulled down with all the strength his adrenaline charged muscles could muster. The technique would spill air from the back of the chute and induce forward drift.

'Jesus! This is going to be tight,' he thought desperately, as he continued to pull down on the lift web, until he could almost touch the edge of the parachute material. It was working slowly, but as he continued to lose height, he knew it would be touch and go if he made it onto dry land in time.

With less than fifteen feet of clear air beneath his boots, Pat silently drifted across the cliff's edge towards dry land. He hit the ground with his usual terrible landing. Rolling onto his feet, relief flooded him. He always thought of the saying he had learned at jumps school years ago.

'Any landing you walk away from, is a good landing.' He smirked to himself at the memory as he twisted and slapped the quick release catch, and stepped clear of his parachute harness. Walking the few short yards to the cliff's edge, Pat looked down at the boiling ocean and crashing waves two hundred feet below him. 'Bloody

231

Hell,' he muttered to himself, as he walked back to recover his bergan and weapon.

'I'm getting too old for this!'

Derek Cordell closed the top secret report, removed his reading glasses, and exhaled deeply. After six exhausting weeks of work at Bakhma, the army engineers and SEALS had found nothing which remotely resembled a finished atomic bomb. They had certainly found the smashed remnants of thousands of centrifuges, and the human remains of hundreds of people who had been trapped when the complex was destroyed.

Highly radioactive containers which had stored uranium 235 had been recovered, but all were empty. The engineers had been helped by members of the U.S. Federal Aviation Authority's top air crash investigation team. Their expertise lay in rebuilding wreckage; to deduce which part of an aircrafts' structure had failed, causing some catastrophic accident. This time though, they had painstakingly pieced together parts of mangled and unidentified machinery and heavy jigs brought up from the flooded halls of Bakhma. The reassembled equipment was then analysed by Dr Manstein's people, who had been sent to Bakhma on secondment from the Los Alamos nuclear weapons research facility. The SEALS reported that there was absolutely no doubt that the complex's self-destruct mechanism had been deliberately activated. They had found the Control room's steel door with a hole cut through it, and the sabotaged locks on both the door and the self-destruct panel. The electrical cabling had been traced to where each demolition charge had been detonated. Most of the written files were beyond recovery, having been under water for weeks, but some document wallets and a few plastic identity badges were salvaged from the dark and flooded tunnels.

Derek Cordell looked at his military intelligence counterparts, who had joined him earlier with Dr Manstein, who now sat beside him.

'Well Gentlemen, you have all read the report. From your peoples own information Dr Manstein, could the Iraqis have completed a bomb?'

The head of the U.S. Department of Energy looked grave. He thought for several moments, and stared at the desk blotter in front of him. He looked up and said.

'When we dropped the atomic bombs on Hiroshima and Nagasaki in 1945, they were both what we would consider rudimentary devices by today's standards of nuclear weapon design. They were our first attempts at

233

making atomic bombs, but they both detonated and proved devastatingly effective. The Iraqis could not be considered to have achieved or advanced their program anywhere beyond our 1945 stage of nuclear weapons development. Given the evidence in front of me, and having discussed the matter in great detail with senior members of my staff at Los Alamos, and those still over in Iraq,' he paused, and chewed his lower lip. 'I must unfortunately conclude that... Yes, Saddam Hussein's people did produce a crude but viable atomic bomb at Bakhma.'

There were gasps around the table. Cordell heard someone close to him quietly mutter.

'Oh, sweet Jesus!'

Dr Manstein terrifying conclusion changed everything.

'Gentlemen, the Gilgamesh project has just taken the most severe twist imaginable. We must now work on a 99% probability that there is a rogue atom bomb out there somewhere. Whoever has it has had over two years to place it anywhere in the world. It could even be a few blocks from where we sit, waiting for the some madman's order to detonate it. This is now a crisis of unimaginable gravity. It is my duty to inform the President immediately.

Please stay in the building, and make yourselves available at short notice for an emergency meeting. '

With that, he stood up and strode out of the room, closely followed by his aides.

The alarm bells which rang in Washington D.C. were heard shortly afterwards in Britain. The American President had authorised release of the latest Bakhma report to the British SIS, and to Mossad in Israel. Both agencies were currently briefing their Prime Ministers on the crisis. The President was also currently considering releasing the information to other friendly states Security Services, but was holding the decision until he had held a three way telephone conference with the leaders of Israel and Gt. Britain.

Shortly afterwards, Sir Alex spoke quietly to all his Heads of Department.

'Well, there we are Ladies and Gentlemen. It now looks almost certain that the Gilgamesh bomb does exist. The P.M. wants a maximum effort on this. As it stands, it's been missing for over two years. We know absolutely nothing about who took it or how it was taken, where it's been for the last couple of years, where it is now, or who currently has it. We are also in the dark as to its future use.

I think it prudent to assume however, there is a very high probability that at some time in the future, it will be detonated somewhere on the mainland of the United Kingdom. '

In the smoke and mirror world of international intelligence and counter espionage, there was usually no clear evidence on which to base firm conclusions. In the secret shadowy world where bluff, double agents and carefully formulated lies were the normal day to day currency, sometimes it was down to the experience and old fashioned hunches of the officers concerned, which carried a situation to a successful conclusion. It could be the little things, snippets of information gleaned from here and there which when added together formed an overall picture of what was truly happening in some overseas arena, currently being scrutinised by the watchful eyes of MI6. It was a 'gut feeling' which prompted C to continue.

'There is every possibility that the bomb has already been delivered to these shores, but something occurred to me after reading the latest from Bakhma , which I think is worth considering. Personally, I don't think a project of this magnitude falls within the remit of some small obscure splinter group. If the bomb is up for sale, its cost would be prohibitive to any but the wealthiest terrorist organisations, of which only one currently comes to mind.'

Heads nodded around the table.

'Al-Qaeda of course,' said one of the department chiefs.

'Precisely that James,' said C. 'They have already shown their willingness to seek out and use radiation as a weapon. We have hurt them financially since 9/11. We have tracked down and sequestrated many, many millions from their coffers, and so have the Americans. As a result, we currently believe their financial reserves to be relatively low. Unfortunately, they have recently become deeply involved in drug trafficking out of Afghanistan, and are rebuilding a vast reserve of money. Now is it not reasonable to assume just for a moment, that this cash is being put aside to purchase the missing atomic bomb?'

'With the added bonus, in their eyes, of adding ruin to western society through spreading heroin addiction?' said another Head.

'Yes Phillip, quite so,' said C, nodding his agreement. 'I think we should keep an open mind on this build-up of funds. I would like your respective thoughts on my table by 9 O'clock tomorrow morning Ladies and Gentlemen. To focus our thoughts, and reinforce the gravity of this situation, I have asked Professor Dunwoody from the Aldermaston atomic Weapons Establishment in Berkshire, to brief us on what they think we are dealing with.'

C lent across to his intercom, depressed a button and said 'Mrs Grey, would you ask the Professor to step in please. '

After a short introduction, Sir Alex handed the meeting over to the Britain's senior atomic weapons design scientist.

'Ladies and Gentlemen, Al-Qaeda has over the last five years made numerous attempts to buy irradiated material from around the world, presumably to create a 'dirty' bomb. Strapping several kilos of some extremely radioactive isotope to high explosive will obviously create a normal chemical explosion, but more importantly, a deadly plume of radioactive fallout which will be carried high up into the atmosphere, and descend over hundreds, perhaps thousands of square miles. The fallout will eventually kill thousands, because long term, the radiation can produce deadly thyroid cancer and leukaemia within its victims. There is also the strong possibility of future birth defects, adverse pregnancy outcomes, and decreased fertility, and so on. We have the evidence of the RBMK

1000 reactor meltdown at Chernobyl on 25th April 1986, which starkly proves the point. In Belarus, subsequent to the disaster, of 500 new births monitored, 499 babies showed defects of one sort or another. To give you an idea of the scale of that disaster, most of the released material was deposited close beside what was left on the reactor building as dust and debris, but the lighter radioactive materials, contaminated with iodine-131 and caesium-137 were carried by the winds over the Ukraine, Belarus, Russia and to some extent over Scandinavia and Europe.' Professor Dunwoody removed a pipe from his pocket, and chewed on its stem. 'Now we come to the device which Sir Alex briefed me on this morning. It would appear from the information, having looked at the blueprints and calculations which were recovered, I think that we are dealing with a device in the 20 kiloton range. '

The Professor chewed on his pipe stem again.

'That's about the same size as the first atom bomb the Americans dropped on the Japanese in 1945. The good news is that at Aldermaston, we seismically monitor any atomic test blasts which occur from time to time around the world. I am delighted to report that we have no evidence whatsoever that such a test has ever been carried out in Iraq. '

239

'So there's a chance it's a dud Professor?' Sir Alex asked hopefully.

'There is always a chance, it's happened before, but I wouldn't rely on that I'm afraid. I would have to advise you that the likelihood is that when they light the blue touch paper, it will go off. '

Sir Alex raised his eyebrows

'Yes, I see Professor. I think it would be prudent to work on that premise. Perhaps you would brief my colleagues on the destructive force of a 20 kiloton bomb, so that we can get the potential threat into some sort of perspective?'

Professor Dunwoody nodded, and absently scratched his chin.

'As you know, atom bombs have only been used twice in anger. The first and foremost blast site of an atomic bomb was the Japanese city of Hiroshima. A 20 Kiloton uranium 235 bomb nicknamed "Little Boy" was dropped from an American B-29 Superfortress on August 6th, 1945. The Aioi bridge, one of the many bridges connecting the delta of the Ota River, was the aiming point of the bomb. The detonation was airburst, and set for just under 2,000 feet. At 08.15 hours, the bomb was dropped from the Enola Gay. It missed its intended target

240

by only 800 feet. At 08.16 hours, in an instant, 66,000 people were killed and 69,000 people were severely injured by the blast wave, and the incredible heat generated by the 20kiloton atomic explosion. The destructive power of a 20 kiloton bomb is equivalent to 20,000 tons of TNT. Not much by today's standards, where we measure yield by the Megaton, but the damage it will do to a city and its population is colossal, nevertheless.'

He paused, as several people within the room reached for their carafes of water, because suddenly, their mouths had become very dry.

The Professor noted this; it was always the same when he gave this sort of briefing. He returned his pipe to a pocket in his jacket, and continued with his chilling monologue.

'The point of total vaporization from the blast measured approximately half a mile in diameter. Total structural destruction ranged out to about one mile in diameter. Severe blast damage carried as far as two miles in diameter around ground zero. At two and a half miles, everything flammable in the area was completely incinerated. The remaining outlying area was peppered with serious fires that stretched out to the final edge, at a little over three miles in diameter.'

241

There was absolute silence in the briefing room. Nobody moved.

'Finally Ladies and Gentlemen, I think we should look at the projected causality percentages from ground zero. On detonation of a device of this size, the blast wave will create a wind velocity of around 320 miles per hour, and within a half mile radius of ground zero, 98% of people will die. Beyond half a mile the wind speeds begin to diminish slightly, down to about 290 mph, but we must assume that 90% of people in that area will also die. Outside a mile of ground zero, large scale buildings will still collapse and the heat will ignite anything which will burn. I'm afraid that a 65% fatality rate will apply in this area. Large numbers of people will be seriously injured of course, probably at least 30% of those who survive the initial blast. Beyond that….'

Professor Dunwoody spread his hands.

'People are still thrown around by 140mph winds with at least 50% fatalities. Most survivors will suffer 2nd and 3rd degree burns. Deaths and destruction diminish proportionately over the next two to three miles, but please remember that any survivors will have also been blasted with massive doses of Gamma, X-ray, Alpha and

Beta radiation, and sadly many will die of radiation poisoning within 21 days of exposure. '

The briefing room remained silent. The Professor's audience were frozen with horror.

'Putting all this into today's context, using the densely packed population of London for example, the final death toll would almost certainly run into millions.' He stopped talking, and surveyed his stunned and silent audience.

'Um…does anyone have any questions?'

No one spoke. The Heads of Department sat silently contemplating the full depths of Dunwoody's terrifying briefing. C brought the meeting to a close.

'Thank you Professor. If we are going to find this bomb, we need to know who has it,' he said. 'With a name, we'll get a face, and then we can begin to track down the culprit. Your thoughts on my desk by 3pm today please, Ladies and Gentlemen.'

Chapter Twenty One

- The Return-

Iraq

Al-Mahdi casually walked into the passport control area at Baghdad International airport, surrounded by teams of noisy Europeans and Americans. Many were travelling back to their security company's base locations after a well-earned break, where they would continue to provide heavily armed close protection for wealthy clients, and the myriad of foreign companies, who were actively involved in rebuilding Iraq's smashed infrastructure. Loudspeakers announced departures and new flight arrivals like any other busy international airport, but security announcements warning all passengers to be vigilant were given even more emphasis at Baghdad International Airport.

Iraqi and U.S. Military Policemen patrolled everywhere; their eyes alert, weapons cocked, ready to instantly respond to any would-be suicide bomber or other threat which might interrupt the operation of the newly rebuilt airport.

Al-Mahdi presented his passport to an Iraqi official at the immigration control counter, who indifferently glanced at the photograph, and then flicked through the various visas stamped inside it.

'You are returning for the first time since the liberation Mr Alhassen?' He enquired.

His eyes downcast, the man before him replied.

'Yes,' said Al-Mahdi sadly. 'My family were butchered by the Ba'ath party dogs. I have been in France for two years, but now it is time for me to come home. '

The immigration officer nodded, and handed back the passport. He was becoming used to the steady trickle of his fellow countrymen and women repeating heart breaking tales of murder and pain, as they returned to their homeland to try and rebuild shattered lives.

'Peace be with you, and upon you brother,' he said, as the miserable man in front of him smiled weakly, took back his passport, and began walking slowly towards the baggage reclaim hall.

Captain Douglas McPherson braced himself as another huge wave crashed over the bow of his ship, sending boiling spray as high as its massive superstructure, where he currently stood on the bridge. The wind was blowing a severe North-Westerly, as his massive 130,000 ton container ship the MSC Roma Star bucked and rolled through the towering waves. The cargo ship's course touched the edge of the massive typhoon which was ripping its way slowly across the Indian Ocean. At times, the bow disappeared completely in froth and spray, but at over 400 metres long, that was to be expected in such high winds and foul weather. What concerned Captain Douglas was the fate of the hundreds of 40foot steel shipping containers, piled high on the forward deck of the Roma Star. They were chained and bolted fast, but if they shifted, or some were lost overboard, the ship would become dangerously imbalanced and faced capsize, despite its massive displacement. He ordered an increase to the huge container ships speed to its maximum of twenty-five knots, and continued the Roma Star's passage through the boiling seas towards their next scheduled port of call, the Iraqi docks at Umm Qasr.

Al-Mahdi drove away from Baghdad International airport in a hired Toyota pickup truck. He followed the signs toward Baghdad, keeping his speed to a moderate level to avoid attracting attention, and being stopped by the police. He drove with little fear of terrorist action.

Attacks on military convoys were a regular occurrence in the lawless stretch between the airport and city, but Al-Mahdi was confident that he would be quite safe in a lone unmarked civilian vehicle, bearing Iraqi number plates.

His plan required a day in Baghdad, procuring everything on a list which currently lay folded against a thick bundle of $100 U.S. dollar bills within a body belt, concealed under his sleeveless shirt. He knew that if he looked in the right markets, and down the correct side streets, everything he required would be found, without too much difficulty. He passed several signs warning of a military road block ahead, and began to slow. Al-Mahdi could see brake lights coming on from vehicles ahead, and a snaking line of cars and trucks, which slowly entered the vehicle check point. His passage was reduced to a crawl, but eventually, he was waved forward by two heavily armed American soldiers, and directed into a side bay, where his vehicle was quickly and thoroughly searched. He produced his passport, and identified himself as a dealer in antiquities, on a business trip to Iraq's capital. An American soldier handed his passport to a bored looking Iraqi Policeman, who checked the photograph, and handed it back to Al-Mahdi, waving him on his way. After passing through two more road blocks, each one more heavily defended by razor wire and sandbagged machinegun emplacements than the last, he was driving through the outer suburbs of Baghdad, towards his first destination.

When the first fax had arrived at his stonemason's yard three months earlier, Jawed al-Maluku knew the Prophet was smiling on him. Work had been sparse since the invasion, and the new customer had agreed his price without question, provided the tight time scale he demanded was met. Married to a senior Ba'ath party Interior Ministry official's daughter, al-Maluku had received numerous lucrative orders for smiling statues of the President over the previous twenty years, which were displayed everywhere in public places, markets and town centres, during Saddam Hussein's reign. When the Government had changed, they cancelled further orders, and refused to pay for the latest batch of life-size figures of the deposed President. When he had faxed back an acceptance, further faxes arrived from France, showing dimensions and pictures of the original which was to be exactly copied, and a generous down payment had been telexed to his bank account in Baghdad, to ensure work began immediately. The order was slightly unusual, but al-Maluku assumed the customer needed to save on weight,

248

and technically, the order posed no problems to his highly experienced artisans.

Al-Mahdi arrived at the stone mason's yard in the early afternoon, having finished purchasing all the equipment he needed to complete phase three of his plan. The yard was littered with partly finished stone statues, wooden packing cases, and piles of chipped stone. Al-Mahdi parked outside the yard's office, and was met by a beaming Jawed al-Maluku.

'Mr Alhassen. Welcome, welcome. Please come into my office.'

Al-Mahdi eyed him coldly.

'I wish to see the statue now, my time is short. I must hurry to see another client later today.'

This was a lie, but he had a long way to drive, and little time or interest in pleasantries.

'Yes of course,' said the stone yards owner, gesturing him towards one of the large wooden sheds nearby. 'This way, please.'

After unlocking the door, the proprietor stood aside, as Al-Mahdi entered. It was pleasantly cool inside, as they walked to the back of the shed, where two large packing cases stood alone in a corner.

'Here Sir, is your order. I am sure you will be pleased,' said al-Maluku, as he opened the first wooden case. Al-Mahdi stared at the statue. It was exactly as he had ordered. Lying cocooned in a thick bed of straw, was an excellent 10 foot replica of the ancient Babylonian God Nergal. Al-Mahdi had chosen that particular deity carefully. In ancient Babylonian mythology, the Lord Nergal ruled Hades. He was worshiped as the evil God of war, disease and pestilence; symbolizing the misery and destruction which accompany the strife of nations. As a consequence of this aspect of Nergal's character, he was also considered to be the God of fire; the destroying element and therefore of all misfortunes caused by an excess of his heat. Al-Mahdi knew that ignorant Europeans wouldn't appreciate the irony, but it had amused him to choose Nergal, nonetheless.

'Yes, it looks good Mr al-Maluku. You have aged it well; it looks properly weathered and very old. The statue appeared suitably chipped and worn, and was covered with the artificial grime of millennia.

'You used the sandstone as I requested? He asked.

'Yes indeed Mr Alhassen, it is exactly as you ordered.'

Turning his attention to the other packing case, Al-Mahdi, said.

'Good, now I wish to see the figure's base. '

The statues large base block was also formed from plain stone, and oblong in shape. The colour and texture of the base was identical to the figure of Nergal, and both seemed to have been formed from the same block of sandstone. When Al-Mahdi looked more closely, he detected the hairline crack of the lid.

'Open it!' He ordered. al-Maluku raised his hands theatrically, and smiling, carefully heaved up one side of the lid, revealing the empty space beneath it.

'It took almost two weeks to drill out the block, and dress the internal edges, but the dimensions you supplied have been followed to the millimetre Mr Alhassen. '

Al-Mahdi nodded. 'Excellent Mr al-Maluku, you have done well. Perhaps we can now go to your office, where I can give you the balance of your fee, and the papers you will need to supply to the freight forwarders, when they collect my order later today? I will take the base in its packing case now, and require some pieces of the same stone to show my customer the colour and texture of the statue, before it arrives at its final destination. '

251

With the statue's hollow base safely secured inside its wooded packing case, and firmly strapped to the back of his pickup, Al-Mahdi arrived at the bomb's hiding place shortly before dark. He had timed the two hundred and fifty kilometre drive from Baghdad perfectly, to avoid the need to use his headlights on the last leg of his journey. They would have shone like the beam of some lonely lighthouse, built to protect a distant rocky shoreline. He drove slowly, to avoid raising too much dust. The lawless foothills of the newly established Kurdish homelands were certainly not a place to advertise an unescorted vehicle, especially when it was driven by an ex-Mukhabarat Colonel.

Al-Mahdi drove slowly into the gloomy cave mouth. Once the Toyota was safely inside the cave, and fully hidden from the outside world, he switched on the headlights. It had taken him hours to conceal the bomb to his complete satisfaction more than two years previously. He was rewarded with the sight of what looked convincingly like a partial roof collapse further inside the cave. There was no obvious sign of fresh disturbance within the cave; no footprints or vehicle tracks anywhere. After the bomb had been completely buried, he had slowly and carefully swept away all trace of his visit, before making his way to the safety of Iran. Abandoning the lorry close to the mountainous border crossing, dressed in ragged civilian clothes, he had melted into the thousands of legitimate refugees seeking sanctuary from the allied bombing.

Climbing out of the vehicles cab carrying a small canvas bag, he walked towards the rock fall. The headlight beams cast deep black shadows against the cave wall, as he reviewed the jumbled pile of rock. Kneeling down, Al-Mahdi opened the bag, and withdrew the small Geiger counter he had purchased earlier in Baghdad. Thanks to the wholesale looting of the Ministries immediately after the 'liberation', almost anything could be found for sale, if the buyer knew where to look, and had enough dollars to pay.

Sweeping the radiation detector around and over the rock pile, the readings appeared to show that the bombs internal protective shielding was still intact. He heard only the slow click, click of the audio radiation dose counter, echoing through the cave. The detection gauge's needle hardly moved, registering only faint background radiation, and falling well within the normal tolerances he remembered from his days at Bakhma. Satisfied, he switched off the Geiger counter and replaced it in its bag.

Despite the coolness inside the cave, he was soon sweating freely, as he began lifting the heavy rocks and throwing them clear.

It was late in the evening and Commander Roebottom was a worried man. On his desk lay a pile of manila case files. They were reports on relatively routine undertakings and all were connected to cases which merely required his signature to progress with the final stages of investigation. What concerned Commander Roebottom most, were the seven red folders piled neatly in front of him. After his meeting with Sir Alex, Harry Roebottom had arranged a comprehensive trawl through the secret and detailed records of several thousand 'possibles' who had come to the attention of Special Branch and the UK's internal security service MI5, in the past two years, and who might fit the criteria of this specific and highly dangerous situation. Finding a suspect was easy enough, but searching for 'sleepers' was an almost impossible task. A sleeper would certainly not be associated with any active radical group; and God knows, he thought, there were plenty of them to choose from. He was looking for an individual, probably a young man born in the UK, carefully nurtured and turned into a fanatic, who now devoutly believed in the justice of his cause. Such a man would be happy to become a martyr and die for his Faith. His ascension to Paradise would have been assured by those who had originally radicalised him. He would almost certainly be a loner, keeping himself to himself, who would have deliberately avoided gaining any notoriety with the authorities.

He'd live a quiet normal life, until the moment he was activated with perhaps, a series of coded passages from the Qur'an, or even a specific name or word, or practically anything which would identify his handler to him. Harry Roebottom tapped his pen on the top red folder, as he considered the complexity of the modern Islamic terrorist threat. Over the past few years, he had seen numerous reports crossing his desk of young British Asian men travelling to their devout parent's homeland in Muslim Pakistan, ostensibly, and quite innocently, to receive intensive tuition at a Madrassa spiritual training school. During their stay however, a few had been identified as suitably vulnerable targets who could be recruited into the Jihad; the holy war against all unbelievers. The Jihadist talent scouts persuaded them to defer their studies, and travel to the border of Afghanistan to a remote fundamentalist guerrilla training camp. Their minders then subjected their unsuspecting recruit to a course of subtle but intensive brainwashing. After unrelenting weeks of immersion, the new recruit was left hungry for revenge and martyrdom against any who their new masters deemed to be the enemies of Islam.

Standing in the washroom on the sixth floor, Cornelius Wilde felt triumphant, but his elation was racked with painful ambivalence. His head remained cleaved by last night's bottle. He was nauseous, but desperate to clear his mind sufficiently to deliver the vital presentation he was about to give. He was furious with himself for being so fundamentally stupid. It was a mistake he would expect from the latest intake at the SIS staff college. How could he have missed something so painfully, blindingly obvious? A nagging doubt danced at the edge of his splitting headache. Perhaps, he though ruefully, Pat Farrell was right after all? Maybe the booze was beginning to affect his mind and his analytical abilities. Cornelius wasn't fully convinced, but a suggestion like that coming from a friend was enough to make any man feel sick.

'Christ!' He though savagely, so was this bloody hangover.

Unpredictable moods swings and heavy drinking were more than his wife could cope with any longer. She had taken the children and walked out just months before, after one last awful row. He remembered some of it. He had said things he regretted, to excuse himself. A letter had arrived from her solicitors a few days later, demanding a divorce. Legal wrangling and the eventual settlement would leave him with penniless and alone.

Cornelius knew he would lose more than just possessions if he didn't get a grip of his life. His family would break up, the job he loved would go, and most importantly, what little self-respect he still clung to would become just another bitter memory.

He splashed his face again in the basin filled with cold water. Cornelius took a long hard look at his dripping face in the mirror. When he could bear to look no longer, he dried his hands on a paper towel, and rubbed the damp tissue across his face.

As usual, important people were relying on him for a breakthrough. Well, he thought smugly, he'd give the bastards that, if that little shit Ingram didn't upset things again. He knew this was probably his last chance before the axe fell, and he was summarily sacked, and escorted under guard from the building. His role was key; but he felt crushed with the weight of the universe pressing down on his shoulders. But then, he though sadly, that was how he had felt since the beginning of his trip down the slippery booze sodden slope. He glanced at his watch. Five minutes left to make himself sober and presentable, before he stood before his peers.

'Hopeless,' he muttered to himself as he donned his jacket and ran fingers through damp hair. He looked back at his reflection in the mirror, and raised an eyebrow.

'Well, maybe not hopeless,' he thought. He might just be able to pull it off yet again and fool the others, but he knew he couldn't deceive himself any longer. A mocking voice whispered to him from somewhere deep inside his splitting head.

'Loser... loser'

Cornelius scowled at himself as he straightened his tie, swallowed another handful of aspirins and left the SIS washroom.

When he entered the briefing room, Cornelius was relieved to see Piers Ingram was absent. There were more important matters to attend to, and he'd analyse that development later. Removing several folders from his briefcase, on a nod from Sir Alex, he cleared his dry throat and began his briefing.

'Ladies and Gentlemen, I have spent days hunting around and trawling through what few personnel records we have available of Saddam's military, and high ranking Ba'ath party members, who as of this date, still eluded capture.' Cornelius Wilde smiled despite a sudden wave of nausea. 'I concentrated on what staff files the Americans found in Baghdad, and think I have come up with one particular man who had the opportunity, background and authority to pull off the theft of the bomb.'

A murmur arose from the SIS Heads. Absently, Cornelius raised a hand to quell the noise and nodded to an assistant, who turned on a projector, flooding the screen with the cruel features of Colonel Jalal Al-Mahdi.

'This man fits the bill pretty much exactly. I've been looking at him for a while. He is Colonel Jalal El Mahdi; nephew of General Ali Al-Majid, better known as Chemical Ali. He seems to be a particularly nasty piece of work.' Cornelius picked up one of the files, and prepared to run through a short biopsy on Al-Mahdi.

'I managed to trace his history with the assistance of the new Iraqi Interior and Defence Ministries. The

Foreign Office lent heavily on them, and they have managed to come up with the following information.'

Cornelius was struggling to concentrate. He ignored a sudden wave of light-headedness, cleared his throat again softly, and began to read.

'Jalal Al-Mahdi was born on 29th August 1964 in the Ba'ath party's private medical clinic in Baghdad. He is the second son of one of Chemical Ali's sisters.'

Cornelius sipped some water, and continued.

'It appears that after finishing High school, he went on to Baghdad University. Considered a very bright student, he was sent on to study ancient Middle Eastern antiquities at the Sorbonne in Paris. He was there for about a year, but rather strangely, he left suddenly, and returned to Iraq. That part of his life remains a bit of a mystery, as we don't have any information on exactly why he left France in such a hurry. We are still waiting to hear from our counterparts in the French secret service on the matter. They seem to be dragging their Gallic heals somewhat, and have been quite reticent and even evasive on the matter.'

Cornelius raised an eyebrow and smiled, 'but we all know what the French are like?'

There were several smiles around the room, and heads nodded silent agreement as he continued.

'Anyway, after his return to Iraq, he was enrolled into the military, and spent the next two years at the Iraq Officers Academy. After graduation, he went into the Iraqi army having passed out as top of his class. Al-Mahdi enjoyed several rapid promotions over the next six years, and from what I can gather, he somehow became deeply involved with Operation Anfal….Something to do with his uncle, perhaps?'

Steadying himself against the table, Cornelius looked up from his notes. 'He was concerned with the trials using poison gas on unsuspecting Kurdish villages. He oversaw development of Saddam's plan, where the Kurds, as a race were to be gassed out of existence.'

Cornelius shook his head slowly and continued. 'He disappeared off the radar completely at this point. At the end of the trial phase of Anfal, his name was suddenly stricken from the army list of officers. It was strange, as I couldn't find any trace of him whatsoever until one of our people remembered seeing his name on some of the Gilgamesh documents recovered from Baghdad.' Cornelius paused from his report, and nodded in the direction of Julie Wallace, who had been allowed to sit in

261

on his briefing. In such senior company, she blushed furiously, but repaid his compliment with her most dazzling smile.

'When we looked at the papers more closely, we found that his signature was plastered over dozens of confidential security reports and standing orders concerning operations at the Bakhma dam project. With this fresh evidence in hand, and given the high degree of nepotism which pervaded the Iraqi Government at the time, I felt I was definitely on the right track.'

Cornelius drained the water glass, and refilled it from the carafe in front of him. His hand trembled.

'I switched tack in my search at this point because new questions came to mind. 'The hung-over analyst shrugged. 'If he was indeed involved at Bakhma, what were his duties? He boasted no scientific credentials, so involvement in weapons development was out of the question. He was no longer serving with the Iraqi army, so what was left? Clearly, with the projects recovered security documents, and bearing in mind his powerful family connections, I was pointed straight at where to look next.'

Cornelius paused and looked up from his notes again, as if searching for hands to rise with the answer. No one moved in his audience. He continued.

'The Iraqi Secret Police, the Mukhabarat were charged amongst other things, with the security of Iraq's secret weapons program throughout Saddam Hussein's reign of terror. Although most of the personal records of serving Mukhabarat officers had been hastily shredded or deleted from their intelligence database, before the American armoured column arrived on the outskirts of Baghdad, I managed to track our man down via of all things, the pay records.'

The aspirins were beginning to ease his suffering, and despite the receding headache, Cornelius was at last, beginning to enjoy himself.

'In their haste to cover their tracks, it appears they simply overlooked removal of salary records for the entire Mukhabarat. The Americans are delighted, and so, of course are the new Iraqi Government. There are plenty of people in the new Iraqi corridors of power with scores to settle with Saddam's secret police, but paradoxically, dozens of their most senior officers are being re-hired by the new regime.' Cornelius slowly shook his head again. 'Their experience and knowledge is unfortunately vital, given the current instability in Iraq.'

The SIS intelligence analysis looked up at his audience.

'So, Ladies and Gentlemen, in conclusion, as a result of this chance find, there is no doubt in my mind that Al-Mahdi was deeply embedded in the Bakhma Gilgamesh project. We can't find any traces of a more senior Mukhabarat officer involved, anywhere within Gilgamesh, and his sudden disappearance neatly coincides with the destruction of the Bakhma facility.'

Cornelius dropped the file on the table before him. It was time.

'I must conclude therefore, that Colonel Jalal Al-Mahdi was head of its overall security, and it was him Ladies and Gentlemen, I now firmly believe who stole the Iraq Atom bomb.'

There was a long pause before C stood up and thanked Cornelius for his analysis.

'Excellent work Cornelius and well done Miss Wallace, for your input.'

He had already made a mental note to review her civil service grading; her support for Cornelius had been invaluable so far, and in C's opinion, she deserved to move forward in her career within SIS. She smiled, and blushed again, as C continued.

'We are now making good progress in this case, but we must not become complaisant. So far, we have managed to identify where the bomb was built, and we now have a prime suspect in its theft. From Cornelius's anylais I doubt that there was a political motive involved, and must assume that the thief or thieves were motivated purely by money. What the bomb is worth is anyone's guess. I think that depends on the buyer's resources, and their willingness to pay the asking price. What we can be sure of Ladies and Gentlemen, is that the price will not be cheap. If it is indeed Al-Qaeda we are dealing with, then I believe that their close connection with the Taliban's narcotics trade will provide the main source of cash. If that is the case, the first question is of course can we stop the flow of money, and block the heroin coming out of Afghanistan?'

Before anyone could answer, C shook his head. 'The answer to both questions is I'm afraid a resounding No! There are simply too many political, economic and geographic barriers to cutting their cash flow at source.'

C sat down, and looked at the concerned faces surrounding him.

'I will take your points shortly, but my gut instinct is that we must find Colonel Al-Mahdi. He is the central key player. If he has already sold the bomb, and we find him, I'm quite sure we will be able to persuade him to tell us who bought it, and if he hasn't sold it, he can be made to tell us where it is.'

C stood up again, and walked across to the projected image of Al-Mahdi, who stared down coldly at them all. He pounded his fist against the screen.

'We simply must find this man!'

Chapter Twenty Two

-The Scorpion -

Iraq - The Forbidden Zone

In the cool depths of the cave, a hunting black scorpion was close to completing its slow, patient stalk. Now just inches away, the unsuspecting cockroach continued its journey across the dark cave floor. With a sudden blur of speed, the fat scorpion seized its prey with powerful pincers and stung it repeatedly. The trapped cockroach frantically struggled for a few moments, as powerful venom surged through its small body. Its efforts to escape were in vain, and moments later, the cockroach gave a last shudder, and was still. The scorpion waited a few seconds more, then began to feed.

Colonel Al-Mahdi removed his heavy gloves, and drank deeply from a bottle of cool mineral water. He had worked hard for several hours, and had finished clearing the rocks away from the bomb, which remained hidden and secure within its original packing case. Having made a visual scan for damage, he switched on the Geiger counter, and once again ran it over the wooden container. He was relieved to see that the readings remained unchanged.

To begin the task of loading the packing case containing the bomb into the waiting statues sandstone base, he wrapped a strong metal chain around the exterior of the bomb's wooden case, and attached it to the towing hook on the back of the Toyota. Having carefully taken up the slack, he engaged the vehicle's low ratio four-wheel drive, and slowly, very slowly dragged the heavy container away from the cave wall. Satisfied that there was now sufficient clearance, he stopped the Toyota, and reversed back a little to slacken the chains.

Checking the crate again with the radiation detector, he began to assemble a strong tubular steel hoist directly above the wooden crate. When he had finished its construction, the triangular engine hoist almost grazed the cave roof, but it needed the height, if it was going to be sufficient for its task. After another long swig from the his water bottle, he looped the towing chain twice around the bombs packing case, and attached the chain to the steel hook which hung limply from the hoists apex. Satisfied that all was ready, he began to wind the lifting mechanisms handle, and the crate began to slowly rise off the cave floor.

The original head of the MI6, Captain Sir Mansfield Cumming RN, always signed himself as 'C. He formed the Service in 1909, and began the long tradition of the head of the Service adopting the initial 'C' as his personal icon.

Sir Alex McLean liked to walk along the embankment, beside the sparkling waters of the Thames. He always found the quiet passage of the cool waters soothed his mind, and helped him to focus on any awkward problem which was presently confounding him. Beside him, walked Commander Harry Roebottom, the tough, straight talking Yorkshire policeman, who headed Britain's Special Branch.

'The real problem we face Harry, is that Al-Mahdi has a two year head start on us.'

In the distance, the two men could see the top of the Millennium wheel; its gondolas filled with excited passengers, enjoying their panoramic view of London.

'There is no doubt, to compound the problem that we are dealing with a clever, cunning and very dangerous man. I really think we would underestimate him at our peril.'

Commander Roebottom nodded.

269

'Aye, the bastard lifted the bomb from under the Iraqi Governments noses, and got clean away with it.'

It was Sir Alex's turn to nod.

'Yes indeed.'

C cast his gaze across the Thames, as noisy seagulls swooped and squabbled over its silvery waters.

'We think we have pieced together how he did it, from details the Americans sent us after they arrived at Bakhma. Apparently, they found an entire convoy of military vehicles parked in a tunnel several miles from the dam. The soldiers escorting it were all dead, and the American forensic team who carried out the autopsies found massive concentrations of hydrogen cyanide in all of them. Apparently, Saddam Hussein had ordered the bombs movement while the Americans were racing towards Baghdad, and we think that Al-Mahdi used that moment to spring his trap. To make matters worse, he covered his tracks by tripping Bakhma's self-destruct system before he left, flooding everything, and killing hundreds of people inside.'

The head of Special Branch exhaled loudly. 'Jesus Alex, he's a ruthless bastard and no mistake.'

C nodded again.

'I'm afraid so Harry. In my estimation next to bin Laden, he poses as an individual, the greatest threat we have faced since the Second World War. Somehow, he gassed the entire convoy, and simply drove the bomb clean away. It was simple, and ruthlessly effective.'

The two men continued to stroll beside the Thames deep in thought until Harry Roebottom spoke again.

'Do we know if he had any accomplices?'

C pursed his lips. 'He might have, but our physiological profile people seem to think he would be quite capable of working alone. Apparently, he had a reputation for meticulous planning, which is borne out not only by the theft, but also by the fact that he has successfully hidden somewhere for over two years, and so far, we haven't a clue where he's been hiding himself, or the bomb.'

They continued in silence, until Roebottom spoke again.

'Given that he worked out the theft so precisely, it follows that once he finds a buyer, he must have already planned how to move it to its target, assuming of course that the buyers want it delivered, and it's not already there.'

271

'Yes, that follows,' said C thoughtfully. 'If he hasn't already done so, he has to move a bulky half ton package from wherever it's hidden to somewhere, in fact, anywhere around the world.'

C watched an open topped pleasure steamer packed with tourists chugging slowly against the rivers powerful tidal flow.

'If the bomb is already in the UK, our chances of finding it are practically zero.' C said gravely. 'But if it is in transit, or due to be moved soon, at least we have a chance, however slim.'

The two men reached the south side of Lambeth bridge and stopped. C smiled, and said.

'Our one advantage, such as it is, is that we now know our man. We have a face, and that's a beginning.'

It was time for the SIS Director's final pitch.

'Sorry Harry, I'm convinced there is an Al-Qaeda connection to this whole business, but I am not suggesting your people get involved in a worldwide search. If and when it arrives on our shores, it would be very useful to know in advance who might be helping him, or taking delivery over here.'

'Ay, it will be some bloody Muslim fanatic of course, and almost certainly a sleeper. Someone already

272

brainwashed, and pre-embedded deep into our society. He will be just sitting somewhere, following a dull, law abiding routine, waiting patiently to be activated.'

Harry Roebottom shook hands with the SIS chief and said.

'Not an easy task Alex, and with everything else, believe me, we're stretched as it is.'

Harry Roebottom stared intently at the SIS chief.

'I promise you though; we'll take a really long hard look'

Al-Mahdi was ready to leave the cave as dawn broke. He was satisfied with his efforts so far, and the crated bomb and its trigger were now securely entombed within the statue's heavy stone base. He had encountered only one problem. The bomb had hung up when the hoist had lifted it to its maximum height. It still dangled nearly two inches below the lip of the open sandstone sarcophagus. Al-Mahdi had stopped for a while, and calmly smoked a cigarette while he pondered the problem. The bomb could not be lifted any higher, and he dare not risk scratching or chipping the side of the stone base by forcing the bomb over its lip. Sooner or later the statue and its base would undergo the scrutiny of customs

273

inspections, and there must be no fresh mark or scratches which might raise the slightest curiosity. He sat on a flat rock beside the vehicle, looking at the suspended wooden crate. After several moments, he smiled and stood up.

'Of course' he said aloud, his voice echoing within the confines of the cave. He walked across to the back of the Toyota. Crouching down, he partially deflated both rear tyres, until the vehicle had sunk down under its own weight by several inches. When he cautiously reversed the Toyota, directly under the suspended packing case, the statues base now cleared it by a little more than half an inch. It would still be close, but sufficient. It had then been a simple matter to slowly lower the heavy crate into the stone base using the hoist. The fit was perfect.

He began shovelling sand into the sarcophagus, filling any air gaps so that if the finished base was hit with a mallet, it wouldn't sound hollow. Once the heavy lid was replaced Al-Mahdi had taken a hammer from the vehicles cab, and finely crushed the small pieces of surplus sandstone he had brought with him from the stone masons yard. Mixing the now powdered stone with cement, dirt and water, he created a thick slurry, which he carefully poured around the tiny gap between the top of the statue base and its heavy lid. Carefully wiping away any excess, he sat down, lit another cigarette and waited. Within an hour, the cement had dried, hiding the narrow seam completely. All that remained was the simple job of re-nailing the wooden crate lid surrounding the statue's base back into place, and firmly re-strapping it the Toyota's cargo floor.

Satisfied with his efforts, he didn't bother disassembling the hoist, or re-inflating the tyres, as his journey to the railhead at Kirkuk would take no more than an hour. From his old army days, he knew anyway that partially deflated tyres increased the vehicles grip on the rough sandy tracks he would be using. He washed and shaved, and discarded his dusty, sweat soaked shirt and trousers. Changing into fresh clothes, he climbed aboard the Toyota, and began his journey to Kirkuk.

The Roma Star had at last sailed clear of the typhoon, and Captain Douglas was feeling confident that he would reach the Iraqi port of Umm Qasr within the next 36 hours, if nothing else interrupted their present cruising speed. Time was money in the worldwide shipping trade, and the Greek owners of the Roma Star took a dim view of delays to their tight schedules. His ship had weathered the recent storm without mishap, but the chief

Engineer had reported some unusual vibrations in the port engines main bearing. His Swedish engineer had assured the Captain that it probably wasn't anything serious, but recommended further investigation when they reached Iraq. When Captain Douglas had enquired how long the bearings examination would take, he was pleased to hear that no more than eight hours would be lost.

'Very well, Mr Johansson, please begin your inspection as soon as the engines are switched off, and we have begun unloading at Umm Qasr.'

The railhead at Kirkuk was already alive and bustling with activity when Al-Mahdi arrived. Loading of the day's first freight train was nearing completion, and the early morning's fresh fruit and vegetables bound for Baghdad were being lifted down from numerous battered civilian trucks and carts, and stacked inside the freight wagons by sweating railway labourers. Wicker cages packed with noisy chickens and honking geese sat crammed on the crowded platform, waiting their turn to be loaded. Al-Mahdi parked the Toyota, and removed the rotor arm from inside the engines distributer cap. Despite the armed patrols of police and American soldiers who guarded the station complex, he had no intention of losing the vehicle and its cargo to some random street gang at this stage of his plan. He walked briskly through the throng of people, to the busy station office, and enquired who was in charge of freight forwarding. When he had paid for his own ticket, and the railway's shipping charge, two extra crisp new twenty dollar bills assured that his cargo was promptly loaded by an ancient forklift truck onto a freight car marked boldly with legend

'Umm Qasr Port.'

Abandoning the Toyota, Al-Mahdi climbed aboard one of the two passenger carriages attached to the train. He walked through the crowded multitude of noisy farmers who were engaged in loudly discussing prices and intent on escorting their valuable produce to Baghdad's popular markets. Entering the small and deserted 1st class compartment, he closed the door and gratefully sat down. The journey to Baghdad was something over 200 kilometres, but the fast freight train would make only two stops before it reached the Iraqi capital. It was scheduled to load cargo at Tikrit; Saddam Hussein's birthplace, and then take on more cargo at the busy station at Sammara.

While living in France, Al-Mahdi had considered the problem of moving the bomb from its hiding place in the mountains of Kurdistan to the coastal town of Umm

Qasr. He had decided to transport the bomb using the railway; it would avoid countless military and police roadblocks.

Since the invasion, the railway system inside Iraq had been heavily rebuilt, after the damage done to it by American bombers and cruise missiles. When the train reached Baghdad, his freight car would be re-shunted and attached to the slow train which would broadly follow the route of the polluted Euphrates River, eventually reaching its destination of the southern Iraqi port of Umm Qasr, on the northernmost shores of the Persian Gulf.

Outside, the train's guard blew his whistle as the last farmers frantically finished their loading and scrabbled aboard. At the front of the train, the engineer gave two loud warning blasts on his engine's horn. Moments later, the heavy cargo train began to move.

Through hooded eyes, Al-Mahdi watched as the untidy sprawl of Kirkuk's dusty streets quickly disappeared, as the train gathered speed and cleared its boundaries. Al-Mahdi closed his eyes. He had laboured throughout the night; he desperately needed to rest. Satisfied that all was in order, he fell into a deep and dreamless sleep.

Chapter Twenty Three

-Umm Qasr -

Southern Iraq

'Tickets please!'

Al-Mahdi woke with a start. He tensed as he realised someone was leaning over him.

'Your ticket Sir, may I see it?' There were two men standing in the isle beside his seat, the Guard, and a uniformed Iraqi Policeman. Recovering quickly from his sudden awakening, Al-Mahdi said.

'Ah yes, of course, my ticket. I have it here somewhere.'

He fumbled in his pockets, found it, and passed it over to the Conductor. It was inspected, clipped and returned to him. The Conductor stepped aside, and the policeman, whose hand rested on his pistol holster, demanded the sleepy passenger's papers. Al-Mahdi appeared nervous as he handed his passport to the officer, whose face remained impassive behind his sunglasses, as his eyes flicked from the passport's photograph to Al-Mahdi.

'What is the purpose of your journey Mr Alhassen?' Enquired the policeman.

'I'm a dealer in antiquities Sir, and I am escorting a shipment to Umm Qasr.'

Deference was always advisable to the Iraqi Police force. Al-Mahdi had no desire to upset this stupid fat fool or make him suspicious. He might spend the rest of the journey to Baghdad in handcuffs. He'd certainly be taken off the train and questioned, and would miss his connection to the docks. The overweight police officer stared at Al-Mahdi for several long moments, suddenly nodded and returned the passport. He said nothing, turned and followed the Conductor out of the compartment. Al-Mahdi breathed deeply. He was pleased; his stolen identity had once again stood up to the close scrutiny of the authorities.

Commander Roebottom replaced the final page, as he finished reading the contents of the last red folder. Numerous lines of investigation and thorough searches of Special Branch's threat analysis database had drawn a blank. During a high level meeting with his most senior officers, it had been suggested that a check of all visitors to

Pakistan, by young Moslem men over the last few years might perhaps flag something worth pursuing.

It was a daunting task, and had taken days to cross reference all the files, but the resulting red folders had been forwarded to his office for further consideration. It could still be any of them, or none of them, but only two of the subjects before him caused any ripples of his old fashioned copper's instincts.

Within the last two years, both young men in the two folders had grossly overstayed their visas in Pakistan, and had reported the loss or theft of their passports to the British High Commission in Islamabad. Most who had asked for assistance in returning to the UK had missed the visa deadline by at most only a few weeks, and had plausible excuses such as illness or simply having forgotten the official date of their return to the UK, but one stood out, who had been missing for nearly six months. His folder contained the man's statement that he had left his Madrassa after several months of religious training, because one night, he had a vivid dream. In it, he had been ordered by the Prophet to join an ageing Mullah who had befriended him during his studies, and accompany him as he toured the remote mountainous villages on the Afghan border, preaching the word of Islam to the faithful.

281

His statement went on to say that he had obeyed the message within the dream. He simply couldn't defy the word of God. His passport had been lost somewhere during his arduous journey through the mountains. After several months, the elderly cleric had contracted Cholera and died, forcing his return.

The other report also seemed unusual, as the young man had missed the deadline by nearly four months, claiming he had met a beautiful Pashtuni girl who he had fallen deeply in love with, and had worked hard on the farm near Kandahar where she lived, while trying in vain to win her father's respect and acceptance of him as a suitable suitor for his daughter's hand in marriage. Eventually the father's patience was exhausted; the man had been beaten by the girl's brothers, robbed of his possessions and threatened with disembowelment if he did not leave.

Commanded Roebottom took out his unlit pipe, and chewed its stem.

Both stories seemed plausible, and put them in the right general location, but both were almost impossible to check further. On the other hand either story could be a complete load of bollocks, he thought ruefully.

Neither had any form in the UK, and both were at best long shots, but they were all he had to offer. Making up his mind, he crossed to his desk and depressed the intercom key.

'Call the Director General's secretary over at Box, and tell her I need to see her boss first thing tomorrow morning.'

The following morning, Big Ben chimed nine, as Commander Roebottom settled himself comfortably into a leather bound armchair, facing the head of MI5.

'Well Harry, what brings you over from Scotland Yard so suddenly, at this time in the morning? It's my people who do the cloak and dagger stuff?'

Harry Roebottom grunted,

'It's the Gilgamesh business James. I had a meeting with Sir Alex over at Vauxhall Cross a couple of days ago, concerning sleepers who might help this Al-Mahdi character, if he brings his bloody bomb to the UK. You know how difficult a task finding sleepers is?'

Mi5's Head shuddered. The ghosts of the Portal Spy ring danced through his memory.

Peter and Helen Kroger, two Soviet agents had penetrated security at the Royal Naval base at Portland in the late 1950s and fed their masters in Moscow high level military secrets and intelligence until their eventual arrest in 1961. Living quietly at their suburban home in Cranley Drive, Ruislip, they had appeared to their neighbours as honest, law abiding citizens. Inserted seven years previously by the KGB, protected by their deep cover, they had been free to carry on their espionage with impunity for years, before their eventual capture.

'Do you have someone in mind Harry?'

'Yes James, I think I've got two targets that might be worth the attention of your people. Sir Alex seems to think that if the bomb is coming. He thinks it might arrive soon, and if it does, we need to see if either of these two men breaks cover.'

He handed the red folders to MI5's chief, who glancing down at them, pressed his desktop intercom.

'Can you ask William Lawrence to come up please?'

The heavy diesel locomotive pulled slowly into the sidings beside Umm Qasr docks. With a loud hiss and a shrill squeal of its pneumatic brakes, the long freight train shuddered to a full and final stop. Al-Mahdi's eyes narrowed, as he stepped down from the passenger carriage into the brilliant sunshine. He called to a passing worker.

'Where is the international export office?' The worker pointed back along the platform.

'It is the red brick building over there Sir. 'He said. Al-Mahdi acknowledged the man's help with a slight nod. Walking briskly down to the end of the platform, he crossed the road running parallel with it, and entered the newly built office block. Finding his freight company's name on the board in the building's foyer, Al-Mahdi walked up two flights of stairs, and eventually found the small office of the firm which he had already engaged to collect the statue from the stone masons yard.

Inside, several clerks sat at computer consoles, busily typing manifest details into various shipping documents. He spoke to the young woman sitting at the front desk.

'My name is Abu Alhassen. You are arranging the shipment of a statue for me.'

The young woman frowned, and stood up.

'One moment please, Mr Alhassen.'

Walking over to one of her colleagues desks, she enquired if the paperwork for his shipment was ready. The clerk nodded, and began sifting through a pile of documents, eventually handing a small bundle to her.

She returned to the front desk, and quickly scanned the top page. She smiled as she handed the papers to Al-Mahdi.

'Here they are Mr Alhassen, all ready for your signatures. I believe we are still waiting for part of the consignment?'

Al-Mahdi regarded her coldly.

'That is correct; the last crate arrived here fifteen minutes ago, aboard the train from Kirkuk.'

'That's fine Sir, I will arrange to have it collected from the train, and placed with the other part of your consignment, which has already been loaded into one of our shipping containers. One moment please.'

She sat down at her desk, and began typing at her computer's keyboard. After a moment, she said.

'Yes, here it is Mr Alhassen; the container is scheduled to be loaded aboard the M.S. Roma Star this afternoon.'

'Yes, we can certainly arrange two teams of watchers, but the problem is, I don't currently have any to spare. It will mean withdrawing them from on-going surveillance operations I'm afraid.'

William Lawrence looked at the open folders in front of him. His department within MI5 was charged with the responsibility of providing 24-hour scrutiny of suspects in MI5's unending war against suspected terrorist groups in the UK.

After the mass murder of 9/11, and the recent suicide bombings of the London Underground, his specialist surveillance teams; known as 'watchers', were already stretched to breaking point. Although relatively low paid, and considered by many high flying 'spooks' within MI5 as little more than grunts, the watchers were nevertheless a vital link in the intelligence gathering chain. They were responsible amongst other things, for physically tailing suspects on foot or by vehicle. Following active suspects without being detected was a highly skilled craft, but MI5's watchers were highly professional and skilled at their job. Inadvertently alerting the target might force them to go to ground, and cause an on-going operation to be fatally compromised. If a target was at home and stationary, then covert observation from an adjacent building or even an unmarked van parked outside in the street might be used. While concentrating on a target, the watchers also provided photographic evidence of his or her meetings, and intercepted all telephone conversations made to other potential players in a terrorist plot. William Lawrence flicked through the folders again

'One targets based in Manchester and the other one in Leeds. 'He thought for a moment. 'It will take at least 24 hours to disengage, brief and redeploy my teams.' He rubbed his chin. 'From memory, I think there is only one category B surveillance operation in progress at the moment.' His face showed genuine concern. 'I'm sure the rest are all top priority A grade jobs. I'd better go and liaise with our Ops people, and see which teams are closest, and who we can spare.'

The head of MI5 nodded as Lawrence stood up.

'Make this a priority William, this operation just might give us the break we need, so use my name if anyone has a problem with their operation being curtailed.'

As William Lawrence opened the Director's door to leave, he stopped abruptly, as something occurred to him. He remembered a confidential Ministry of Defence memo which had arrived on his desk 24 hours earlier. Turning back to face his boss, he said.

'If it is really awkward to disengage our own, can I have your authority to use some of these new Shadow Squadron people?'

The Director tapped a pen on his desk. He had seen the memo too. The men in the new Shadow Squadron were reservists, only recently trained by his MI5 officers, and untried at the highest level of operational surveillance.

'Hmm, I don't know David? They're new on the block, and if they perform badly, we might lose the one lead which will crack this awful case wide open.'

William Lawrence shook his head slowly.

'I wouldn't have suggested it at all Sir, but with the way things are just now, whichever team I withdraw, there will be a huge hole left in the net.'

The head of MI5 knew the dangers only too well. With more than two hundred known Islamic groups currently under surveillance throughout the U. K., any one of them might be planning a home grown spectacular, which could ultimately cost the lives of hundreds, if not thousands of innocent civilians. It had been hard intelligence provided by David's people which had foiled a recent plot to detonate a bomb inside a tube train, as it passed under the river Thames. The resulting flood would have been catastrophic within the crowded underground network. Time was against them, a nuclear strike on London was unthinkable.

'All right David, it's certainly worth further consideration.' The Director chewed his pen for a moment, and then he said. 'Let me see the personnel files of the SAS people you are suggesting, and I'll give you my decision.'

Pat's file read like an adventure novel. Twice decorated for bravery while serving with the regular SAS, credited with singlehandedly destroying a Iraqi Surface to air battery during the first Gulf War, and countless other close fought, and in one case close run battles, the man was a living legend.

The Director picked up another folder. Spike Morris. Only 23, Morris was an ex-regular Paratrooper who carried a glowing report from his old Commanding Officer. He had gained some covert surveillance experience in Northern Ireland and had an active tour of Afghanistan under his belt while still serving with 2 Para. Several misdemeanours recorded by the local police for fighting in Aldershot, but nothing, the Director mused, which was out of character with highly trained, bored young men with nothing else to pass the time in a dull garrison town.

The Director chose another folder, and raised an eyebrow as he read. The Rt. Honourable Francis Randolph Lane. An ex-Eaton and Harrow schoolboy, Lane had close family ties to the Royal Family, and was currently working as an overpaid Merchant banker in the City. After passing their selection and serving with the reserve SAS for two years, he had successfully completed the tough sniper course at the Warminster School of Infantry, setting a new pass mark record, having beaten some of the best shots in the British army along the way, before being awarded his converted snipers badge.

Choosing another manila folder, the Director raised his eyebrow again. Danny Morris; also 23, currently living and working at his father's garage, in London's tough East end. His father was known to the police, and rumoured to have had close links to the vicious Kray brothers, when they ruled their Shoreditch gangland Manor in the '60's. Despite his ancestry, Morris was a highly skilled mechanic, who apparently, ran marathons as a hobby.

The Director had seen enough. He was aware that the failure rate during selection of these tough SAS men was in excess of 90%, and regulars or not, they had all passed the gruelling test marches alone, across the barren wilderness of the Brecon Beacons and Black mountains in south Wales. These were certainly not ordinary men, far from it. These reservists had earned the right to be trusted with the security of the nation. The Special Air Service Regiment's untarnished reputation for excellence and courage made his mind up for him. True respect was a rare commodity in today's society he thought, but these men had earned it.

Current budgeting restrictions and operational pressures constantly threw up manpower problems, and he had become resigned to making compromises. But this time, he decided it was an acceptable risk. The Director picked up a telephone from his desk, and dialled an internal number.

'Ah yes, hallo David. It's concerning these SAS men. If you must use them, it's with my blessing.'

The afternoon sun sparkled on the warm blue waters as local dhows peacefully fished off the shores of the northern Persian Gulf. Al-Mahdi stood silently watching his container, as it was hoisted by one of Umm Qasr's heavy cranes up and away from the quayside, high onto the Roma Star's cargo deck. It swung in the gentle offshore breeze, as the crane's operator stopped its slow decent. With great precision, he gently lowered the steel container the last few feet onto the ship, where it was firmly bolted to the container below by the ship's Formosan deckhands. Like a slumbering whale, the huge container ship floated still and silent as it was loaded.

With the aid of a local Pilot and a small fleet of tugs, Captain Douglas had safely docked his ship early that morning, where it was now securely moored in its deep-water berth. Only a small part of the Roma Star's current manifest of containerised cargo was bound for customers in Iraq, and had already been unloaded. The containers which now stood neatly stacked on the quayside were crammed with lumber and building materials imported from China, cheap furniture and electrical goods from India, bicycles from Korea and thousands of other foodstuffs and items from around the world which would soon appear in the shops and bazaars of scattered Iraqi towns, villages and cities.

Captain Douglas stood on the bridge, watching as his deck crew secured the last container aboard ship. His Chief Mate reported all deck cargo was secure, shortly after his engineering officer had finished making his report concerning the port engines main bearing. After a thorough examination, he had found no sign of damage, and concluded that the vibration was caused by nothing more than a loose inspection casing. Captain Douglas was delighted with the news, as he had been deeply concerned that engine trouble would delay leaving Umm Qasr.

The next leg of his scheduled route entailed hugging the coast around the Saudi Arabian peninsula, sailing through the Red Sea, and up to the Suez Canal. With over twenty five years of experience, he knew that it was a straightforward navigational exercise, sailing 3,600 miles at an average speed of twenty-five knots should take him 6 days, but he would, as always, take extra care through the narrow and crowded Straits of Hormuz, whose lawless waters separated Iran on one side, and the Oman on the other. With that potential delay in mind, he allowed a week's steaming to reach the canal, which would keep him exactly to his tight schedule.

His white coated Formosan steward knocked on the wall beside the open bridge door, and stepped inside. In heavily accented English he said.

'Your new passenger is aboard Sir, and I have showed him to his cabin.'

Captain Douglas nodded.

'Thank you Takk, make sure he is comfortable, and for heaven's sake, keep him off my bridge!'

Takk smiled. 'Yes Sir, of course, Sir.'

He bowed slightly and grinning, left the bridge. Takk knew what his Captain thought of passengers. Shipping companies augmented their income by providing cabins for occasional passengers, but Captain Douglas considered them nothing more than a bloody nuisance, who got in the crew's way, and irritated the life out of him with their damned silly questions.

As the ship got under way, safely established in his cabin, Al-Mahdi looked out of his small porthole, across the gentle swell of the Persian Gulf, at the slowly receding Iraqi port and the barren Iraqi coastline. He had planned to accompany the bomb aboard ship for the first part of its journey, as this would remove even the remotest chance of him being recognised if he returned to Baghdad, before he could make good his escape. There was a soft knock on his cabin door.

'Yes!' He barked, angry at the surprise and being torn away from his train of thought. Takk opened the door, and politely asked if everything was in order. Al-Mahdi eyed the steward with contempt.

'Yes, everything is as it should be. During the passage, I will take my meals in my room, and do not wish to be otherwise disturbed. Should I require anything I will ring for you, is that clear?'

Takk made his usual respectful bow, and said.

'Yes Mr Alhassen, I understand fully.'

As Takk turned and stepped out of the cabin, Al-Mahdi said something more.

'I also require a transistor radio, so that I can listen to music.'

Takk nodded and closed the door. Al-Mahdi wanted a small radio, but his interest in music was minimal. He wanted the radio to monitor the English and Arabic news channels, in case the American dogs went public with what they must now surely know of Gilgamesh.

Chapter Twenty Four

-The Face of God -

Leeds England

Muhammad Saleem Rana shivered as he stepped off the bus in Richmond Avenue, unaware that his journey from Leeds Grand Mosque was being closely monitored. The skies above the grey Yorkshire city were heavily overcast. A cold, steady rain fell onto those unlucky enough to be caught out in it. Since his return from Afghanistan, Muhammad Rana had struggled to reacclimatise himself to the harsh winter climate of northern England. He turned up his collar and with his head down, struggled through the wind and rain, which threatened to turn to sleet, if the temperature fell by just a few degrees more. In one of the large side pockets of his coat, sat a package which had been handed to him by a stranger in the Mosque. As he brushed passed, and handed Rana the package, the stranger whispered a quotation which Muhammad Rana instantly recognised, having committed it to memory months earlier while in the camp in Afghanistan.

'To God belongs the East and West, wheresoever you look is the face of God.'

Rana felt a rush of pure exultation when his coded activation taken from the Qur'an was spoken softly to him. This was the key passage he had waited so patiently for. At last, his mission was beginning, and his time of martyrdom would soon be at hand.

When he had stepped down from the bus, Rana didn't notice the nondescript saloon car which pulled in thirty yards behind him. A man had opened the passenger door, and quickly climbed out. He ran his fingers over his face, appearing to brush off the rain, but in fact he was speaking softly into the microphone, which he wore concealed on his wrist.

'Tango Bravo, the target is Out, Out and foxtrot (on foot), I have the trigger. Comms check over.' Spike whispered, as he began following Rana.

His message was answered quickly; he received the reply through the small and discrete earpiece he wore in his ear.

'Tango Alpha, roger that, strength five. Out.'

The saloon pulled out into the traffic stream, and passed him and the target, as Rana walked on, towards his family's home in one of the many nondescript backstreets of Leeds.

The old order of family loyalty and obedience had been scoured away from him, while he had lived in the camp in Afghanistan. The Mullahs there had constantly told him:

'You are now involved in Jihad - the Holy war against the Kafir (non-believers), and anything which must be done to destroy the infidel dogs who oppose Islam is clearly countenanced within the Qur'an.'

As part of his indoctrination, one heavily scarred cleric went on to say.

'Three paths are open to us in the Holy war against the enemies of Islam. We must subjugate them, convert them or kill them!'

Rana had listened intently as he was subjected to weeks of twisted spiritual teaching, which exposed him to a remorseless torrent of unrelenting hatred against the West, and he regarded with growing wonder the carefully selected verses from the Qur'an which were repeatedly read to him. He had memorised many, but two always came to mind when he sought comfort and reassurance of the righteousness of him mission.

"Those who believe fight in the cause of Allah, and those who reject Faith fight in the cause of evil: so fight ye against the friends of Satan" (Qur'an 4:76)

* * * * * *

"Slay the idolaters wherever ye find them, and take them captive, and besiege them, and prepare for them each ambush." (Qur'an 9:5).

* * * * * *

These and other passages had become his creed. The verses and indoctrination began to coalesce in his mind, until the men in the camps had him in exactly the mental condition they wanted. He became consumed with hatred, ravaged with a desperate hunger for revenge against those who defied the words of the blessed Prophet. There was no confusion or ambivalence in his mind any more. These men lived by the word of Allah, and if he was to enter Paradise, they must be obeyed without question.

During weeks of bitter fighting in Afghanistan's White Mountains that followed, he had shown no mercy to the hated Kafir. Mohammed Rana thought it trivial; deliberately lying to his father, family and friends when he eventually returned to England, about overstaying his time in Pakistan. His father had accepted his explanation, when his son had told him about the dream he had experienced.

'I believe it was a vision father, Allah spoke to me through the blessed Prophet, peace be upon him. I felt sure you would understand that I was called to serve the Faith, and felt it was impossible to disobey.'

His devout father had nodded, placing his hand on his son's shoulder. With a tear in his eye, he had said.

'Truly, it was a blessing, you followed your heart, and by that, the word of God. You did what you had to, and I am proud of you, my son.'

Rana knew that the pious explanation for his long absence was simply a lie taught to him by one of the men who escorted him to Islamabad, but it had served its purpose.

'Thank you father.'

He stifled further thoughts on the subject. He was a true warrior of Islam, and must always crush unworthy and impure thoughts of disloyalty to the Jihad.

'The target has turned left, left into Headingley Lane, Tango Charlie.'

A young man wearing a dark bomber jacket and jeans was sheltering in a shop doorway beside the junction

301

of the two roads. Frankie Lane lifted his wrist, and looked at his watch.

'Roger that, I have the trigger Tango Bravo.' He muttered quietly into his microphone.

Waiting for Rana to pass him on the other side of the street, Frankie stepped out into the rain and began to follow his target, as Danny disappeared into a gloomy side alley, to await immanent pickup by the second car being used in the rolling surveillance operation.

When he reached his family's small terraced home in Manor Mount Terrace, Muhammad Rana extracted his key and opened the front door. He heard his mother call from the kitchen.

'Is that you Muhammad? Dinner will be ready in twenty minutes.'

As he quickly climbed the stairs, he called down.

'OK, Mother, I'll be down in a minute.'

In the privacy of his bedroom, Rana took off his wet coat, and extracted the package. Ripping off the brown paper covering, he stared intently at what he found. The package was a brand new mobile phone; a pay as you go which could be bought on any high street, anywhere in the country. It was a cheap and basic model, which lacked the sophistication of many high end phones. Turning over the box, he saw that six words had been neatly written on it.

'Do not use. Charge and wait.'

'Port ten, all ahead, dead slow.'

Ordered the Suez Canal Authority Pilot, as he carefully manoeuvred the massive Roma Star and maintained its position, relative to the large bulk grain carrier, which steamed slowly in the distance, ahead of him. The massive container ship was part of the day's only northbound convoy. Within the Suez Canal, only one deep-water shipping lane exists, with several passing areas along its entire 195 kilometre length. Only three convoys would transit the canal on a typical day, two southbound and one northbound. The first southbound convoy entered the canal in the early hours of the morning from Port Said and proceeded to the Great Bitter Lake, where the ships anchored just outside the main shipping lane, to await the passage of the northbound convoy. Further south, the northbound convoy steamed past the second southbound convoy, which had moored temporarily near the canal bank in a bypass, in the vicinity of El Qantara.

'Mid-ships. Steady as she goes.' The Egyptian Pilot ordered.

The orders were repeated by the Roma Star's helmsman. He glanced across the bridge to Captain Douglas.

'For such a big ship, she handles well Captain.'

The Roam Star's Master nodded, as he concentrated on watching the grain carrier through his binoculars, as it steamed slowly, 1,000 metres ahead.

'Aye Pilot, she's a good ship and serves me well. With luck, if all goes to plan, we should be clear of the Canal, through Port Said and into the Mediterranean by nightfall.'

'No, nothing, absolutely nothing at all has surfaced yet.' William Lawrence said to the assembled heads of British Intelligence at MI5's headquarters, within Thames House.

'Our people and our SAS friends have had the two potential sleepers that you know about under 24 hour observation for 48 hours, but so far they have nothing unusual or suspicious to report. Both men are at least maintaining the appearance of leading perfectly ordinary, normal lives. One teaches at a school for the disabled in the centre of Manchester, and the other is studying Physics at Leeds University. Both men visit their own local

Mosques every day, and their families check out with not a sign of criminality between any of them.'

Commander Roebottom raised his hand a few inches from the table and interrupted.

'Special Branch has been making some intense but very discrete enquiries around the country, but so far no other new leads have emerged. If Al-Qaeda is planning another Spectacular soon in the UK, there's not even the slightest sign of it among the rank and file.'

Sir Alex McLean spoke next.

'I have had my people making enquiries too, but I'm afraid I have nothing interesting to report either, except that according to our most recent calculations, we now estimate that including the latest harvest, this year's profits from the heroin trade to the Taliban and their Al-Qaeda allies; coming out of Afghanistan, are approaching half a billion US dollars.'

Someone whistled softly

'Makes my bloody police pension fund look pretty damned silly,' snorted Commander Roebottom, shaking his head.

Sir Alex smiled. 'Mine too Harry.' He looked suddenly serious. "I have spoken to the NSA and a number of other friendly Intelligence agency heads, and their people are all in the same boat. No one seems to know anything. Our main player, Jalal Al-Mahdi still remains at large, and it seems to me Gentlemen, our hands are firmly tied through a serious lack of any concrete intelligence. As I see it, we have no option but to maintain our vigilance, and wait for someone out there to make a mistake.'

Heads nodded gravely around the table as he continued.

'Our political masters don't want to go public with this Gilgamesh situation, and for once, I am in complete agreement with them. I've no doubt that they don't wish to appear impotent in the eyes of the electorate, or create a panic, but from our point of view, it will avoid showing our hand, such as it is, to whoever might be trying to smuggle the bomb.'

He looked across at MI5's Director.

'May I suggest that we advise COBRA to maintain the news blackout, and we continue surveillance on our two possible sleepers? Our Ports and Airports are being closely watched, and we're listening at all the right keyholes around the UK. Now all we can do is sit, watch and wait. '

'Aye,' said Commander Roebottom, 'And hope we get lucky.'

Chapter Twenty Five

- Marseille'-

France

'All stop!'

Although encountering several heavy squalls, which were to be expected at this time of year, it had been a most unremarkable crossing from Port Said. Thankfully, the ship's only fare paying passenger had remained in his cabin throughout the passage from Suez. Takk had grinned broadly when he reported to his Captain that Mr Alhassen had reported feeling very seasick as their passage across the Mediterranean had begun, and that he wished to be left alone.

'There we are Captain; I now return full control of your ship to you. Welcome to the port of Marseille.'

The Roma Star's Master nodded towards the French harbour Pilot. On the quayside, dock workers were manoeuvring heavy hawsers into place, intent on making fast the latest arrival to France's largest Mediterranean container port, before the harbour's huge cranes began to unload and reload the Roma Star's cargo decks once again.

Al-Mahdi stepped onto the quay, thankful to be once again on dry land. He had heard nothing concerning Gilgamesh on the radio during his passage from Umm Qasr.

'The fools,' he thought. 'They will know of it soon enough.'

Following the signs to customs and immigration, he presented his stolen passport and the documents from the French Interior Ministry which gave him temporary permission to reside in France. The immigration official read the documents carefully, and signalled to a police officer.

'Please take this Gentleman to the waiting area, while I verify his details.' Al-Mahdi was led away, into an area signposted - Restricted: Staff Only.

The immigration officer shouted to the man patiently waiting his turn, in the growing queue.

'Next!'

Ten minutes later, the immigration officer finished processing the last inbound passenger, and casually looked at the Alhassen papers again. On the Ministry letter, there was a long case file reference number. He tapped the number into his computer console, and a few moments later was routed through various Government servers to the Alhassen case file, recorded on the central Interior Ministry immigration database in Paris. He compared the man's photograph on the computer screen with the passport photo. Satisfied that they represented the same man, he cross-checked the other personal details and the man's residential address. Officially, his full status remained undecided, but it all seemed in order, Alhassen did have the right of entry.

He said to a colleague. 'I'll be back in a few minutes,' and walked off down the corridor to the area set aside for holding those who needed to be vetted before being given permission to walk on French soil. He unlocked the door, and stepped inside the small interview room, where Al-Mahdi sat calmly smoking a cigarette.

'Mr Alhassen, thank you for your patience, I must ask you a few questions before I can allow you to enter France.'

Al-Mahdi eyed him coldly, and said nothing.

'Please confirm your date of birth, your work and residential address in France.'

Al-Mahdi correctly answered the questions without hesitation. When he had stolen Alhassen's identity and passport several years earlier, he had memorised the condemned prisoner's details, shortly before the man's execution in Abu Ghraib prison. It had been Alhassen's misfortune to closely resemble the Mukhabarat Colonel.

'And which area of Paris would that be please? Al-Mahdi's face remained impassive,

'Why, the Latin Quarter of course. Close to the Jardin des Plantes.' He sighed

'I do not wish to be rude Monsieur, but I have a train to catch. Will this take much longer?'

The immigration officer hunched slightly forward; and shrugging his shoulders in traditional Gallic style he said.

'Ah, Monsieur Alhassen, these matters take as long as they take.' Putting on his reading glasses, he glanced again at Alhassen's passport.

'Now Monsieur, what exactly was the purpose of your visit to Iraq?'

Al-Mahdi sat on the crowded train. He had been the last passenger to board, jumping onto the train as the guard blew a long blast on his whistle. He had thrown two twenty dollar bills to the driver of his taxi, as it screeched to a halt on the station's forecourt, after a high speed dash across the city to the railway station. He had constantly glanced at his Rolex, desperate to catch the last train of the day, which would carry him across France. It had taken a supreme effort, but he had managed to control his growing anger at the delay caused by the petty immigration official sitting in front of him, at the Marseille dockyard. Both men knew his papers were in order, and Al-Mahdi would have shot the man for his insolence, if they had been in Iraq before the invasion. But he was not in Iraq, and things were done differently in France.

His plan had worked perfectly so far. The bomb had been extracted from the dangerous mountains of Kurdistan, transported clear across Iraq under the very noses of the stupid Americans, and shipped safely to France. Al-Mahdi presumed that the Intelligence services worldwide must by now be on high alert, and actively searching of the bomb. It would be too obvious to transport it to its final destination with papers showing that the statue had come directly from Iraq. His whole plan hinged on simplicity. The bomb would soon be collected from the docks in Marseille by a local haulage company, and stored temporarily at their depot on the outskirts of the city. When he returned to his shop in Paris, he would make fresh arrangements for it to be collected by a different freight forwarding company,

311

returned to the docks and reloaded onto another container ship pending its final seaborne journey. This way, the initial movement from Iraq would be taken out of the loop completely, as if it had never happened, and new headed notepaper from Alhassen's Antiques would simply show the statue and its base to have been exported from France.

Smiling to himself, he lit a cigarette and ordered coffee from the restaurant car, as the train thundered on through the night towards Paris.

Chapter Twenty Six

-Drone -

The Tribal Homelands

Flying at 20,000 feet, the American built MQ-1 Predator was invisible to the naked eye. The unmanned aircraft continually swept the wild Tribal Homelands of northern Pakistan with its unblinking high resolution cameras. During each of its long 35 hour reconnaissance flights, the drone's mission was to search out and investigate anything suspicious within its vast mountainous search area. Via an on-board satellite link, its Central Intelligence Agency pilot sat in safety over 100 miles away from the barren Tribal Homelands, flying the aircraft entirely by remote control, from a heavily guarded allied ground base. Infrared detectors would instantly alert the pilot if the on-board sensors picked up the tell-tale heat signature of a man or vehicle far below. Once the cameras zoomed in, if a potential target was identified as hostile, it could be destroyed by either of the two deadly Hellfire missiles which the drone carried slung beneath its wings.

'Found anything?' The replacement pilot enquired when the handover began at the start of his shift.

His long sweep of the Afghanistan and Pakistan border had revealed nothing of intelligence or broken the monotony of the flight.

'Naw!' Said the tired pilot, who had remotely flown the bird for 12 long and boring hours. As he rubbed his tired eyes he said. 'Nothing at all moving down there.'

The fact that the General Atomics Predator was a technological marvel was undisputed, but critically, it lacked one vital capability. Although its sophisticated radar and electronic heat seeking eyes could penetrate the densest clouds or the darkest night, they could not see through the solid rock of the mountains below. Unaware of the imperative target directly beneath it, the Predator flew on through the clear blue skies, maintaining its cold and lonely vigil.

Oblivious to the dangers above, hidden inside a deep subterranean network of caves, Osama bin Laden spoke to his most trusted Captains. They had all spent many days travelling to the secret meeting place, for the honour of being close to him, and to hear the words of their leader. By the light of numerous oil lamps and

314

spluttering candles, he looked one by one into the cruel faces of his battle-hardened veterans.

Satisfied at last, he addressed his followers.

'The wars in Afghanistan and in Iraq make millions of dollars for big corporations, either weapons manufacturers or those working in the reconstruction, such as Halliburton and its sister companies. It is crystal clear who benefits from igniting the fire of this war and this bloodshed: They are the merchants of war, the bloodsuckers who run the policy of the world from behind the scenes. President Bush, Prime Minister Blair and their ilk, the media giants, and the U.N. All are a fatal danger to the world, and the Zionist lobby is their most dangerous member. God willing, we will persist in fighting them. In today's wars, there are no morals. We believe the worst thieves in the world today and the worst terrorists are the Americans and their running dogs. We do not have to differentiate between military or civilian. As far as we are concerned, they are all targets. Very soon they will all reap the whirlwind of their blasphemies against the word of Islam. Our fiery sword will smite them...'

Jamal Al-Mahdi had slept well after his return to Paris. During the train journey, he had called the cell

315

phone number originally given to him by his Al-Qaeda contact, and arranged an early meeting for the following morning.

At the arranged hour, he saw the man who had come to his shop, months ago. The two men strolled along the tree lined banks of the Seine, passing groups of noisy students and young lovers who walked entwined, oblivious to the world around them. Talking in whispers, Al-Mahdi and the elderly Asian finalised the bombs ultimate destination, and the arrangements for its handover.

The two men sat down on a deserted riverside bench. His contact passed Al-Mahdi a briefcase and told him to open it. Al-Mahdi placed the leather brief case on his knees, and pushed its two catches apart. With a click they sprung open, and he slowly lifted the lid. Inside, were two fat brown envelopes, and a French EU passport. Keeping it low and hidden behind the brief case lid, Al-Mahdi flicked the passport open. He was immediately impressed at the care which someone had been taken with the passport photograph. Great skill had been used to re-scan and digitally alter Al-Mahdi's appearance from the original. His new face showed him as an older man, clean shaven with white hair and gold rimmed glasses, and wearing what appeared to be a hearing aid in his left ear.

'Very good.' Said Al-Mahdi. His new name was common among Arabs - 'Abbas Jassim Ali. He mouthed the name softly to himself, committing it to memory. His contact stared across the river, watching the busy flow of Parisian traffic on the opposite bank, his face impassive.

'You will find the glasses and hearing aid in one of the packages and a bottle of white hair dye in the other. You have nine days before the handover. Be there on time, your life and much, much more depends on it.'

The deadly threat hung silently in the air between them for a moment. Al-Mahdi nodded. Without uttering another word, the contact stood up and with the aid of his cane slowly walked off along the towpath, beside the peacefully flowing waters of the great river.

Lowering his binoculars the Renseignements Generaux Inspector spoke to his sergeant.

'That's it Henri, the meeting is over.'

Both French internal security agents were sitting in their car, parked on the opposite bank.

'Khalid defiantly passed the briefcase to the other man. Did you get enough photographs of both of them?'

317

Henri Bonnaire nodded, patting the long telephoto lens of his camera. He removed the cigarette from between his lips and said.

'Yes chief, plenty of side on and full face.' He thought for a moment and shrugged.

'The light isn't good, the damned sun is still too low, but I think they should be OK.'

It was his Inspector's turn to shrug.

'It's just routine so don't worry.' The low morning sun had made it difficult for him to make out too much detail. He looked at his watch. 'Come on, it's time to go back to headquarters. I need some coffee.' He sighed. 'I've got a mountain of paperwork to catch up on.' He started the Citroen's engine. 'Let me see the photos when you have them ready. I'll include them in my report, before it goes upstairs.'

Al-Mahdi returned to his shop, but left the sign hanging in the window showing closed. He locked the door from inside, and climbed the narrow stairs at the back, which led up to his small apartment above the store. He removed the packages and passport, but before he locked them away in a cupboard, he studied the passport photograph. He smiled to himself. The transformation

318

would be easy enough. Now he had the bomb's destination he must make arrangements for its final shipment. It was also time for him to book a flight in his new name, to make the handover in person. His plan was almost completed, and soon, Abbas Jassim Ali would become a very, very rich man.

It was late in the afternoon when Henri Bonnaire walked back into his office. The basement room was thick with stale cigarette smoke. His Section Chief sat at his desk, hunched over his computer's keypad, furiously pounding it with his usual two fingered style. A cigarette dangled from the corner of the Inspector's mouth, and ash fell onto his shirt as he looked up and spoke.

'Where the hell have you been?'

As his sergeant opened his mouth to explain, impatiently he waved his hand and said.

'Forget it, where are the damned photos you took this morning?'

Bonnaire sighed and said.

'They didn't come out too well Chief. I'm sorry, the sun...'

Bouchard glanced at the top picture of the two men they had been watching earlier in the day. The sun's glare blurred the pictures almost beyond recognition.

'These are no bloody good!' He snapped, glancing at the others. 'If I didn't know that was Khalid I would never have recognised him, and as for the other man?' He shrugged. 'It could be anyone?'

Bonnaire stared at the spoiled pictures.

'I could send them back to the lab, and ask them to do a workup; perhaps they can reduce the glare and sharpen the faces?'

Claude Bouchard threw the sheaf of photographs back onto his desk blotter and exhaled hard.

'Yes, do that Henri.' He glanced up at the wall clock. It was late on Friday afternoon. The technical department was closed at weekends, which meant he wouldn't get the damned pictures back until Monday lunchtime, at the earliest. Without identifying the second man, he had nothing positive to send to his Superintendent on the second floor.

'OK, I'll hold onto the report concerning this morning for now. Run the photos upstairs Henri, before they close, and ask the lab boys to start working on them as soon as possible on Monday morning. Oh yes, Henri,' he smiled 'For heaven's sake, say please!'

On Monday morning, Al-Mahdi rose early, and began his transformation from Abu Alhassen to Abbas Jassim Ali. He carefully followed the directions on the bottle of dye, and was rewarded after 30 minutes with a thick head of snow white hair. He checked his appearance in the mirror, and satisfied, dressed in the expensive new suit he had bought two days earlier. His suitcase was already packed with more new clothes. He put on the gold rimmed spectacles, and inserted the hearing aid into his left ear. Holding up the open passport beside his new reflection, his eyes flicked from one to the other. Al-Mahdi had decided that Abbas Jassim Ali would be a rich businessman on vacation, and he saw no reason not to enjoy acting the part.

Satisfied that his appearance matched the passport photograph, he placed it into his breast pocket. Glancing at his watch, he put on his overcoat, picked up his suitcase and opened the shop door. The street was deserted, except for a stray dog which sniffed inquisitively at some overflowing dustbins on the other side of the road. Locking the shop door, he walked up the narrow side street to the main road, and after waiting for a few minutes, hailed a passing taxi.

'Charles de Gaulle airport.' He said to the driver, as he bundled his suitcase inside.

Claude Bouchard felt the loss of his dear wife most at weekends. His house was filled with the ghosts of their happy life together. Since the cancer had taken her away from him a year earlier, he hadn't changed anything at home. It was just too painful to even think of throwing out her precious things. During their many years together, they had never been blessed with children, and Claude's retirement was only two years away. There were no grandchildren to bounce on his knee, and the thought of having to sit at home alone, without his beloved Michelle appalled him. Most men were sorry to begin their work after two days of rest after the weekend, but Claude was happiest when he could leave thoughts of his dear Michelle behind, and bury himself in his Nation's security work at the Renseignements Generaux.

After nodding to the uniformed security guard at the building's main entrance, Bouchard went straight to the photo lab to enquire if they had started work on his pictures. He didn't like loose ends, and although Khalid's surveillance was just another routine follow and report job, the annoying delay in finishing the paperwork had played on his mind over the weekend. Bouchard had been given the task, as Khalid had come to the R.G.'s attention when the man's face had appeared several times in surveillance photos relating to other men, with known affiliations to Al-Qaeda, that the R.G. were currently focused on.

'It's the first job on my list Claude.' The lab technician said as he pulled on his white lab coat. 'I had a quick look at the photos on Friday.'

He pulled a face and smiled 'I'm sure I can improve the quality. It might take an hour or so, but I'll let you know as soon as I have something.'

Impatiently stubbing out yet another cigarette, Claude Bouchard stared at one of the worked up photographs.

'I know this man,' he said looking at the partially restored picture through a large magnifying glass an hour later. Eight pictures were spread across his desk, and he had closely inspected each one in turn.

'It was in the past, but I'm sure that I've seen his face before.' He rubbed his chin, deep in thought. When had it been? Certainly not recently, no, he knew it was a long time ago. There was something familiar about the cruel features of the man sitting on the riverside bench, talking to Khalid. Henri Bonnaire looked over his Chief's shoulder and gave a mock shudder.

'He looks the sort of man Madam Guillotine would have dealt with, before they stopped chopping heads off. '

Bonnaire stared at the face for several moments longer, then something clicked in his memory.

'That's it, Henri.' Bonnaire's fist pounded the table. "You're a genius, I *do* know this man.'

He stood up, and gathered the photos.

'I need to get over to records,' he yelled over his shoulder as he dashed across the office, and threw open the door. 'You're good with the technical stuff, so run his face through that new face recognition software we've just got; I want to know where he's living.... If he's who I think he is, he shouldn't be in France at all.'

His journey to Charles de Gaulle airport had been uneventful, although the taxi driver seemed to think the A1 AutoRoute heading out of Paris was his own personal racetrack, and had appeared intent on creating a new personal best time to the airport. Al-Mahdi swung his suitcase onto the scales at the Air France check-in desk inside the Terminal Two building. He showed his ticket and new passport, and was asked to make his way to gate number 7, where his flight was just about to board. Nodding to the girl behind the desk, he walked calmly through the busy concourse and presented his boarding pass to the attendant at the crowded boarding gate.

Claude Bouchard had finished spluttering his request to his Superintendent, to open the sealed file over at records, after the clerk had refused to release it to him. He explained to his superior about the prostitute's murder years before, and that he was positive that the man was Jalal Al-Mahdi, the nephew of Chemical Ali, who was currently under sentence of death, awaiting execution in Baghdad. He remembered that the whole business had been hushed-up at the time, following orders issued by the Interior Minister himself.

The Superintendent looked at each photo in turn, and then at his Inspector.

'Even if it is the man you think it is I don't have the authority to permit you to open the record Inspector

Bouchard. As you said yourself, the case was sealed on the explicit orders of the Minister himself.'

Claude Bouchard opened his mouth to protest.

'But Superintendent, I...'

The Superintendent held up his hand.

'No, you may not continue this line of enquiry without a full Government clearance. I will inform the Ministry of course, and make a request through the proper channels, but for now we must leave it there I'm afraid. I'll keep the photographs. Good day to you Inspector.'

The Superintendent picked up the telephone after Bouchard had left his office.

'Put me through to the R.G. Commissioner... quickly!'

Claude Bouchard slammed the door of his office, after he had smoked a cigarette, angrily pacing up and down outside the headquarters building, hoping the fresh air would help calm him.

'Stupid bloody bureaucracy.' He growled as he slumped back into his chair. Henri Bonnaire caught part of what his Inspector was muttering to himself.

'Proper channels,..make a request,..bloody clearance..'

Inspector Bouchard looked at his sergeant.

'What the hell are you grinning at?' He snarled.

'Oh sorry Chief...but I've found him. At least I think I have.' He said, pointing to his computer screen.

Bonnaire leapt from his seat and rushed behind his sergeant's desk. He stared at the flickering screen.

'That's him Henri; I'll put my damned pension on it!'

His sergeant breathed a huge sigh of relief.

'I didn't find anything at all in the Criminal records database, so I thought I'd better try immigration. That new software found him after several minutes. He's been living here in Paris for the past two years, over in the Latin Quarter under the name of Abu Alhassen.'

Inspector Bouchard thought for a moment

'If he's come into France on a false passport, then we can arrest him.'

Bouchard grabbed his coat.

'Come on then you smug little bastard, this guy wouldn't come back to France just for fun. He's up to something serious, if he's associating with the likes of Khalid and his friends. Let's go!'

Al-Mahdi settled comfortably into his seat aboard the Air France Boeing 747. The smiling stewardess fluttered around him and the other passengers in the upper 1st Class cabin, ensuring their seat belts were correctly fastened, and enquiring if they required a newspaper during the flight. She politely informed them that once they had taken off, complimentary champagne would be served and a light breakfast was available to those who required it.

Having completed the mandatory safety briefing to her passengers, she sat down and strapped herself in for take-off. As the heavy plane taxied toward the main runway, the aircraft's Captain spoke to his passengers.

'Ladies and Gentlemen, this is your Captain speaking. Welcome aboard flight FR 156 to London Heathrow International... '

Marcel Devereaux, the R.G.'s Head of Service whistled softly to himself as he replaced the telephone receiver.

'Merde!' he thought 'There will be a terrible scandal over this if the press gets hold of it; the Élysée Palace could be in for some very serious trouble.'

Months before, he remembered that the meeting with the Interior Minister had been a stormy one. He had argued vociferously against a further cover up, after the Americans had passed on the information that Al-Mahdi was suspected of involvement in the theft of an Iraqi atom bomb, but the Minister had overruled and dismissed his arguments with his usual haughty manner.

'From what you have told me, my dear Commissioner, I find no evidence of this Al-Mahdi person having any current connection with France. From your briefing, I can see no firm proof that the bomb exists at all.'

He had a meeting at the Élysée Palace shortly with a delegation of Ministers from France's ex colony of Chad, and this damned Policeman seemed intent on making him late. If his busy schedule was upset, his plans for the evening would be ruined. The Minister's wife was away in Lyon visiting her family, and his Mistress had promised him something special for tonight.

Barely concealing his growing irritation, the Minister of the Interior said. 'As a matter of National security, may I suggest Commissioner, that perhaps you quietly circulate his photograph to your Heads of Department only, and inform them that you are to be alerted by them personally, should any sign of him become apparent?'

The Minister paced as he spoke, stopping beside the tall windows with his hands clasped behind his back, watching a motorcycle dispatch rider arriving in the courtyard below.

'If we launch a full-scale manhunt, the press might well dig up his past, and I think that might not reflect well on the dignity of France, in the eyes of the rest of the world.'

Commissioner Devereaux held his tongue

'Wouldn't reflect well on your Ministry or one of your predecessors, you mean, you slimy little bastard. 'He thought bitterly to himself, but his face remained impassive. The Minister stared intently at Devereaux. His mind was made up.

'I formally order you Monsieur Commissioner, to avoid any co-operation with other nation's security agencies concerning this whole Al-Mahdi affair.'

Two months later, the R.G.'s Head of Service sat angrily in silence as his driver weaved through the Parisian traffic as they returned to headquarters, following his latest difficult meeting with the Minister of the Interior.

330

'Damn these bloody politicians. 'He thought miserably. 'If they had not decided to release a vicious murderer to avoid losing a deal with the Iraqis, Al-Mahdi would still be languishing in a French jail. This whole business would never have happened in the first place. '

To his surprise, his fresh appeal to track down the fugitive had met with some limited success this time; the Minister had agreed that if Al-Mahdi was arrested over his forged documents, he should be immediately handed over to the Government's 'Action Service.'

Devereaux knew that the Minister had in effect signed Al-Mahdi's unofficial death warrant. The thugs of the Action Service was well known for their brutal methods, and Devereaux was in no doubt that after being tortured for information just in case there was a bomb, Al-Mahdi's lifeless body would be fished out of the Seine shortly afterwards. The press would be told it was just another drugs related gang murder; the man had carried no identification, and the matter would be quickly forgotten.

When Inspector Bouchard and Henri Bonnaire arrived outside Al-Mahdi's shop in the Latin Quarter, Alhassen's Antiquities was closed and appeared deserted. After several minutes of hammering on the door, the owner of the cafe next door looked out into the street to see what the commotion was about. Flashing his R.G. Identity card, Bouchard demanded to know where Abu Alhassen was. The cafe owner shrugged.

'He was away for a couple of weeks, and then he came back. Perhaps he has gone away again?'

The cafe owner's wife appeared behind her husband, carrying a broom.

'I think I saw him early this morning. It was still dark outside, but maybe it was him. If it was, he was carrying a suitcase, when he walked past our place.'

'At what time did you see him Madam? Sergeant Bonnaire enquired.

She glanced at the clock above the door and pursed her lips.

'Maybe, six o'clock?'

'Well, that's as far as we can go,' Claude Bouchard said as they turned into the main traffic stream. 'He's had all morning to disappear. He could be anywhere by now.' He sighed 'I'll write it all up, and send it upstairs. If the Superintendent wants us to keep an eye on the place, he will tell me.' He slowly shook his head. 'Come on Henri, it's you turn to buy the coffees...'

Chapter Twenty Seven

I spy

-London -

The porter gave Al-Mahdi his key and quietly left the room. Walking around the sumptuous suite of rooms he had taken at the Dorchester hotel on Park Lane, in London's exclusive Mayfair, he admired the antique furniture, beautiful marbled bathroom and was delighted with the overwhelming luxury which surrounded him. Walking across the thickly piled carpet, he stopped and looked out of the large bay window, at the green rolling expanse of central London's Hyde Park.

'I must get used to this style of living.' He thought to himself, smiling.

When his aircraft had landed at Heathrow Airport, he followed the other passengers holding European Union passports through the EU immigration hall. His French passport was inspected and returned to him. Having followed the others to baggage reclaim and found his suitcase, Al-Mahdi took a black taxi from the rank outside the Terminal into the very heart of London. His precious shipment was due to arrive in three days' time, but for now, he was intent on enjoying a small part of the down payment which Al-Qaeda had already paid him.

As a Muslim, alcohol had always been forbidden to him, but he had thought hard about the dramatic change his life was undergoing during his voyage on the Roam Star, as it steamed across the Mediterranean. Why should he deny himself anything? When his business was concluded, would he not be one of the richest men in the world, who could buy literally anything he desired? He picked up the ornate bedside telephone, and dialled room service.

'Send a bottle of your finest champagne to suite 9.'

A cool female voice responded

'Of course Mr Ali, I will see to it immediately.'

When Sally's telephone rang later that evening, her pimp, known in the local underworld as Cassar, told her to prepare herself for a wealthy client, who would be arriving at her apartment shortly.

When Cassar had first met Sally and installed her in the Mayfair apartment, he made a point of contacting the right people in all the prestigious hotels in central London, whose customers might require her services. He had established a comfortable arrangement where he paid a generous commission to those who sent him business.

Sally was proving to be a very good investment; Cassar had already also received several lucrative referrals from other satisfied customers. The Arab clientele he served could afford the high price he demanded, and he made sure he squeezed them for everything he could. A few minutes earlier, he had received a call from a senior Porter at the Dorchester, who told him that a guest had enquired where he could find a high class blond woman.

Anyone who could afford the Dorchester would pay a little extra for Sally he thought, as he lifted the telephone, and dialled her apartment's number.

Twenty minutes later, Al-Mahdi rang her entry phone buzzer. He was feeling the effects of the alcohol, effects he had never experienced before. It fanned the flames that had begun to burn inside him after drinking several glasses of the vintage champagne. He had not had a woman for some time, and with his new riches, he decided it was his duty to begin enjoying some the pleasures that came with great wealth. She would obey him, or suffer the consequences.

That morning, Rana had opened his front door, carrying an overnight bag. A minicab was waiting for him in the street outside.

'Leeds Mainline station.' He said to the driver, and got in beside him.

'Charlie one. The target is Out, Out; mobile in a minicab index P132 HXA, towards Headingly Lane, I have the trigger.'

Pat was sitting in the driver's seat of the white transit van. He started the engine, and pulled away from his static OP in Manor Mount Terrace. The minicab drove on towards the station, with the van shadowing at a discrete distance. Spike Morris and Frankie Lane, in Charlie one were waiting in their unmarked car, and pulled out immediately after the mini cab had passed them.

'Charlie Two, I have the trigger.'

'Charlie One roger that.'

Pat gave up his pursuit and pulled off the main road. Danny sat beside him, studying a road map.

'Looks like he's heading for the main railway station Pat.' He said, following the route on the map with his finger. 'Take the next right, and then right again, we should be able to get ahead of them, if we're quick.'

Rana sat immobile as the cab entered the station's busy forecourt. His new cell phone had rung suddenly the previous evening, while he was revising for a mid-module physics exam. In the privacy of his bedroom, he had listened intently to the stranger's voice who spoke his orders.

'You will take a train to London's Kings Cross St. Pancras tomorrow at 10am. When you arrive in London, you will call the following number from a public call box. You will say: Ali calling. Is my Uncle there? You will then receive further instructions. Destroy this phone.'

Rana committed the number to memory, switched off the phone and began packing his overnight bag.

At Felixstowe harbour, the two man Customs and Excise rummage crew were busy searching inside yet another container. The sniffer dog had shown no interest in any of its contents, and had already been taken elsewhere to continue its search for narcotics. The Customs officers had almost finished opening and resealing various boxes and crates chosen at random inside the container. One of the officers checked the manifest documents attached to a large wooden crate.

'Here's a good one George. It's a stone statue of an ancient Babylonian God.' He thought for a moment. With his curiosity aroused he said 'We'd better take a quick look.'

Using a crowbar, he deftly levered open the crate's wooden lid.

'Strewth, he's an ugly bugger!'

From his weathered eagles head, Lord Nergal's demonic eyes stared coldly up at him. The Customs man suppressed a shudder and checked the manifest details again.

'French import destined for the British Museum in London.'

He checked the dimensions and weight.

'Looks OK, but pass me the rubber mallet will you?'

Tapping the statue along its length, he was rewarded with the same dull thud. Satisfied that the statue was solid stone, he replaced the lid, and hammered it closed. Ignoring the crate containing the statues base, he climbed out of the container.

'Come on George, that's enough, there's another forty odd more to do from this shipment alone before we can call it a day.' He said breaking the seal on the next container and wrenching open its heavy steel doors.

Commander Roebottom was sitting at his desk at New Scotland reading a report. His telephone rang. Absently, he picked up the receiver.

'Roebottom.' He answered in his usual gruff manner.

'Hallo Commander, David Lawrence here. Thought you would like to know that one of your sleepers has just jumped aboard the 10.05 train from Leeds to London. Might be nothing, he could be off to visit a sick aunt or something, but it seems a bit odd. We checked with his University; he was supposed to be sitting an important exam this morning, and he's skipped without so much as a word. Bit strange, because if he's had to miss a lecture in the past, he's always called in and let them know beforehand.'

Roebottom sat bolt upright. His old fashioned copper's instincts set alarm bells ringing. Given that they had so little to go on, this was something; a break from normal routine; behaviour which was out of character. It was defiantly worth following up.

'What time is the train due to arrive in London?' There was a short pause while Lawrence referred to his notes.

'Ah, yes, here we are. The train should arrive at Kings Cross St. Pancras at 12.41. That's in about ninety minute's time. Our SAS friends are on the train, watching Rana. I've tipped off the Metropolitan Police Commissioner, and arranged a full CID surveillance team, who are on their way to the station as we speak. If he gets off the train beforehand, I'll let you know, but I think it's prudent to assume he's heading straight for central London. Oh yes, there's another thing that's a bit odd.... He's only bought a one-way ticket.'

Pat was sitting at the end of the carriage next to Spike, as the intercity express train thundered along the high speed track, southbound towards the London Terminus. Rana was sitting several rows ahead of them, staring idly out of the window at the passing Hertfordshire farmhouses and lush countryside, oblivious to the covert Special Forces team surrounding him. At the other end of the crowded carriage, Danny and three more Shadow Squadron troopers sat apart from each other, but all had taken isle seats as, weeks before, the MI5 officer had been

340

trained them to do. If Rana moved, one of the men would stay with him. The other members of the Leeds surveillance operation, who had managed to scramble aboard the express when Rana had left his home town, were dotted along the adjoining carriages as backup.

Spike looked down the carriage and stared at the back of the target's head.

'Christ Pat, this is boring. After the last few days, I don't know how the spooks that do this for a living, can stand it.'

Pat smiled. 'You just got to have patience. It comes with the job and a lot of practice.'

Spike snorted. 'I guess you're right. When I've got my head stuck in a wiring loom at the Telephone Exchange, looking for a fault somewhere among thousands of bloody connections, patience is just as necessary as a voltmeter, or a good pair of pliers.'

Pat nodded. 'You've got it son. You finish your training soon, don't you?'

Spike raised an eyebrow. 'Blimey Pat, how did you know?'

Pat smiled. As Troop Commander, he needed to know all the skills his men possessed. It might make the difference between success and failure on a future job, or

341

even save their lives one day. He'd read a copy of Spike's latest British Telecom. assessment. They knew they had a rising star in their midst. Spike's affinity with things electronic surprised even his highly skilled instructors. Few men are blessed with a gift, but if something took a current, transmitted and received, or did something cunningly electrical, Spike, Pat knew, was in his element.

'I like to keep my beady eye on all of you Spike. I did a course on it once, down in Hereford.'

Spike glanced sideways at Pat. He was never sure if his Troop Commander was serious.

During one recent explosives exercise, Two Troop had been invited by a local Council, to demolish an old wartime coastal battery position on the Devon coast. To Pat's great annoyance, the compressor they needed to power the pneumatic drills through the thick reinforced concrete walls had developed a mechanical fault, and sat quiet and useless. Unable to drill through and under the steel reinforced concrete, the plastic explosives couldn't be placed properly, and the job looked doomed. As Two Troop stood around the silent machine scratching their heads, Danny Thomas had found an adjustable spanner from somewhere, set to work, and within fifteen minutes had the compressor at full power again, purring like a contented kitten. Probably can't change a light bulb, Pat thought to himself, but if an engine was involved, he's call on Danny's services without hesitation.

Along the length of the train, concealed speakers suddenly announced their arrival at London Kings Cross St. Pancras Terminus in fifteen minutes.

Pat rolled his neck casually. 'Nearly time to stretch our legs again.'

The 12.41 express from Leeds rolled to a final stop at Kings Cross St. Pancras station at precisely 12.45pm. All along the crowded train carriage doors opened, disgorging passengers onto the crowded terminus platform. Rana stepped down from the train, and followed the crowd's flow towards the ticket barrier.

'Hallo Charlie four, this is Yankee one, have you still got the trigger on the target?'

Pat heard the call from the waiting detectives. He had also just stepped down from the carriage, but couldn't speak for fear of compromise from the surrounding throng of commuters. Instead, with his hand in his pocket, he pushed and released his radio's transmit button twice, signalling the affirmative. As Rana approached the barrier, Pat received another message, this time from a female voice.

'Charlie four, this is Yankee two, I have the target in sight. Turn left after the barrier, I have the trigger.'

Pat and his team understood. They must break contact as soon as Rana reached the end of the platform. Click, click.

Once he had handed over his ticket at the barrier, Muhammad Saleem Rana stopped for a moment, and looked around for an information sign, which would lead him to a public telephone. He failed to notice several travellers innocently waiting for their trains, idly killing time by window shopping within the station's busy concourse, reading newspapers or sipping coffee at the bistro style cafes which were dotted around the station. Although he didn't notice, they were all highly focused, and intent on watching his movements. Each detective had been assigned an exit, and would support Yankee two in her rolling surveillance, switching with her, the moment she signalled it was necessary.

Rana walked through the concourse until he found an empty public phone booth. He picked up the receiver and dialled the number he had committed to memory the night before. On the third ring the connection was made. There was silence from the other end, so he said.

'Ali calling, is my Uncle there?'

There was a pause, and then the distant voice said.

'Buy a ticket to Hammersmith, on the Hammersmith & City underground tube train. Get off at Ladbroke Grove, and wait under the bridge at the entrance to the station. You will be met there.'

The conversation ended with an abrupt click as the messenger hung up. Rana replaced the receiver, picked up his grip and followed the public information signs to the London Underground ticket booth. Purchasing his ticket, he walked off in search of the correct platform, followed closely by Yankee two, and at a discrete distance, several other Yankee call signs.

Pat assembled his team in a coffee shop on the station concourse.

'Right lads, well done. We've handed the target over to the plods, and that's us done. Stand down and go home. I've spoken to the others on my mobile, who weren't on the train with us. They're on their way back on the train to London now. It's time to stand down and get away home.'

345

Yankee Two remained in her seat reading a magazine, as the underground train pulled into Ladbroke Grove station. When Rana suddenly stood up and moved to the carriage door, the other three members of the police surveillance team casually stood up in different parts of the carriage, and slowly made their way towards the other sliding doors. The tube train came to a full stop, and most of the passengers got off, intent on their own journeys, taking no interest in their fellow travellers. Rana followed the exit signs as he walked along the platform. Placing his ticket into the automated barrier, he passed through the small concourse, and stood on the pavement outside, his nose wrinkling at the exhaust fumes from the busy traffic stream in Ladbroke Grove.

A young Asian man engaged in a conversation on his cell phone walked up behind him. He stood next to Rana, waiting for a break in the traffic, so that he could cross the road.

'Are you looking for Uncle Ali?' The man whispered.

Rana didn't show the surprise he felt. He nodded.

'Yes I am.' He replied.

'Get ready then. 'That was all the young man said. Moments later, a black Ford Cortina screeched to a halt in front of Rana, and the rear passenger door flew open.

'I am Uncle Ali!' He bundled Rana into the back of the waiting car. Uncle Ali jumped in behind him, as the car's driver stamped on the accelerator. They sped away from the station towards the Harrow road in a cloud of acrid blue tyre smoke.

'Oh Shit!' Hissed Yankee four to Yankee five, as they dodged past several startled pedestrians and ran out onto the pavement.

'We've lost him, damn it... He's gone.... '

Chapter Twenty Eight

Ground Zero

Central London

William Lawrence replaced the telephone receiver ten minutes later, and stared at it with horror for several moments.

'Christ!'

He had managed to control a moment of panic as he listened to the news about Rana's disappearance. He knew that losing a suspect was always a possibility during a surveillance operation, and as far as he was concerned, this was all the proof he needed that they were now dealing with a highly trained terrorist cell. The snatch was too slick and professional to be anything else, he thought. Their one vital lead was gone, and the terrorist Spectacular was coming soon, Lawrence was now convinced of it.

'Better go and break the news to the Boss, and face the music.' He thought miserably, as he stood up and left his office. He walked a short distance along the panelled corridor. He stopped, straightened his tie and knocked on the Director General's door.

The mood of the hastily assembled security chiefs was sombre. The emergency meeting had brought no good news; the whole situation had taken a considerable turn for the worse after the incident at Ladbroke Grove. The local police had reported a black Ford Cortina had been found abandoned and burning on some waste ground several miles from the station, shortly after Rana had been snatched. As the car burned, a witness had reported seeing a white van leaving the area, but its number plates had been obscured by the smoke.

The Director General of MI5 spoke to the others.

'I think it fair to assume that the terrorist cell responsible for lifting Rana was following a simple security failsafe when they took him. By suddenly whisking him away, they removed any threat of being followed beyond Ladbroke Grove, if Rana did have a tail on him. There is no reason to assume that they knew we were on to him, they just removed any possibility of anyone following him to their hideout.'

Several members of the meeting nodded their agreement.

'Aye, these men are showing signs of being well trained.' Commander Roebottom said. 'I expect it's likely that they are hidden somewhere in the general area of central London. I would think they wouldn't risk a long journey through London to its outer suburbs or beyond. They might be hiding within a large Asian community like Tower Hamlets or Newham, or perhaps in the Brick Lane area in the East end. One the other hand, they could be posing as innocent students, sharing a flat or house almost anywhere in London.'

No one spoke for a moment. All the assembled security chiefs knew that with a surface area of over 600 square miles, and a diversely cosmopolitan population counted in the millions, Greater London was the perfect place for a small group of fanatical terrorists to hide.

'Has anything at all come up from Customs or the Ports?' Sir Alex McLean enquired.

'No, nothing I'm afraid.' Said the head of Customs and Excise, whose department were amongst other things, responsible for searching Gt. Britain's imports for illegally smuggled contraband and drugs. 'If we had ten times the manpower, we still couldn't search every item which comes into the country. We have been looking more closely at anything bulky and heavy recently, but.' He held his hands up in supplication. 'Realistically, even working flat out with the resources we have, I doubt more than fifty per cent of the UK's total imports have been searched thoroughly in the last month. The sheer volume of goods coming into the country is simply, well, immense.'

Sir Alex raised an eyebrow.

'Dear me,' he said. 'That gives the terrorists an even chance of slipping the damned bomb into the country.'

'Yes,' said the customs chief gravely 'I'm afraid it does.

Following a good night's sleep after the Leeds job, Pat Farrell had decided to take a rare day off, and had slept late. He was still in his dressing gown when his doorbell rang. Pat answered the door. Two men stood outside. Holding up a police warrant card, one of the men said.

'I'm Detective Constable Morgan and this is my colleague D.C. Adams. Are you Pat Farrell?' Pat's faced betrayed his surprise.

'Yes, that's me, what's this all about then?'

The detective said 'Can we come in Mr Farrell; we need to ask you some questions?'

'We're here concerning a serious assault in Mayfair last night on a prostitute by the name of Sally McCaffey. Do you know her Mr Farrell?'

Sitting in his flat's small lounge, Pat's face clouded with concern.

'Sally, yes I know her. Christ, what's happened?'

The detective ignored the question and said.

'Your name was in her diary, with the word taxi underlined beside it. We managed to trace you through the Carriage Office. What exactly is your relationship with Miss McCaffey?'

Pat sat back on his chair and exhaled hard.

'Yes, of course I know her. She's a friend,' he paused, 'well, sort of.'

He explained the incident months previously at Kings Cross, and the recent fleeting meeting on the taxi rank outside the London Hilton. After more questioning, the police officers eventually appeared satisfied with his explanation.

'Where is Sally now?' Asked Pat, 'And how badly is she hurt?'

The detective closed his notebook.

'Miss McCaffey is still unconscious in hospital, so we haven't been able to interview her yet. She's in St

Thomas's.' The detective stared at Pat for a moment. Suddenly, both his expression and tone softened.

'Look, these enquiries are always difficult. There's usually a pimp involved somewhere, particularly with high class hookers, but getting the girl to name them always takes time while we're trying to find the attacker. The girls usually live in a weird fantasy world where they imagine their pimp secretly loves them, or at least is their best friend. They usually try to protect him from us. It just gives their attacker more time to disappear.'

The other detective shook his head sadly. His face was sour.

'Pimps are real scumbags. The truth is they couldn't care less about their girls. He's made no effort to pass on any information to us anonymously or otherwise about the 'client' who attacked Miss McCaffey. He's just keeping his head down to protect his own miserable skin.'

The two CID policemen stood up. D.C. Adams said.

'Well, thanks for your help Mr Farrell, if I need anything more, I'll be in touch. We'll see ourselves out. '

Pat Farrell found Sally lying asleep in a hospital bed, in a small side ward close to the busy casualty department, at St. Thomas's. He had trouble recognising her. The pretty girl who had recently paid her debt to him so happily was a real mess. Sally's face was heavily bruised, and both her eyes were discoloured and badly swollen. Her lip was cut, and her right arm was suspended on a bedside frame, encased in white plaster. Monitors beeped slowly around her. Pat stopped a passing Doctor and asked how she was, explaining that he had just heard of her attack, and was a close friend.

The young Doctor picked up her chart, and quickly scanned her notes.

'She was found unconscious by the ambulance crew late last night in Mayfair. The injuries appear to be the result of a very nasty beating.'

He read through the next page. 'She has a broken nose and a hairline fracture to the left side of her jaw. There may be damage to her vision, but we'll know more when the swelling around the eyes has gone down. Her facial injuries are consistent with being repeatedly punched. She has multiple contusions all over her body, probably from being kicked, and her right arm and several fingers are broken. Worst of all I'm afraid, she was violently raped by her attacker.'

Pat's face was a mask of stone as he nodded at the Doctor.

'Nothing life threatening though Doc?' He said hopefully. His blood ran cold as he looked at Sally's poor battered face.

'No. It appears she's been very, very lucky. We haven't found any evidence of internal damage or haemorrhaging. The scan showed slight swelling of her left kidney, but that's usually consistent with being kicked.'

He looked through the notes again.

'It will take a while, but she should pull through, providing there no complications or permanent damage to either eye.'

The young Doctor's bleeper went off as he replaced the chart.

'Sorry, I must go, I'm on call,' he said, switching off the beeping device attached to his belt. He walked out of the room, and away down the busy corridor to the nearest house phone.

Pat stood alone, staring down at Sally. He had seen enough bloody battlefield casualties during his army career, but being wounded was an occupational hazard and went with the job. He had never seen a defenceless woman with injuries like this, especially someone he knew personally. His eyes blazed and he ground his teeth with anger.

'Poor little cow.' Pat thought angrily, when he walked out of the hospital. 'Some fucker is going to pay for this!' He took out his cell phone, and dialled a number.

'Hallo Spike, give Danny a call will you, I need a favour from both of you... '

Chapter Twenty Nine

'So that's the story boys.' Pat said to Spike and Danny, as they sat huddled in Pat's favourite pub off the Harrow road. 'I need to grab the pimp, and get the name of the bastard who hurt Sally.'

Pat narrowed his eyes as he stared at his two most trusted troopers.

'This isn't an official job in any way, and if you don't want to get involved then that's OK. No hard feelings.'

'What are you going to do with this bloke, the one that hurt your friend?' Asked Spike. Danny nodded his agreement to the question.

Pat smiled. 'I'm not planning on slotting him, if that's what you mean?' He said, looking intently at them both.

'After what the bastard did to a defenceless woman, he deserves a good kicking, Then I'm going to hand him over to the police. Nothing more than that, I promise. It's just some old fashioned rough justice, that's all.'

Both men stared at their beer glasses for a moment. With Pat's assurance, it felt right. Danny looked up first and nodded.

'Yeah, I'm in.'

Spike thought for a moment and smiled,

'I'd better come along too Pat.' He nodded towards Danny 'He'll only fuck it up if I don't.'

Under the soft Soho street illumination, central London's historical red light district maintained a subtle air of sleaze, despite the recent efforts of Westminster Council to clean up its tawdry image. Most of the dingy strip clubs and sex shops had gone, driven out by huge punitive Council licensing fees, but dotted among the entrances of smart new bistros and trendy wine bars, some doorways still led down poorly lit stairways to 'private' clubs, whose customers sort pleasures of a more physical nature.

'That must be him,' said Pat. 'The bloke dressed like a Chicago gangster, over there by the white Mercedes.'

Spike and Danny both nodded.

'Yeah, got him Pat,' said Danny.

Pat had been busy after he left Sally. He used his cab drivers knowledge to visit the right places, and ask the right questions of the girls who worked the streets. When they saw his cab drivers badge, their reluctance to talk to a stranger eased. There was an old Victorian saying known to most London taxi drivers and prostitutes alike.

'Whores and taxi drivers both earn a living from the gutter.'

It explained their unspoken kinship and change in attitude towards Pat. Some knew Sally McCaffey, and had already heard enough through the hooker's grapevine to know what had happened to her. In their book, Pimps were supposed to protect their girls, and keep them away from the known hard-core weirdo's that prowled the back streets of London.

No-one seemed to say anything good about Cassar. He had been a strictly small-time pimp before he met Sally. Cassar ran a small string of girls in Soho, and another in Kings Cross. He had a reputation for enjoying slapping his girls around, if he suspected them of withholding his cut of their earnings. Rumour had it that he'd slashed a girl's face with a blade once to 'encourage' the others to pay a fat percentage of their earnings to him, in order to remain under the wing of his dubious protection. Sally was his ticket out of the gutter; his springboard into real money. Getting a description of her pimp had been easy.

'Short, fat and greasy.' They were the most common descriptions.

'Dresses like he's Malta's answer to Al Capone.' Sneered one girl. Two girls who worked for him in Kings Cross readily suggested where he was most likely to be found after dark.

'He likes to hang around the Spaniard's bar just off Brewer Street most nights.' Said one.

'That's where his Soho girls work from.,' added her friend.

Pat had briefed Spike and Danny on the target area and Cassar, based on the information he had gathered. Pat decided to implement his plan that night.

'Right boys, you know the drill - Speed, Aggression and Surprise. Put your masks on, and duck down.'

'Yeah, yeah, we know, we know. 'Said Spike with a grin, pulling the black woollen ski mask over his face.

The small Soho cul-de-sac was dark and deserted; the late night revellers had long since deserted Brewer Street's fashionable watering holes for their homes and a warm bed. Pat eased his taxi forward, until he was parallel with Cassar.

'You book a taxi in the name of Cassar mate?' Pat enquired, keeping his head down and hidden in the shadows.

'Yeah that's me, but I ain't ordered no taxi.' Pat lifted a sheet of paper into view.

'You must have mate, your names here on the order, look here.'

Cassar stepped towards the taxi. He had almost reached the driver's door.

'Look man, I'm telling you, I ain't ordered no...'

The taxi's rear passenger door burst open, and two hooded figures erupted from it. One punched Cassar hard in the stomach, knocking the wind out of him. As he doubled up, the other hooded figure pushed him to the ground and shoved his hands behind his back, securing them both together with a thick cable-tie noose. Before Cassar even thought of calling for help, his mouth was covered with a broad piece of gaffer tape, and he was dragged into the back of the cab. The door was pulled shut behind him. Danny pulled a pillowcase over the prostrate pimp's head.

'*Go!*' Spike hissed, while he sat heavily on their prisoner.

Pat didn't rush his exit; no-one notices a London cab, or its driver, by day or night on the capital's streets.

'Nine seconds? Hmm, could be better. 'He whispered.

Pat wasn't sure, but he could have sworn he heard someone in the back mutter.

'*Bollocks!*'

Pat and his team's boots crunched softly on the gravel as they frogmarched the hapless Cassar from the taxi, into the entrance of the dark and deserted Wapping warehouse. They dragged him up four flights of creaking wooden stairs, scattering groups of rats, who angrily squeaked and hissed at the intruders before scampering into dark corners. Cassar groaned and rolled his head as they reached the top floor. Spike and Danny both had him in powerful arm locks, and his initial struggles had quickly stopped when they added a little more pressure to their iron grip.

'Right, over there, put him on the deck.' Said Pat, whose face was now hidden behind his own a ski mask. All three were careful not to use each other's names.

Spike and Danny had learnt that lesson when they had helped Pat and the rest of the Troop kidnap the Assistant Chief Constable of the Devon Constabulary three months earlier, as part of a joint police and Special Forces exercise. When they had lifted the A.C.C. in a daring roadside ambush, the highly trained police dog tracker teams had failed to catch the kidnappers, or rescue their Boss, after miles of difficult cross-country tracking, much to the A.C.C. 's anger, and Two Troop's collective glee.

Until the early '60s, the steel girder which jutted out above the dark, murky waters of the river Thames had been fitted with a pulley, which helped the stevedores lift heavy crates from cargo barges moored to the waterfront beside the warehouse. It was long gone now; the entire riverside trading estate was empty; its buildings nothing more than neglected shells waiting for eventual demolition and redevelopment. The only lights they had seen since entering the derelict estate, were reflected along the opposite bank of the river, glittering and sparkling off the dark water.

Pat walked softly to the open loading bay and threw a length of rope over the girder. While Danny knelt on Cassar, Spike firmly secured his ankles together with two thick cable ties. Pat crouched down beside the shivering pimp, and tied one end of the rope securely through the cable ties and then firmly around his ankles. The other end of the rope was lashed tightly to an iron ring embedded in the wooden floor.

'Take off his hood and swing him out.' Ordered Pat. Danny and Spike pushed the struggling pimp to the edge of the loading bay.

Spike whispered 'One, two, three!'

They launched the unfortunate Maltese over the edge. His terrified screams were muffled by the gaffer tape. The rope was short; he dropped only a few inches. Swinging gently in the cool river breeze, he hung like a gutted shark, his feet in the air, and his head pointing down at the dark lapping waters 70 feet below.

Somewhere in the distance, a river boat's horn hooted forlornly across the river. As its echoes faded Pat spoke quietly.

'We're going to ask you some questions Cassar. 'He paused for a moment, and looked down at the river. 'You have upset some very important people. I'll let you work out what will happen if you fail to answer me, or if we think you are lying to us.'

Pat pulled out a large hunting knife, and rested it on the taught rope beside him. Cassar eyes bulged as he let out another muffled scream.

'When we remove the tape from your mouth, if you call out, no-one will hear you. Answer my questions truthfully and you will live, but if you lie to me, you will die. Do you understand the rules?' He hissed, tapping the flat side of the blade on the rope. Cassar nodded frantically as he looked at the knife, and then into the cold, glittering eyes behind the mask.

When the white van had arrived at the cell's base in Loveday Road, a quiet turning off Ealing Broadway, Rana had fully recovered from the shock of his sudden pickup, by two members of the terrorist cell. Any nervousness he had felt had melted away, and been replaced with growing exaltation. The cell's driver had shown him upstairs to the room where he would sleep.

'We will pray soon, and then we will eat.' He said. 'After that, we will tell you of the plan.'

Inside the pre-war semi-detached house, the floors and walls were bare. Black plastic sheeting had been taped over the windows. Rana felt a deep feeling of relief. At last he was isolated among men who would assist him fulfil his destiny; his holy quest to gain martyrdom in the holy war against the Kafir.

The fire had first been ignited during his time in the camp in Afghanistan. It smouldered during the long months he had waited patiently at home in Leeds, for the call to Jihad. His Al-Qaeda masters knew the last 24 hours would act as the catalyst, and rekindle his devotion. His fanatical desire to attain Paradise, by punishing the infidel non-believers for their persecution of his Muslim brothers around the world, was to him, almost at hand.

After the men had washed thoroughly, Rana was given the privilege of leading the groups' evening prayers. The men's meal afterwards was simple lamb and rice, washed down with bottles of plain mineral water. The man who had first named himself as Uncle Ali introduced Rana to the other members of the group. Each of the seven young men had spent time in the camps in Afghanistan. Some had been born in the UK, but the older man, Uncle Ali said, was a Syrian, acting as their quartermaster and link with Al-Qaeda.

He was also responsible for planning and co-ordinating their forthcoming strike. Rana's eyes stared in wonder, and his mouth fell open as the Syrian told him of the existence of the atomic bomb, and the plan to stab at London's black heart.

'You will prepare and detonate the bomb. It is a great honour for you. You will be driven with the bomb into the heart of London, and you will explode it.' He placed his hand on his chest, and spoke to them all.

'You, my friends, are the chosen. Your martyrdom videos with be released on the internet even as you fly to Paradise, and your names will be remembered and honoured forevermore; the men who slew millions of the hated Kafir, at a single stroke. The great warrior Saladin himself will prepare for you all, a seat at his own table in Paradise. The honours and delights which await you cannot be imagined, but very soon, you will begin to enjoy them for all eternity.'

He looked at each of the men in turn, who returned his stare expectantly. 'Insha'Allah. All of you will be welcomed at the gates of Paradise as exalted heroes. The blessings of the Prophet, peace be upon him, are with you all.'

'Well done both of you; that was a very slick job tonight. You both did extremely well.' Pat said over his shoulder, as he drove them back into central London.

Danny and Spike both grinned. 'What was all that about a chainsaw Spike?' Asked Danny. When they had the information they sought, Spike had pulled in and untied the whimpering Cassar, but had replaced the pillowcase as he bent forward with a warning.

'You will forget tonight. It never happened, see.' He hissed. 'If you go to the police, or warn your customer, we will find you again, and cut you into little pieces with a chainsaw. Stay down on the floor and keep your hood on for ten minutes. One of us will be watching you. If you disobey, you will die. Do you understand?'

Cassar had groaned and nodded, vowing to himself that an immediate move back to Malta was a very sensible career move, on the grounds of his future health.

Spike laughed. 'Seemed the right thing to say.' He shrugged 'Just getting into the role.'

Pat turned his eyes skywards, away from the dark and deserted road for a moment.

'It's too late to lift the target tonight; I want to do a recce. first anyway. We know he's staying in a suite at the Dorchester hotel, but I want to get a closer look at the hotel's layout first, and find out exactly what he looks like, and where his suite is. I'll scope out the situation later on.'

Pat yawned. 'After we've all had some sleep.'

Chapter Thirty

Al-Mahdi was awoken next morning by someone knocking repeatedly on his hotel suite door. He rose from his bed, slipping on a thick towelling robe. He was expecting a visit from his Al-Qaeda contact today, but checking his watch, it was only 08.30. If it was him, he was two hours early. His suspicions aroused, Al-Mahdi paused before opening the door.

'Who is it?' He demanded. The reply came swiftly.

'Package delivery to suite 7; and I need a signature please.'

Al-Mahdi thought for a moment. He looked through the door's spy hole. He could see only one man, dressed in a black bomber jacket and blue jeans standing in the corridor outside, who appeared to be busy looking from the address on the package to the number on his door. The man had a green oval medallion hanging around his neck, similar to the one worn by the taxi driver, who had brought him from Heathrow several days earlier.

'Who is the package for, and where is it from?'

369

There was a pause. Al-Mahdi continued observing the man through the spy hole. He saw him turn the jiffy bag over and shrug to himself.

'Sorry, it doesn't say, just says suite 7.' Al-Mahdi relaxed slightly. It seemed innocent enough. He unlocked the door and opened it.

'Who are you?' Demanded Al-Mahdi.

'I'm a cabbie mate; I got this job off the radio. Pick up from a tourist firm in Piccadilly and deliver to suite 7, Dorchester hotel. Compliments of the management, I suppose?'

Al-Mahdi nodded and opened the package. It was full of brochures advertising London attractions.

'Very well.' He said, and moved to close the door.

'Sorry Guv, can you sign here please?'

Pat's heart was racing as he rode the elevator down to the exclusive hotel's lobby. He had bought the jiffy bag earlier, and had filled it with freely available colour brochures from the London Hilton before driving the short distance back up Park Lane to the Dorchester. His cab drivers badge had easily got him past the hotel's front desk. It was a common occurrence, the reception staff were perfectly used to London cabbies popping into the hotel, and making small deliveries to their guests. A signature confirming delivery was also quite a normal practice, as the contents could sometimes be of important commercial or business value.

When the suite door had opened, Pat's blood felt as though it had turned to ice in his veins. He had recognised Al-Mahdi instantly. It had taken a supreme effort not to show any emotion or reaction. Although he had expected to see the face of Sally's attacker, he had been confronted with much more than he had bargained for. He had to forget Sally for now; this had to be phoned in. Taking the steps outside the hotel three at a time, he sprinted back into his taxi, which was parked at the back end of the Dorchester's rank. He thought for a moment, and then dialled a number on his cell phone. Pat recognised the voice of the Chief Clerk, who worked in the Orderly room at 21 SAS. He said.

'Hallo Stan, its Pat Farrell. Can you put me through to the Adjutant, quickly please?'

The white van backed slowly into the small garage which was attached to the side of the Al-Qaeda safe house. The Syrian switched off the engine.

371

'Shut the doors quickly. 'He ordered, climbing down from the driver's seat.

'Did your contacts provide what we wanted?' One of the young men asked expectantly as he bolted the two garage doors together.

'Yes, everything you will need is in the back of the van.'

The young man smiled, failing to suppress his excitement. At the Syrians first meeting of the day, the final arrangements for the bomb's delivery had been agreed with Al-Mahdi. He would deliver the device and trigger, within two hours of receiving confirmation that the balance of his payment had been received by his bank in Switzerland. The money would be transferred from a holding account to Al-Mahdi when a coded message was given to one of the Bank's Directors by the Syrian. That would not be done until the Syrian physically took possession of the bomb and detonator.

The second meeting later that morning was with his Chechen suppliers in London's East End. It had gone well too, thought the Quartermaster. He knew the East Europeans by reputation to be very dangerous men, willing to cut throats or shoot anyone suspected of double cross. He had handed over a briefcase full of cash to them, when the order was fulfilled. To the hard faced Chechens, this was purely a business transaction, where no questions were ever asked of the customer. An order was placed, the money was paid, and the goods were delivered. That was the end of the matter as far as they were concerned.

Since the fall of the Iron Curtain, despite the best efforts of Interpol and numerous national police forces, shipping guns and ammunition to Europe's underworld had become a highly lucrative business. The Chechen Mafia reasoned that after all, money was money, wherever it came from. Guns were a highly sought after commodity, of great value, much the same as women imported for prostitution, people trafficking operations or drug smuggling.

The Syrian watched as the boxes were unloaded and carried through the connecting door into the house. He had carefully checked the guns before paying for them. When he was satisfied that they were genuine, and would work properly when the time came, he had given the Chechen the briefcase. The money was quickly counted. With a curt nod, the deal was concluded. The van now stood empty, and the terrorists were assembled in the largest room downstairs. The Syrian nodded to two of his men.

373

'Go upstairs and prepare the camera.' To the others he said.

'In the wooden boxes are 500 rounds of ammunition. Take them out, and load all the magazines. When you have finished we will begin recording your martyrdom videos.'

These films would be released to the world's media tomorrow afternoon, immediately after the detonation, when the centre of London had been reduced to a smoking, radioactive funeral pyre.

Al-Mahdi received the call he was expecting from Switzerland shortly after five that evening. His banker, Herr Borgman confirmed the sum of $45,000.000.00 had arrived, and was now, as agreed, held on one of the bank's special escrow accounts, pending the call from Mr Alhassen's customer, who would clear the final transfer of funds into his personal account. Al-Mahdi smiled as he replaced the receiver.

'The fools,' he thought, 'if they only knew what was about to happen.' He walked to his suitcase, and extracted some papers. Finding the telephone number he required, he dialled the transport company who had collected and moved his shipment from Felixstowe harbour to their outer London hub.

Commander Roebottom said.

'Thank you for coming at such short notice Ladies and Gentlemen. There has been a development of the utmost gravity in the Gilgamesh business, which requires our immediate attention. Following the telephone call earlier today from a member of 21 SAS, we have found Al-Mahdi, the man who stole the Iraqi bomb.'

There were excited gasps around the table, among the Heads of Britain's security agencies.

'Through an extraordinary stroke of luck, he was identified, due to another entirely separate matter, by one of Brigadier Lethbridge's people, and is presently staying at the Dorchester hotel in Mayfair, under the assumed name of Abbas Jassim Ali. We contacted MI5, who have instigated a high level surveillance operation on him. The latest report has him still in the hotel, but they intercepted the following telephone call about an hour ago.' He nodded to his assistant, who switched on a tape recorder.

'This is Mr Ali from Al-Hassan's Antiquities; you are holding a consignment for us in your London depot.' He read the consignment number to the clerk. 'There has

375

been a minor charge to our requirements. The British Museum is not quite ready to receive delivery, so I need the shipment made instead to our warehouse in Ealing. Please arrange delivery for 10'oclock tomorrow morning to Unit 16, Croft Industrial estate, Brookman road, Ealing.'

The clerk confirmed the address, reading it back to Al-Mahdi.

'That is correct. At 10 o'clock tomorrow then. Goodbye.'

Commander Roebottom's aide switched off the recorder. There were looks of collective relief on the faces of his audience.

'So there we have it. 'The Special Branch chief said. 'We now have Al-Mahdi pinpointed, the current location of the bomb, and its delivery address tomorrow. I am assuming that Al-Mahdi is not planning on exploding the damn thing himself. Judging from his current luxurious lifestyle, he has recently come into a very large amount of money, and is planning I think, on spending it over a very long time in the future.'

There were several grim smiles around the table.

'No, I think the final detonation is the job of our missing sleeper, Muhammad Saleem Rana. With his scientific background, I believe he is the trigger man. I am also assuming that the sleeper has the backup of a full terrorist cell, of unknown size behind him. Given the cost to Al-Qaeda and the importance of the entire operation, we must assume they are armed, and willing to die to protect the bomb.'

Commander Roebottom nodded towards Brigadier Lethbridge.

'Perhaps you would like to pick it up from here Brigadier?'

The SAS Brigade Commander nodded.

'Thank you Commander. My people are looking at the plans of the building within the industrial estate now, and we will formulate our strategy accordingly. I am due to brief the Prime Minister and his COBRA emergency committee at 07.00 hours tomorrow morning on our final attack plan. If they agree and accept everything, and hand control of the situation over to us, we will implement our attack on or around the time the bomb is delivered to the terrorists. Out timescale is very short, but we will close down the entire operation at the industrial unit tomorrow morning in Ealing.'

One of the security chiefs faces clouded with concern.

'Surely you're not going to allow delivery of the bomb to the terrorists, and then try and lift the whole lot?'

Brigadier Lethbridge chewed his bottom lip for a moment as he contemplated the question. He fixed the intelligence head with his steely blue eyes.

'No,' he said firmly. 'That's not quite what we have in mind at all.'

Twenty minutes before Commander Roebottom stood up and gave his appreciation of the latest developments concerning the impending terrorist threat, Spike Morris and Danny Thomas were standing at the bar of their local pub, chatting to two pretty girls they had just picked up. When the girls decided they needed to visit the Ladies, Spike and Danny exchanged quizzical glances.

'Why do they always go together?' Danny wondered aloud.

'Dunno mate, it's one of life's little mysteries, but it looks like we're both on a promise?' Spike said with a broad grin.

'Yep. Let's get a few more pints in, and then take them out for an Indian, down at the Star of Bengal.'

His friend nodded his agreement. 'Sounds like a plan. It's good to me buddy.'

As Danny put his pint glass down on the bar's counter, his bleeper went off.

'Oh shit, not now!' He said looking horrified. 'They can't be serious?'

Spike grinned, and was about to say something sarcastic when his bleeper went off too.

'Oh bugger, and me!' He said miserably, switching it off and draining his glass. He caught the eye of the barmaid.

'Rosie? Do us a favour and tell those two lovelies something's come up, will you?'

Rosie smiled.

'Tell them we're really sorry, and we'll catch up with them another time.'

The plump barmaid sighed theatrically and nodded. Both young men pulled on their jackets as they headed through the door, into the cold night air.

Chapter Thirty One

- Op.Windmill -

Ealing – West London

01.00 Hours: - Operation Windmill

The lights blazed throughout the Territorial SAS base in Chelsea. Everywhere within D block, HQ squadron support teams scurried about the business of mounting a co-ordinated attack on a highly dangerous terrorist cell in nine hours' time. Individual radios and their battery levels were being checked, ammunition was being ferried up from the ammunition bunker, and the quartermaster's stores were being readied. All sixteen members of Two Troop were currently seated over in the Training Wing block, receiving an initial but detailed briefing on the general situation, including a mass of background intelligence from senior MI5 and MI6 officers.

Once the historical and global picture was painted, Brigadier Lethbridge's second in command, Colonel Hunter, outlined the ground Two Troop would be working in, in just a few short hours time. He began by describing the industrial estate's location, and its relationship within the general area of Ealing, using a large scale map projected onto a white screen at the front of the classroom. Satisfied with the general explanation, he switched to a more detailed map of the industrial estate. Having explained the maps scale, he continued.

'The estate's main entrance is on the Southwest side next to Brook Road here,' he said. 'There are a total of twenty six individual business units which make up the Croft Industrial estate. They are grouped together in three to five units per block. There are a total of seven blocks in the immediate area we are concerned with; the biggest are two manufacturing units. One makes plastic fittings for the motor industry, and the other makes paper cups.'

Colonel Hunter pointed them out on the screen using a laser pen.

'There are seven smaller storage and distribution units. They range from motor parts factors to coffee vending machine suppliers. Two units are currently empty, and finally, we have the unit we are interested in. '

He paused for a moment as he checked the marked map on the desk in front of him.

'This is the one. 'He said. 'Number 16.' He circled the unit on the screen with his light pen.

'As you can see from the map, it's at the back end of the estate, over by the railway tracks which, in fact, comprises part of the outdoor section of the London Underground Central Line. The boundary is a 6 foot chain link fence, and Ealing Broadway station is about 600 metres away, over here.'

Once again, using the light pen, he indicated the direction of the western terminus of the underground's Central line.

'As you can see, the estate is surrounded on three sides by residential housing. Any questions, so far?'

A question came from one of the Troops two snipers.

'I'm assuming me and Frankie will be covering the outside area during the assault Boss, but is there an embankment along the railway line? If so, is there any dead ground behind it?'

Colonel Hunter looked at his maps for a moment.

'Good question Terry. The maps I've got don't show enough detail to answer that one, but I'll have the answer for you in about two hours, when the Troop gets a situation update, and we review individual tasks.'

Terry nodded.

'OK, Roger that Boss.'

Colonel Hunter went on to outline the general attack plan of Operation Windmill, and then handed over to the Quartermaster, who walked to the front of the classroom carrying what looked like a padded body warmer. With a smug smile on his face, he said.

'Right lads, as you all know, the body armour you've been training with is heavy and inflexible. I'm delighted to say that I've got something special for you which has just finished its Ministry of Defence acceptance trials, and arrived from Hereford two days ago.'

Without apparent effort, he lifted the sleeveless black vest onto the table and undid the front Velcro fastening.

'This Gentlemen, is called Dragon Skin. It's the latest body armour from an American company called Pinnacle Armour. Its incredible protection comes from a thin skin of small, over laced and interconnected composite ceramic and titanium discs, which sit under the outer layer of normal material. It's lightweight, only about 7lbs, protects all your vital organs, and it has the added advantage of being extremely flexible. I've seen the test videos, and this kit will even stop high velocity 7.62 armour-piercing rounds, fired from point blank range. During part of the demonstration, Pinnacle placed a shot up vest on the ground with a fragmentation grenade under it. They blew the grenade electrically, and nothing went through into the test dummy.'

There were whistles of appreciation from the troop. Spike looked at his mate Danny with a broad grin.

'Terrific, I'll take one!' Was all he said.

'We'll issue a vest to each of you at the end of the briefings, and you can start getting used to them by wearing them when you start rehearsals shortly. '

02.00 Hrs: Operation Windmill.

After being issued with their new protective body armour, Two Troop moved back to the main building, where they changed into their black, fireproofed boiler suits and military jump boots. Wearing their belts kit and body armour, they made their way down to the armoury, and signed out their weapons. Each man was issued with his Heckler & Koch MP5 submachine gun, and the usual backup 9mm Browning semi-automatic pistol.

'Straight back up to the main drill hall lads when you're done here lads, and we'll start the practice walk throughs.' Said Pat, as his Troop filed through the armoury.

Upstairs, the full-scale warehouse layout had been marked out with white tape, which was pinned securely to the wooden floor. Pat stood in the middle of the large drill hall, with the Troop sitting on the floor around him with their weapons cradled in their laps.

'We've no time to build a full-scale replica of Unit 16 lads, so the mine tape has got to represent the target buildings walls. The window locations are marked with the tape being over sprayed in red, and the doors locations in green. To orientate you all, the loading bay at the front of the building is over there. 'He said, pointing towards the back of the hall.

'Terry and Frankie, as you know, you're providing sniper cover outside, but I want you to watch everything, so you know what's happening during the assault.'

Both men nodded.

'There are three entrances. 'Pat said. "One's the loading bay with a big metal roller door for vehicle access. The second is the normal pedestrian door beside it on the left, and there's an emergency fire escape door at the back of the building.' He added, pointing in the opposite direction across the hall.

'Part of the plan is for the assault teams to go in using explosive entry from front and back simultaneously. I want you Charlie, with Dinger, to smash in the skylight on the roof when the attack starts, and drop eight CS gas grenades through the hole. Try and spread them out as much as you can, right?'

The SAS Corporal nodded 'Yeah, no problem Pat. We'll have the lot in as soon as the doors are blown.'

'Fine.' Replied Pat. 'Once they're in, you can give us some fire support from the roof.'

Pat looked at his men. 'I've split you into two assault groups of four. I'm calling them front and back, to keep things simple. 'Yorkie, you'll lead your patrol in as the front assault group, and Don, you'll lead the back assault team, coming in through the rear.'

Spike sniggered 'Nothing new there then Don?'

The burley Scottish Corporal glared at the young Trooper as the rest of the Troop laughed.

'Watch it you!' He growled.

'Sorry Corporal.' Said Spike, intent suddenly on inspecting his boots.

'All right, settle down lads.' Pat said, holding up his hand. 'I know you're all keyed up, but this is serious, and there's still a lot to cover, so belt up and listen.'

03.00 Hrs: - Operation Windmill

Business had been tough for Ted Williams over the last few months. The economy was locked in a downturn, and heading towards a recession. His company's last quarter sales figures were very disappointing; down nearly 14% compared to the previous year, and as a result, his business was beginning to struggle. Getting a call from Ealing Police station at 2.30 in the morning hadn't helped to lighten his mood, as he walked yawning into the station's entrance.

'I'm Ted Williams from Rapid Coffee Supplies over on the Croft Industrial estate. I got a call from you lot about half an hour ago, saying I had to come in, because something had happened near my unit?'

The desk sergeant behind the counter contemplated the bleary eyed man standing in front of him for a moment, then nodded towards the line of chairs behind him.

'If you take a seat Mr Williams, I'll get someone to come down to talk to you.'

As Ted sat down, Basil Hues from the plastics firm a couple of doors up from Ted's unit walked in.

'Hallo Bas, did they get you out of bed too?'

Ten minutes later, Ted Williams and Basil Hues stood up and shook hands with the smartly dressed civilian, and the police Superintendent, in one of the small interview rooms inside Ealing Police station. The civilian, who had identified himself simply as Mr Brown, had explained that their keys and alarm codes were needed, due to a suspected terrorist threat in the industrial unit, situated between them both on the Croft estate.

'Thank you for your co-operation Gentlemen. Please make sure you stop your people coming into work this morning. The gas leak story should do the job, and we'll let you know as soon as it's clear for you to go back to work. Please don't discuss this business with your wives or anyone else. Security is vital in these cases, and we must keep everything under wraps for now. I'm sure you understand?'

As the two men were shown out of the Police station by the Superintendent, William Lawrence handed the keys and codes to the Watchers surveillance team leader.

'Right Jimmy, get your people over to the Croft estate, and start putting your equipment into both their units.'

04.00 Hrs: - Operation Windmill

'OK, that last walkthrough was good; everyone got it exactly right. Now we've got to start speeding things up. When the doors go in, I want everyone inside the building with within six seconds.' Pat looked at his men. 'Surprise will come with the thunderclap of the explosions. Anyone inside the building will be stunned by the concussion for several seconds, that's why we need speed. Once they realise what's happening, we've lost the edge unless we're in really quick.'

Two Troop eagerly nodded their understanding.

'The guys with the frame charges have got to get them into position quickly and quietly, so they're ready when we get the final Go from the Boss. Any questions about anything so far?... No? Right then, back to work.'

Shortly after 4am, in their safe house in Loveday Road, Rana moved around the upstairs bedrooms, shaking each cell member in turn, and whispering.

'Wake up man; it's time for dawn prayers.'

The excitement he felt at his immanent ascension to Paradise had caused him to sleep only fitfully during the night. As his moved around the group, he slowly passed a string of thirty-three Shubha prayer beads through his fingers, muttering a different name of Allah, as he touched each bead in turn. On this special day, the beads made him feel even closer to God than ever before. He wanted to be in a perfect state of Islamic grace when the time came, so it was imperative that the ritual of early morning prayers were followed to the letter.

05.00 Hrs: - Operation Windmill

'Right lads, you all know your jobs, and you know exactly what each of you has to do. It's time to get some scoff. You may not feel like it,' said Pat with a grin,' but trust me, you'll feel better when you've eaten something, and got a hot brew inside yourself.'

'Too late to apply for a transfer to the Cavalry I suppose?' said Mickey Green.

'Never too late Mickey, probably take you about a month mate.'

Mickey grinned... 'OK Pat... Just thought I'd ask. '

When breakfast was over, Two Troop went to draw their ammunition while Pat and two of the Troop started building the frame charges which would, when the assault began, blow in the doors of the unit. Using the dimensions lifted from the industrial block's scale drawings, Pat cut the narrow plastic bars to size. Screwing the pieces firmly together, and cross bracing the corners Pat quickly had a pair of sturdy oblong frames, which would fit neatly around the edges of the unit's doors. Satisfied that the frames were ready, Pat and his men began filling the pre-formed hollow channels within each frame with plastic explosive. Similar to Semtex and American C4 plastic explosive, the British army used its own PE4 for demolition. The explosion would be more than powerful enough to easily cut through heavy steel plate, so the wooden doors would simply disintegrate under the powerful blast.

391

'Pack it in tight boys; you know the drill, don't leave any air gaps.' Both men nodded.

Pre-packed in fat 8oz sticks, the PE4 was completely stable and safe to handle, but had to be kneaded repeatedly to make it pliable.

'We'll fit the detonators just before kick-off, so leave me a good gap at the bottom.'

When the filling was finished, the two troopers bound the frames with masking tape to keep the explosives in place. Pat made a last inspection. Nodding with satisfaction that the frame charges would do the job, Pat rubbed his hand over his face and said.

'OK, good job, you're moving out a 06.00 hours, so get away now, sort your ammunition out, then take a break with the rest of the lads. Tell Spike, Danny and Mickey Green to report to me.'

While he waited for his troopers, Pat thought over his own special part in the assault. He rubbed his chin absently. It worked once before, long ago I suppose, but it's been quite a while since anyone pulled it off,' he thought ruefully as he waited.

06.00 Hrs: - Operation Windmill

With a full Battalion of the Irish Guards stationed in barracks close by in Lower Sloane Street, it was not unusual for army vehicles to use the almost deserted roads around Chelsea in the early hours of most mornings. The Guards regularly sent vehicles to their Ceremonial duty stations at Buckingham Palace, the Tower of London and Windsor castle. The few civilian delivery vans going about their business, paid scant regard to the small three vehicle military convoy driving up Sloane Street towards Knightsbridge. Two Troop's Squadron Commander, Major Peter Howard sat beside his driver in the lead Land Rover, navigating with a dog-eared London street map. Both men were bare headed, and their camouflage uniforms bore no badges or insignia.

'We'll head up towards Shepherds Bush first, so take a left at the top and head towards the Albert Hall.'

His driver nodded. 'Roger that, Boss.'

At the end of Sloane Street, The Land Rover turned towards Kensington, closely followed by two of his squadrons'4 ton lorries.

'We need to be in Ealing before seven.' He said, glancing at his watch, 'Better step on it.'

08.00 Hrs: - Operation Windmill

A nondescript white van entered the Croft estate shortly after 8am. It drove slowly around the car park, and coasted quietly through the warren of industrial units. As it reached the chain link security fence at the far side of the estate, it turned, and began to prowl its way cautiously back towards unit 16. Satisfied that all was in order, the Syrian ordered the van's driver to stop, as they reached their unit. He turned to the men sitting in the back of the van, and ordered them to stay where they were, until the van was safely inside. Climbing down from the van, he unlocked the access door, and stepped inside. Quickly checking the unit was deserted; he unlocked and opened the steel roller shutter. Urgently waving the van inside, the Syrian slammed the rumbling shutter down firmly behind it.

Although he was unaware of it, the Syrian was not the only one watching the arrival of his men inside the building. In the operations room on the second floor of Ealing Police station, several senior Security officers were gathered round television screens which William

394

Lawrence's men had installed several hours previously. Two hidden cameras fed the screens, beaming live feed images of the terrorists, as they climbed down from the rear of the van. When the MI5 technicians had entered the adjacent units several hours previously, they had quietly drilled through the connecting walls, and fitted tiny microphones and fibre optic surveillance cameras, which fed the real time images directly into the police Control room.

'There's eight of the bastards!' Major Howard said, his face grim. The men watched as one of the terrorists withdrew two large sports bags from the van, and began distributing weapons to each member of the cell.

'Yes, I'm afraid we thought they would be armed.' David Lawrence replied. 'With an operation of this magnitude, Al-Qaeda was bound to do their utmost to protect their investment. It looks like a peaceful resolution is highly unlikely Major Howard, and your men will have to deal with the situation.'

Behind them, a telephone rang. One of David Lawrence's men picked up the receiver. He listened for a moment and said.

'Yes, I understand, I'll pass the message on.' He turned to the others. 'Al-Mahdi has left the Dorchester in a taxi. Two of our vehicles are following him. He collected a suitcase from Paddington Station's left luggage office, and he's just passed Lancaster gate, heading west along the Bayswater road. His tail will keep us informed of his location, but it looks like he's heading towards Ealing. '

Chapter Thirty Two

- COBRA -

Whitehall London

'The COBRA Committee is the United Kingdom's emergency response team for national crises. It is an acronym for - Cabinet Office Briefing Room 'A'.

Chaired by the Prime Minister, its membership includes the head of MI5, the Metropolitan Police Commissioner, and the Civil Contingencies Secretariat, as well as other senior Ministers.

In the heavily protected underground bunker in Westminster, Brigadier Lethbridge had finished briefing the COBRA committee on the details of Operation Windmill. If the Prime Minister decided to hand over the situation to the army, the results would be violent and bloody. One of the Ministers, responsible for London, and well known in the media as a left wing pacifist said.

'Surely even at this late stage, we can avert the necessity of a bloodbath? Clearly, the alleged suspects are walking into a trap, and the Brigadiers men are going to execute them. Humanity demands that they must be given an opportunity to surrender, and then the Courts can deal with them.'

The Prime Minister nodded towards his Minister, noting the other nodding heads among the Committee. He thought for a moment

'What is your opinion on that James?' He inquired, looking towards MI5's Director General.

'Well Prime Minister, it is our experience that normally, suspected members of Al-Qaeda cells will surrender themselves quite quietly when Commander Roebottom's Special Branch officers move in and arrest them. They tend to be unarmed, low grade foot soldiers, and have little fight in them when they are lifted. It's true that they have been known to put up a struggle, but it is a rare occurrence.'

Commander Roebottom interrupted.

'Aye, but I lost two of my men in Dulwich recently, and another officer, stabbed and killed during a raid on a Manchester flat at the beginning of 2003. My men were searching a house, looking to arrest an Algerian suspect. During the course of the search, one of the occupants of the house managed to get free, snatch up a kitchen knife and stabbed a number of my officers,' he said. 'One died from his injuries.'

The Prime Minister nodded 'Yes, I remember the incident Commander.' He said sadly 'It was a tragic loss.'

MI5's chief looked at the Prime Minister and said.

'It is my considered opinion Prime Minister, that we are dealing with a totally different entity here. From the pictures we have received from Ealing, our friends at Vauxhall Cross believe they have identified six of the men so far. They suggest that four may be currently wanted in Kenya and Somalia for involvement in Al-Qaeda related bombings, which have killed hundreds of innocent civilians in both countries. One is Rana of course, our sleeper from Leeds, who we believe to have received training in an Al-Qaeda camp in Afghanistan. I think it fair to assume he has been brainwashed, like so many other suicide bombers. Finally, there appears to be a Syrian man named Abu Sallim, who is suspected of being a major player for logistics within Al-Qaeda. The Americans want him badly; they suspect he was involved with terrorist procurement in the United States prior to 9/11 attack.'

The Director General looked across the table to the Minister of London affairs.

'These men already have plenty of blood on their hands Peter, they are heavily armed, and have been selected no doubt because they are more than willing to die to protect the bomb, and its trigger man. We also have Al-Mahdi of course, who we suspect of being at the very least, directly involved for the deaths of thousands of innocent Kurds in Iraq.'

The Prime Minister paused for a moment. He must tread carefully. He suspected, although internal enquiries had failed to find those responsible, that several leaks which had severely embarrassed his Government in the national press over the past few years, had originated from the offices of the Minister for London.

With an election due in eighteen months, he had no wish to alienate 2 million potential Muslim voters in the UK, with an alleged 'shoot to kill' policy. If there were deaths as a result of this business, a Coroners Court would ask too many embarrassing questions, which might ultimately jeopardize his position, and trigger a vote of confidence against him in the House of Commons. The party's majority was already slim in certain key marginal constituencies, and his political enemies within his own party, would relish the opportunity to stab him, when his back was turned.

'Et tu Brute?' He thought miserably. The ensuing political bloodbath might finish him. Suppressing a shudder he looked towards the Director of the SAS, hoping to find some support for the decision he must make shortly.

'Brigadier Lethbridge, drawing on your considerable experience in these matters, what is your opinion on the prospect of getting them to surrender, and avoiding unnecessary casualties?' he asked.

The Brigadier stroked his chin thoughtfully, and then answered.

'Well Prime Minister, that's a very good question. Strangely enough, I discussed just this matter, when I was invited to a Sergeants Mess function in Hereford recently.' The Brigadier knew these damned politicians wouldn't like what he was about to say, but he was going to say it anyway.

'As you are all aware, the SAS has fought many times against terrorists. They can be broadly be broken down into two categories, fanatics, and non-fanatics. You will no doubt remember the London Balcombe Street siege in '75? A gang of armed IRA bombers were surrounded in a flat in Marylebone, with nowhere left to run. They had taken an elderly couple hostage, but were eventually told by the police negotiator that their options had run out, and the SAS were going to be sent in, and they would all die. Directly as a result of that call, they

401

surrendered shortly afterwards. They were hard-core, professional Irish Terrorists, but had no desire to meet their maker early. They were deeply committed to their cause of course, but not fanatical in the true sense which we are now faced with.' The Brigadier scratched the side of his nose, then he continued.

'The men currently waiting for the bomb in the Croft estate are different from the IRA, because they are true fanatics. They have all been radicalised by their past experiences, no doubt with the help of the Camps in Pakistan and Afghanistan. They are currently waiting for a weapon which they are absolutely committed to using, to kill millions of innocent people, whose only crime is that they happen to live in London. These men are utterly devoid of any form of compassion towards their victims, be they men, women or children. They are devout Muslim soldiers, who have been utterly convinced that they will make it to Paradise for evermore, if they die, fighting and killing the hated Kafir, in their Great Holy war. Given the choice of rotting in a British prison for the rest of their lives, or taking the fast track to heaven, I can only suggest one conclusion. They cannot be reasoned with; they cannot be diverted from their aims or beliefs…. In my experience, and those of the men who work for me, there is ultimately only one way you are going to avoid the friendly casualties which will surely come... and that Ladies and Gentlemen, I'm afraid,... is to kill them all!'

Major Peter Howard had just finished checking with his men by radio, that everything was set and ready when the telephone call came from Whitehall.

'Peter Howard. 'He said casually. He listened for several moments before he suddenly exploded.

'They have got to be fucking joking Boss!' He said angrily, staring in utter disbelief at the mobile cell phone.

'We lose the element of surprise so those bastards get the chance to chuck in the towel?' He shook his head, feeling a knot forming in the pit of his stomach. 'My men have got to go up against eight heavily armed, fanatical nut cases, but only after warning them that we're outside first?'

'I'm afraid that's about the size of it Peter.' Brigadier Lethbridge replied from beneath Whitehall. 'The final decision came from the very top. These are the Prime Ministers direct orders. The COBRA Committee voted, and recommended to him that we give them a chance to surrender. Unfortunately, he agreed with them. Personally, I think it's ridiculous, but those are our orders, and sadly, that's how we must play it.'

403

There was silence at both ends for several moments.

'Alright Sir, I'll tell the men.' Major Howard said slowly, fighting to regain his composure. 'I assume the rest of the plan has been accepted?'

The Brigadier sighed. 'Yes Peter, if they make a fight of it, you're to go straight in, and the assault plan will be implemented exactly as we planned it. Just make absolutely sure they fire first ...do you understand me?' There was another pause. Major Howard smiled as he said.

'Yes sir, I believe I understand you completely.'

Shortly before 10 O'clock Al-Mahdi sat in the back of the taxi, as it approached the Croft estate. Sitting on the floor in front of him was the suitcase, containing the trigger to the bomb. In his breast pocket, were his French passport, and a first class, one-way Cathy Pacific airline ticket to Hong Kong.

He had been deeply concerned throughout his planning that the Al-Qaeda men would double-cross him, and had removed the trigger the day after the statue and its base had cleared customs, and been delivered to the London hub. He had temporarily hidden it at Paddington Station.

His flight was due to leave Heathrow at 2 o'clock that afternoon; his timings had been carefully planned. Al-Mahdi would leave the taxi just before arriving at the rendezvous point, keeping the trigger device in the cab. He would meet with his customers, and wait for the bomb to be delivered at 10 O'clock.

Only when he received confirmation that the balance had been transferred into his account in Switzerland, would he hand over the trigger. The taxi would then take him directly on to Heathrow. His driver had agreed the diversion to Ealing, and then on to the airport, perfectly happy with the bonus he had been offered, and glad to be clear of London's congested traffic for the morning. Al-Mahdi smiled to himself. He would be quite safe, and long gone before those Al-Qaeda madmen exploded the bomb in the centre of London.

Chapter Thirty Three

The Killing Fields

Brook Road - Ealing

It was close to 09.50 hrs when William Lawrence 's radio crackled into life.

'Yankee one. Tango one is Out, Out, and approaching the Croft estate main gate on foot.' The MI5 Watcher released his send switch as his car pulled in and stopped at the corner of Brookman road.

'Roger Yankee one, this is Sierra 1, we have the trigger. Confirm he is not carrying his suitcase?'

'Yankee one. No; that's a negative, it must still be in the taxi.'

Commander Roebottom whispered to William Lawrence urgently.

'Tell him to break off and watch the taxi, but don't approach it yet.'

Fishburn nodded and relayed the message, using his radio link from the Command centre in Ealing Police station.

'I'll pass on Al-Mahdi's arrival to my men.' Major Howard said.

As soon as they arrived in Ealing, having received the all clear from the Watchers, the SAS assault teams had deployed straight into the Croft estate. Carrying their frame charges with them, one team had concealed themselves in the coffee distributors inside unit 15, while the other quickly disappeared into unit 17.

Their orders were to lay low and keep out of sight until they received the Go command from Major Howard. The assault group's two snipers were hidden in adjacent buildings on the estate, with a clear field of fire of the front of the target block. Charlie and Dinger had followed their part in the assault plan, climbing onto the flat roof of the block, and were currently lying prone and still near Unit 16's skylight. Major Howard warned his men of Al-Mahdi's arrival, and received a double click, as he asked each team in turn if they understood. He thumbed the microphone once more.

'All stations this is Alpha one, roger that...Stand By. Stand By. *Out.*"

Inside unit 15, Yorkie tapped his knee gently. His men looked at him, as he took out his respirator, and held it to his head. The others understood, and following his example, fitted them in place. They had all heard the order to 'Stand By' via their individual earpieces. Tom Shelby was closest to the door. It was his job to go outside and place the frame charge, when they got the word. He looked down at his gloved hand. It was shaking. Like the others, the tension was pumping an overdose of adrenalin through his bloodstream. Moments before he had made his first parachute jump at RAF Brize Norton, he had felt similar feelings; a churning fusion of raw excitement and cold fear. He knew his nerves wouldn't stop him doing his job though. He had lost count of the practice assaults he had made in the past months; it was just that this time, like Dulwich, it was a real deal. Yorkie looked across at the young Trooper; he had seen Tom looking at his shaking hand. Yorkie tapped his thigh again. When Tom looked towards his team leader, Yorkie gave him a quizzical look, and a thumbs up sign. Tom smiled back, and returned the signal with a nod, and a nervous grin.

Al-Mahdi knocked on the door of Unit 16. It opened several inches.

'What do you want?' Said the voice behind the door.

'I am Colonel Jalal Al-Mahdi, formerly of the Iraqi army and the Mukhabarat, and I have some merchandise for you. I believe you are expecting me?'

The door opened wide enough for him to enter, and Al-Mahdi stepped inside.

Commander Roebottom watched the screen as Al-Mahdi met the terrorists inside the Unit.

'He wouldn't be here if the deal was already completed. 'He said rubbing his chin. The hidden microphones picked up the flow of rapid Arabic between Al-Mahdi and the Syrian.

'What are they saying Abbas?' His interpreter listened intently into his earphones.

'Al-Mahdi is saying that... the item is close by, and he will hand it over, when the call is made, and ...when the money is transferred Sir. The other man is saying ...err...Yes that is as agreed.'

Abbas held his hand to his earpiece.

'Now he's telling Al-Mahdi to wait over in the corner, out of their way until the bomb arrives.'

Commander Roebottom stared intently at the screens.

'Christ, he must have the bloody trigger in the taxi.' He looked at William Lawrence. 'Tell your men to lift the suitcase now David, and get the driver clear.'

Al-Mahdi reached into his expensive Burberry overcoat, and removed an ornate gold cigarette case. He extracted and lit one of his favourite Turkish cigarettes, using the matching lighter he had bought in Mayfair's fashionable Bond Street, the previous day. His cold eyes appraised the men inside the unit, as they nervously waited for the lorry, which would soon bring them one step closer to Paradise. Al-Mahdi listened as he watched; some men spoke rapidly to each other, in raised voices which betrayed their heightened state of tension. Others, he noticed, stood immobile and alone, muttering quietly to themselves, as they nervously fingered their prayer beads and weapons. Al-Mahdi knew only too well that he must stand quietly, to avoid causing even a single spark which might ignite the powder keg of charged emotion around him. He must be very careful; this was a dangerous place, at a very dangerous time...

Major Howard checked his watch. It was 9.55 hrs.

'It's time Commander.' He said gravely. Commander Roebottom looked at his own watch and nodded.

'Aye, you're right.'

It was almost time to close the terrorists down. He nodded to his aide. 'Get the last roads blocked off, and send the lorry on its way.'

For the last hour, the local police had been quietly evacuating the immediate area around the Croft estate. Grumbling residents had been extracted from their homes and ferried to the safety of the local Town Hall, having been informed of a highly dangerous gas leak. The signals between West Acton station to Ealing Broadway on the Central line had been set to red, effectively stopping any trains from passing by along the electrified tracks at the back end of the estate.

Hours earlier, when the assault plan was finalised, Peter Howard had suggested that he should drive the lorry, but Brigadier Lethbridge had immediately vetoed the idea.

'No Peter, you are responsible for co-ordinating the assault. I want you in the Control room, running the show, not risking your neck. Find a volunteer.'

411

Sandy Robertson, Pat's squadron sergeant Major agreed to take on the job. It made sense; he had a Class One Heavy Goods Vehicle license anyway, and had gained plenty of experience of Hub deliveries in his earlier years, when he drove for a delivery company. Dressed in a civilian jacket and jeans, he climbed into the lorry's cab and started its heavy diesel engine.

'Hell of a way to take a trip down memory lane.' He thought ruefully to himself, as he dipped the clutch and selected first gear.

'its coming!' hissed one of the gunmen, who had been ordered to keep watch at the window. 'It's here, the lorry. It's here!' he yelled excitedly.

The other members of the cell crowded around the window talking and whooping at each other, as the lorry pulled up outside.

'Calm down, all of you!' shouted the Syrian. 'Hide your weapons, and act like men, not feeble children.'

The chastened cell quickly obeyed, scuttling around the unit, secreting their guns wherever they could.

'Open the roller door, while I talk to the driver.' He said.

As the heavy steel roller door began to rise, he ducked under it and walked towards the driver, who was climbing down from his cab. Sandy Robertson nodded towards the Syrian, and looked down at his manifest.

'I've got two crates for you mate. I'll open the back and get them down. Where do you want them then?'

The Syrian regarded the driver coldly.

'Put them just inside the door.'

The Syrian stood at the rear of the lorry, surrounded by the others while the first packing case was unloaded. His head sat squarely in the cross hairs of the telescopic sight, mounted on Frankie Lane's sniper rifle. Frankie knew his orders were to wait until they fired first, but if there was trouble now, he would drop the first bastard he saw making a move on Sandy.

'Fuck it,' he thought. 'They can sue me afterwards'. He pressed the send switch on his throat mike. 'Alpha one, this is Alpha five, packages are being unloaded. No problems, but I have a clear shot, over.'

In the Control room, Major Howard snatched up his handset.

'Alpha one, roger that, do not engage, I say again, do not engage. *Out!*"

Frankie Lane sucked air through his teeth, and continued to watch through his hi-powered sight, as the unloading continued.

Sandy Robertson slid the dolly arms out from under the second crate. The trolley clattered noisily over the concrete as he pushed it out of the unit, and rolled it onto the hydraulic tail lift at the back to his lorry.

'Right mate, sign here, and they're all yours.' He said cheerfully, handing the shipping docket to the Syrian. Signing the form, the Syrian walked back into the unit.

'Shut the door.' He said as he walked over to Al-Mahdi.

Outside, Sandy Robertson started the lorry's engine, and pulled away from the unit.

The Syrian eyed the ex-Mukhabarat Colonel coldly.

'When I have the trigger, I will make the call, and you will be paid.' He said.

Al-Mahdi tensed'

'No!' He snapped angrily. 'It was agreed the money would be paid to me, and then I would give you the trigger.'

The Syrian smiled mirthlessly at Al-Mahdi.

'Then we must learn to trust each other brother, mustn't we?' He spoke again, without taking his eyes off Al-Mahdi. 'Ali, go with the Colonel, and bring back the device.'

Al-Mahdi glared at the Syrian, but he knew he was cornered. With so much at stake, he feared he was being double crossed, but he had to agree to the change. If he wanted to get paid, he could see no other choice.

'Very well,' he said through clenched teeth 'We will trust each other... brother.'

Al-Mahdi turned, and strode across the unit towards the front door.

'They are going to get the trigger Sir,' said their interpreter, as the men inside the Control room watched Al-Mahdi and one of the gunmen leave the Unit. Brigadier Lethbridge, who had arrived just minutes earlier, following a high speed dash from Whitchall, said.

'We'll spring the trap when those two come back, and are still out in the open.'

Al-Mahdi's instincts alerted him that something was wrong before he reached the taxi. When he had arrived, the estate was alive with vehicles entering and departing, and men working outside, around several of the buildings. Now, as he walked to the gate, there was no-one; the area was quiet and deserted. The man with him appeared not to have noticed. Ali followed slightly behind, with his machine pistol concealed under his jacket, intently concentrating on Al-Mahdi, and nothing else. As they walked up to the taxi, Al-Mahdi saw that the road outside the estate was equally deserted, and the driver was gone.

'There is something very wrong. 'He hissed, as he looked into the rear of the cab. The suitcase was gone. 'Someone has taken the trigger!' He gasped, turning sharply towards his escort, whose faced betrayed his rising panic.

'We must go back and warn the others. Quickly man, it must be a trap!'

Both men began to run back into the estate, towards unit 16. Al-Mahdi's mind churned as he ran. Without the trigger, the bomb was useless, and the chances were that they would kill him for his failure. If he entered the building, he was finished. He had to escape before it was too late.

Always fearing a double cross, he had taken what precautions he could. Suddenly slowing, he reached inside his jacket sleeve, and pulled out the cut-throat razor, which he had taped to his forearm, shortly before leaving the hotel. With a lunge, he slashed hard at the gunman's neck. Ali stumbled forward, with a sudden look of shock and surprise on his face. Instinctively, his hand went to the gaping wound on his neck, and the look on his face changed from shock to horror, as his fingers felt the powerful surge of blood pumping in rhythmic spurts from his severed jugular. He felt himself falling forward in slow motion, as his mind desperately tried to grasp what had just happened to him. Fighting to stay conscious, he saw Al-Mahdi's blazing black eyes staring down at him, and the bloody razor in his attacker's hand. With a gurgling howl of rage, he swung his submachine gun towards Al-Mahdi, and pulled the trigger...

'Shots fired, shots fired!' Yelled Frankie Lane into his throat mike, as he watched from inside his second floor observation point. He couldn't see where they had come from, or what had happened, but the burst was very close, and there was no mistaking the short vicious staccato rattle of sub machine gun fire. The assault teams had heard the gunfire too. That was the signal they had been waiting for. From inside their gasmasks, Yorkie and Don both were screaming towards their men.

'Go! Go!'

At the front and back of both adjacent units, pairs of men rushed outside and slammed their frame charges against the targets doors, simultaneously pulling the short delay igniters. The three second fuses spluttered and smoked as the SAS troopers frantically threw themselves backwards and rolled into the scant protection of the open doorways. Both deafening explosions rocked the building. Inside, the terrorists closest to the doors were blown off their feet by the blast's shock waves. One terrorist was blown through the front window. As he tried drunkenly to get to his feet, he was killed by a single shot to the head from Frankie Lane's sniper rifle. The blasts had blown the skylight into a million pieces, and within moments Charlie and Dinger were busy hurling CS gas grenades into the smoking hole in the roof, adding to the chaos below. Seconds after the doors were blown in, Pat Farrell, Spike, Danny and Mickey Green launched their part of the attack, and sprang their own surprise. Sheltered from the worst of the blasts by the thick timbers of the two crates, they heaved the wooden crate lids aside, coming into the aim as they appeared from inside the crates, and began firing in all directions at the coughing terrorists.

418

The two assault teams entered the smoking remnants of the unit's doors, moving quickly into the swirling smoke and gas filled interior. The noise was deafening as Danny and Spike both fired at one terrorist who appeared through the smoke in front of them. The impact of all sixty rounds lifted his lifeless body and threw it backwards against the far wall, where it left a long bloody smear. Pat Farrell fired a long burst into Rana, killing him instantly, after Rana had swung his submachine gun towards Yorkie Blake. Mickey Green had seen the Syrian's muzzle flashes through the smoke, and fired towards them. His bullets sparked and ricocheted harmlessly off the steel cabinet in front of him. One of Don's men saw that Mickey's bullets were having no effect, and charged towards the Syrian, firing as he ran. The Syrian screamed as the Trooper reached him, but the Trooper's gun jammed before he could take the final shot. With a curse, he threw the submachine gun down at the Syrian and drew his pistol. Two rounds double-tapped at point blank range exploded the Syrian's scull like an overripe melon. Blood and brains splattered the wall behind what was left of his head.

Two of the remaining terrorists who were sheltering behind an overturned table fired towards the

419

crates, their bullets ripping shards of wood from both of them.

One of the bullets found its mark, sending Danny spinning out of the scant cover of the crate.

'Man down!' Screamed Spike.

'Leave him!' Shouted Pat. There was nothing they could do during the fire fight.

Coughing and spluttering, with their eyes streaming from the irritant gas, the two remaining terrorists broke cover and ran towards the rear exit, only to be hit by an avalanche of fire from the rest of the Troop. The firing stopped as suddenly as it had begun.

Pat Farrell yelled 'Cease fire. Stand Still!'

Every member of the assault teams froze, their hearts still hammering, with every man breathing hard, as if he had just sprinted two hundred yards.

'Are they all unaccounted for?' Pat shouted as he clicked a fresh magazine into place.

'That's all of them Pat.' Yorkie answered.

Pat looked down at the wounded Trooper.

'Roger that. Mickey, use your medic kit and help Danny. The rest of you, check the bodies, I want a full count before I call it in.'

He climbed out of the crate.

420

Ignoring Mickey as he knelt beside his unconscious friend and began to rip open a fat field dressing, Pat's voice echoed through the unit.

'Anyone else hurt? There was silence among the team. Pat nodded, and turned towards Yorkie.

'How many dead Tangos?'

'Six inside, and one outside Pat. They're all dead.'

Pat thumbed his throat mike.

'Hallo Alpha One this is Alpha Two. Assault completed. Seven enemy dead. One friendly casualty. *Over*.
'

Standing in the Control room, Major Howard looked at the others.

'We're still missing two,' he said.

'Al-Mahdi, and one of the terrorists didn't make it back to the unit before the assault started.' He thumbed the microphone send switch.

'Alpha One this is Alpha Two. There are still two unaccounted Tangos, somewhere outside.'

The message crackled in Pat's earpiece.

'Alpha One. For God's sake find them!'

Pat and the others in his team stiffened. He acknowledged the order and spoke again into his throat mike.

421

'Hallo Alpha four and Alpha five, did you see where they went, over. '

Mickey gave no signal about Danny's condition, he was too busy. Pat desperately wanted to know if Danny was alive, but there was no time.

Both snipers answered Pat in the negative, but Frankie Lane said.

'The initial shots came from outside, close to me, over.'

Pat thought for a moment 'Roger that, both of you stay put, and keep your eyes open. We're coming out to take a look.'

Pat called to his men 'Reload and get outside, we've got to find them.' Pat allowed himself the luxury of another quick glance towards his wounded man.

It didn't look good, Danny hadn't moved.

'Mickey, stay with Danny, and radio for the medics.'

Al-Mahdi winced as he hobbled towards the deserted perimeter of the estate. The 9mm bullet had smashed through his calf, just as he had kicked the gun from Ali's dying hand. Knowing his carefully crafted plans lay in tatters; his only imperative now was to escape from the police and soldiers who would surely come after him. Fighting to control his rising panic, and pausing only to snatch up the smoking submachine gun, Al-Mahdi had thrown himself into cover as the explosions had suddenly rocked the estate, and the short, vicious fire fight had begun. Limping heavily, he used the cover of the pall of smoke which billowed and eddied around the adjacent buildings to bypass the fighting, and get himself closer to the perimeter fence. Hot tears of pain ran down his burning cheeks, as he struggled towards his only chance of escape.

Clear of the choking CS gas which still lingered inside the unit, Pat ordered his men to remove their gas masks. They began searching the immediate area outside. The troopers fanned out through the smoke, their weapons held ready. Spike found Ali's body within moments of beginning the search for the missing terrorists.

'Oh Jesus Christ! Over here Pat, quick!' Spike recoiled in revulsion at the dead man's horrific neck wound, and the wide pool of blood which surrounded the body. Pat sprinted over to where his man stood, transfixed.

'All right Spike, get a grip of yourself.' Pat cast his gaze around the body and saw the dead man's weapon was missing. There were splatters of blood on the ground, leading away from the body.

'There's a blood trail. Use your radio and recall the boys. Send the Troop after me.' Pat yelled, running into the dense smoke. 'And tell them the bastard's armed and wounded!'

Al-Mahdi's breath came in ragged gasps as he reached the chain link fence. His injured leg throbbed and burned as he desperately looked along its length, hoping to find a gap.

Beyond the fence was a mesh of high brambles and bush which would hide his escape. Seeing no other way to reach them, he began to climb, hooking his fingers through the mesh, finding strength borne out of fear and desperation. The old security fence wasn't high; less than three metres, but was crowned along its entire length with a single strand of barbed wire. Its rusty barbs snagged his coat as he pulled himself over it. Frantically ripping the material free, Al-Mahdi overbalanced, and fell heavily into the brambles on the other side. He lay gasping on the ground for a moment, as the fresh wave of agony coursed through his wounded leg. Staggering drunkenly to his feet, he pushed through the tangle of brambles and branches, suddenly breaking free of its clawing grasp.

In front of him was a steep embankment, leading down to a railway track. To his right, along the shining tracks was a line of tall signals fading into the distance, their lamps all set at red. Down to his left, was a siding, on which sat a silent, deserted train. With no cover to the right, he knew his only chance was the protection of the red train. Sliding and staggering down the embankment, he groaned with pain, as he skidded to a halt at the bottom of the cutting. Grasping his gun tightly, Al-Mahdi's feet crunched on the track's ballast as he hobbled and limped towards the protection and cover of the train.

The fresh blood trail stopped abruptly. Crouching down beside the fence, Pat Farrell listened intently, casting his head left and right, straining his senses for the slightest sound of movement in the undergrowth out in the waste ground beyond. He heard nothing, but over the fence, the vegetation was flattened and crushed, and there was clear sign that someone had very recently forced their way through the brush, without attempting to cover their tracks.

425

'Got him!' Pat thought triumphantly, as he began climbing the fence in pursuit of his fleeing quarry.

Al-Mahdi stopped between the carriages, and lent on the cold metal of the steel couplings. He was beginning to feel dizzy and exhausted. His trouser leg below the right knee was soaked with blood; it dripped slowly into a small puddle on the ground beneath him. Like a hunted animal, he shivered as he cautiously glanced back along the track, seeing sudden movement at the top of the embankment. One armed man, dressed in black was moving cautiously towards him along the top of the bank. Al-Mahdi waited, hidden between the carriages. Just a few more steps he thought, and the enemy would be almost level with him. His free hand touched his breast pocket containing his passport and ticket.

'I will kill this dog,' he thought 'and still make my escape.' He slowly raised the gun and looked along the sights. Breathing deeply, he waited a few more seconds for the target to come even closer. Muttering a curse, he pulled the trigger.

From his concealed position, Al-Mahdi's short, deafening burst hit Pat Farrell squarely in the chest, spinning him backwards into the low brush. The bolt clanged shut against an empty breach, as his gun fired the remaining rounds in the magazine. With a savage snarl of victory, Al-Mahdi limped away from the train and began to climb the steep embankment.

Panting hard, he reached the top. The body was lying spread-eagled on its back a few metres in front of him. Discarding the empty submachine gun, Al-Mahdi felt in his pocket, and pulled out the razor he had used on Ali. He cautiously advanced towards the body, but suddenly froze in astonishment, as the corpse began to move. It sat up, and pointed a gun at him. The dead man spoke to him in a horse whisper.

'Stand still, or I'll kill you!'

For a moment Al-Mahdi remained frozen. It was impossible; it made no sense. Al-Mahdi had seen the bullets hit. He had killed this man.

'No, you are dead, this cannot be?' He said, lifting the razor.

If he had known that years of military training had honed Pat Farrell's reflexes to the speed of a snapping mousetrap, in that moment, he could have saved his own life. Just obey and stand perfectly still. But Al-Mahdi didn't know, and the previous moments had reduced him to little

427

more than a wounded, frantic beast. As he came onto the balls of his feet to strike, Pat fired.

Years before, Pat's intense training on the close quarter battle ranges at Hereford had taught him that two bullets gave two chances to kill, but thirty were better. His vicelike grip held the bucking machine gun as it roared, emptying in a vicious three second burst into the centre of Al-Mahdi's chest. Al-Mahdi's face contorted and he mouthed a silent scream, as the wall of bullets smashed him backwards. Cart wheeling to the bottom of the embankment, his body bounced over the first rail, and his outstretched arm touched the inner electrified rail close beside it. His bullet-ridden torso arched as 420 volts of direct current surged through his wildly thrashing body. Sparks flared from Al-Mahdi's fingertips and eye sockets as he was enveloped in a cloud of oily black smoke, as his body flamed and burned.

As Pat stood up, he heard rapid footfalls behind him. It was Spike who reached him first. He had followed after alerting the Troop, and had been frantically climbing over the fence when he heard the distant burst of gunfire.

He stopped abruptly when he saw the burning corpse lying on the rails below. Spike looked in awe at his

Troop Sergeant. He noticed the line of ragged bullets holes which were stitched across Pat's chest. Pat's dragon skin armour had saved him.

'Christ Pat, looks like you managed to kill him... twice!'

With a wolfish grin, Pat looked away from the smoking corpse lying across the rails at the bottom of the railway embankment. He fixed his gaze the young Trooper and pointed to his chest.

'Yeah, but the bastard only killed me once.'

Epilogue

'Thanks Rosie.'

Pat lifted the brimming glasses, and carried them carefully to the table where some of his men sat, deeply engrossed in conversation. The pub's bar was crowded with the usual Friday night commuters, relaxing over a quick drink before going for their train, homeward bound for a well-earned weekend break.

Spike looked up a Pat and whispered.

'Daft, isn't it Pat. None of these buggers know how close they came a couple of weeks ago?'

Pat nodded.

'And they probably never will mate.'

The Cabinet had decided to D notice the whole affair, imposing a total reporting ban on Operation Windmill and the entire story behind it.

Pat and his men had been first to know that their role would never be publically acknowledged, but had been pleased by two other items of news, which were for SAS ears only, during Brigadier Lethbridge's debrief. He told them that B squadron's crack Seven Troop were also to be trained into the CRW role, and following the success of Windmill, the whole ethos of Shadow Squadron was to be overhauled and expanded. New training was being planned, and new equipment would be with them soon. There was even talk of medals, and a special exercise in Kenya for Two Troop, but for now, that was only rumour control.

Pat stared at Spike, and shrugged.

'Unsung heroes matey, it goes with the badge.'

Danny nodded and grinned. His arm was still heavily bandaged and remained in a sling.

'Yeah, it's bloody typical.' He said, pointing towards his injured arm.

'I can't even tell my old mum what a hero her little boy's been.'

'You pratt, you should have ducked.' Laughed Spike. 'Want another beer?'

As Pat smiled at the exchange, the crowd by the bar parted. There was movement towards them, Pat turned.

'Hallo Cornelius, how's our new intelligence liaison officer?'

To Pat's delight, Cornelius looked clear eyed and sober. He was well groomed and his voice was steady and clear.

'I'm doing very well thanks Pat, now I'm back in favour, over the river. Would you like a drink?'

Pat's eyes clouded momentarily as they flicked to the glass in Cornelius's hand.

The analyst smiled and put his free hand over the glass.

'It's just orange juice. I'm off the hard stuff. My Doctor changed my meds. and I'm feeling much, much better. I haven't touched a drop in weeks.'

Pat smiled, his face relieved.

'Good one Cornelius... You're looking smartly dressed for the end of the day?'

Cornelius suddenly looked serious.

'I'm meeting my wife for a meal in half an hour. I haven't seen her for months, but I called her today, and told her about signing the pledge.'

His face reflected his apprehension. 'She's agreed to the meet, and who knows, maybe now I'm on the wagon, I can still save my marriage, if I can patch things up with Jennifer?'

Over the background noise of the busy pub, Pat raised his glass.

'Good luck mate.'

As Cornelius smiled his gratitude and opened his mouth to reply, Pat's bleeper suddenly went off, quickly followed by the others.

'Sorry Cornelius, we've got to go. '

Pat looked at his men, who were hurriedly finishing their beer and standing up.

Cornelius sighed.

'It's all right. I understand Pat. When duty calls... '

-The End-

Also by David Black

Dark Empire

Shadow Squadron #2

Sgt Pat Farrell and Two Troop are back in action, in this dark and compelling sequel to The Great Satan!

Pat and his reserve SAS Troop are on a training exercise in Kenya when they are suddenly ordered into the primordial jungle of the Congo, on what should be a straightforward humanitarian rescue mission.

Unfortunately, nothing is straightforward in Africa. Pat and his men find themselves trapped, and facing the disastrous prospect of no escape from the war ravaged, blood-stained country. Hunted by Congolese national forces, and a legion of savage, drug-crazed guerrillas, things don't always go to plan...even for the SAS!

www.david-black.co.uk

Available from Amazon in Kindle format and paperback

Also by David Black

Playing for England

What makes a man want to join the reserve SAS?

The SAS - The famous British Special Forces Regiment; whose selection process boasts more than a 90% failure rate.

David Black's third book - **Playing for England** gives the reader a fascinating, first-hand insight into the rigours of the selection and training process, of those few men who earn the privilege of wearing the sandy beret and winged dagger cap badge.

Join David as he patrols the dangerous streets of Londonderry, and then embarks on an adventure which leads him to the bleak mountains of south Wales, and the seemingly impossible rigours of SAS selection.

http://www.david-black.co.uk

Available from Amazon in Kindle format and paperback

Also by David Black

Siege of Faith

Far to the East across the sparkling waters of the great
Mediterranean Sea, the formidable Ottoman Empire was
secretly planning to add to centuries of expansion. Soon,
they would begin the invasion and conquest of Christian
Europe.

But first, their all-powerful Sultan, Suleiman the
Magnificent knew he must destroy the last Christian
bastion which stood in the way of his glorious destiny of
conquest. The Maltese stronghold... garrisoned and
defended by the noble and devout warrior monks of the
Knights of St. John of Jerusalem...

A powerful story of heroism, love and betrayal set against
the backdrop of the cruel and terrible siege of Malta which
raged through the long hot summer of 1565. The great
Caliph unleashed a massive invasion force of 40,000
fanatical Muslim troops, intent on conquering Malta
before invading poorly defended Christian Europe. A
heretic English Knight - Sir Richard Starkey becomes
embroiled in the bloody five month siege which ensued;
Europe's elite nobility cast chivalry aside, no quarter asked
or mercy given as rivers of Muslim and Christian blood
flowed...

http://www.david-black.co.uk

Available from Amazon in Kindle format and paperback

Also by David Black

EAGLES of the DAMNED

It was autumn in the year AD 9. The summer campaigning season was over. Centurion Rufus and his battle-hardened century were part of three mighty Roman Legions returning to the safety of their winter quarters beside the River Rhine. Like their commanding General, the Centurion and his men suspected nothing.

Little did they know, but the entire Germania province was about to explode...

Lured into a cunning trap, three of Rome's mighty Legions were systematically and ruthlessly annihilated, during seventy-two hours of unimaginable terror and unrelenting butchery. They were mercilessly slaughtered within the Teutoburg, a vast tract of dark and forbidding forest on the northernmost rim of the Roman Empire.

Little could they have imagined, as they were brutally cut down, their fate had been irrevocably sealed years earlier by their own flawed system of provincial governance, and a rabid traitor's overwhelming thirst for vengeance. But how could such a military catastrophe have ever happened to such a well trained and superbly equipped army? This is their story...

http://www.davis-black.co.uk

Available from Amazon in Kindle format and paperback

Also by David Black

COMING SOON !

Inca Sun

Sir Richard and his giant servant Quinn begin their next
great adventure, aboard the Privateer '*The Intrepid*', in **Inca
Sun**, sailing off the dangerous waters of the Caribbean and
South America coastline. Their heretic English Queen,
Elizabeth I has secretly commanded Sir Richard to prowl
the high seas in search of King Phillip of Spain's
fabulously wealthy treasure convoys. They sail twice a year
from the New World for Spain laden with gold and silver
ripped from the Conquistador's mines in Peru and Mexico;
dug from the dark earth by their cruelly treated Inca and
Mayan slaves.

What Richard doesn't know when he accepts his latest
Royal commission is that his arch nemesis - Don Rodrigo
Salvador Torrez has become Governor of King Phillip II's
Mexican province of Veracruz.

One thing is certain, mere gold cannot pay the debt of
honour that exists between the two men since their first
encounter on Malta during the great siege. The only
currency which will settle the terrible debt will be the
loser's noble lifeblood....

http://www.david-black.co.uk

Printed in Great Britain
by Amazon.co.uk, Ltd.,
Marston Gate.